The Best of Galaxy's Edge

The Best of

Galaxy's Edge

2013–2014

an imprint of

Rockville, Maryland

ISBN: 978-1-61242-236-7

www.PhoenixPick.com
Great Science Fiction & Fantasy
Free Ebook Every Month

Published by Phoenix Pick
an imprint of Arc Manor
P. O. Box 10339
Rockville, MD 20849-0339
www.ArcManor.com

Contents

Introduction

by Mike Resnick

So one day I'm talking to Shahid Mahmud, the publisher of Arc Manor/Phoenix Pick, and he remarks wistfully that he would love to start a science fiction magazine, but of course magazines don't make any money these days.

I reply that I'd love to edit one, but I just got through co-editing *Jim Baen's Universe*, which had everything going for it and still went the way of all flesh. (Well, of all phosphors.)

And he stares at me for a long while, and finally asks if I'd be crazy enough to edit one. And I stare back and say, only if we can find someone crazy enough to pay me. And, I add, certain that I was putting the final nail in the coffin, I wouldn't agree to do it unless it could be a showplace for new and lesser-known writers.

That conversation took place three years ago. The first issue of the magazine came out in March of 2013. It's October of 2014 as I write these words, and damned if *Galaxy's Edge* isn't still in business, still getting great reviews, and doing better than ever.

From the outset, I realized that we couldn't buy *all* new stories by new writers each issue. A magazine titled *Unearth* did that maybe a third of a century ago, even published William Gibson's first story ... and you haven't seen it around in maybe a third of a century minus a few months.

We needed some Names (note the capital "N") for the cover, to attract readers, and I came up with a format whereby I would buy four reprint stories an issue from the biggest Names in the field, and we'd serialize a novel by another huge Name ... and this would allow me to buy five or six new stories by new and lesser-known writers for each issue.

Our reprints—by Robert Silverberg, Mercedes Lackey, C. L. Moore (we unearthed a story she wrote for her college magazine which hadn't seen the light of day for 83 years), Robert J. Sawyer, Kristine Kathryn Rusch, Kevin J. Anderson, Jack McDevitt, Kij Johnson, Larry Niven, Andre Norton, David Brin, Nancy Kress, and that whole crowd—not only have attracted readers, but it seems, based on our fan mail, that most of these reprints are new to well over half our readership.

Anyway, running those reprints has allowed us to buy from more than three dozen new and newer writers in our first eleven issues. The best of them are in this book (as well as a few new stories by our established friends who just happened to have something ready to go when I had a hole to fill).

Some of these stories are by writers who are going to join the ranks of the Names pretty soon. There's Brad R. Torgersen, who has picked up a Campbell nomination, a Nebula nomination, and three Hugo nominations during his first four years in the field. There's Tina Gower, winner of the $5,000 Writers of the Future Gold Award. There's Nick DiChario, a two-time Hugo nominee. And Bob Jeschonek, winner of the International Book Award. And one of them, Ken Liu, may have been a newcomer when he wrote his story for this book, but he's a bona fide star these days, a recent winner of the Hugo, Nebula and World Fantasy Awards.

Nor are the newer writers limited to our particular land mass. We've got stories by Bulgaria's Sabina Theo, Italy/France/Scotland's Gio Clairval, and Finland's Leena Likitalo.

But I didn't select their stories for their names, their homes, or their credentials, but solely for their quality. They're all in the pages up ahead, just waiting to please you. So maybe it's time to go take a look at them. I think you'll be glad you did.

8

I, Arachnobot

by Brian Trent

"Be careful, Jimmy!" the old woman says. "It might bite you!"

"It's a robot, Nana. It can't bite me."

"I've seen it bite flies!"

"But not a human being."

The woman with the silver hair and brown eyes anxiously peeks over Jimmy's shoulder to examine me. I've seen her before—in an abstract way while I fashion my webs outside her window—but now I see *her*. The person. The inhabitant of Room 18 in Sheldon Springs Retirement Home.

The nametag on her paisley blouse reads: MILDRED.

She begins a nervous pace, fidgeting and tucking her hair behind her ears as I sit helpless on Jimmy's palm, the tools in his other hand operating on my thorax microchip access-panel. Tools the same color as Mildred's hair.

"When I was a little girl on Anacreon," Mildred mutters, "there was a spider living outside my window. It built webs from the flowerbox to the awning. Anacreon has two suns, did you know that? At twinrise, their combined light seemed to set the web ablaze in two different colors ..." Mildred hesitates, drawing a finger to her mouth like a child who has forgotten an important detail. "I've already told you that story, haven't I, Jimmy?"

"It's okay, Nana."

My eight metallic legs claw uselessly at the air. My eye-cluster swivels and adjusts to regard my tormentor, Jimmy, as he brandishes one last tool—a pair of tweezers—to insert something into me.

A final click reverberates throughout my frame. Jimmy closes my thorax, slips his tools into a small case, and flips me right-side up.

"That'll do it!" he trumpets.

Again, Mildred peers over his shoulder and clutches his arm. "What did you do, Jimmy?"

The boy lifts me to his mouth.

Is he going to eat me? I do not wish to be eaten.

"Now listen here, arachnobot!" he declares in a rich, authoritative tone. "From this moment on, you are an artist. You are to continue making webs, but I've given you a little upgrade. You are to build webs which will make Grandma Millie happy. Every sunrise, you'll make her a new web!"

He plucks me from the table and returns me through the open window to my shimmering, dew-heavy web of liquid protein micro-fabricated strands. I orient myself in the web's center to watch the two humans in the room.

Jimmy hugs the old woman. "Now you have something to keep you happy until my next visit," he says. "Goodbye, Nana."

"Jimmy?" Mildred glances to the photographs on her nightstand. Her face crumples in quiet agonies. "You're not Jimmy. My Jimmy has been dead a long time, hasn't he?"

"It doesn't matter. I'll visit you next month, when I return from the conference. I love you."

Not-Jimmy goes out into the corridor, while Mildred paces anxiously around her room.

My web.

My web isn't good enough for her.

By sunrise the next morning, I've rewoven it into a silken paisley fern.

May is humid, hazy, and dominated by flies.

As the arachnobot of Sheldon Springs Retirement Home, I follow a set of orders not so different, perhaps, from the genetic compulsions of actual arachnids in the vicinity: Spin webs to capture flies. Digest them into the protein polymers I will use to make more webs to capture more flies.

Following this set of commands are the hard-wired underpinnings of my very existence:

1. A robot must never harm a human being or, willingly and knowingly, allow a human being to be harmed.

2. A robot must obey orders given to it by human beings, unless those orders violate the First Law.

And now my newest command sits weightily upon me:

Now listen here, arachnobot! From this moment on, you are an artist. You are to continue making webs, but I've given you a little upgrade. You are to build webs which will make Grandma Millie happy. Every sunrise, you'll make her a new web!

Mildred, I notice through her bedroom window, likes to read books with pictures. She touches pages and new images appear. A landscape of canals. A ringed world swollen on a cratered horizon. Sometimes the pictures bring a smile to Mildred's face. Sometimes they bring tears. I study her expressions. When she conjures the picture of a toad holding a crudely painted flower, she smiles and touches the screen with a quivering hand.

I could make a better flower than that.

By nightfall, she is sleeping with the book on the bed beside her. Its cover-screen fades to display the title: *Memories of Stars and Family.*

Sunrise awakens her. Mildred rubs her eyes, squinting toward the glittering, dangling flower in silk I've woven. Suspended between sill and latch, it glows radiant orange in the rising sunlight.

A ten-degree angle adjustment, I note, would be better.

Mildred approaches the glass. She is wearing pajamas with stars and crescent moons on them.

"How beautiful! Did you do this, little spider?"

I shiver pleasantly from the happy notes in her voice.

"I saw flowers like this when I was a child on Anacreon. I've seen a thousand worlds since then, but it always comes back to the first one, doesn't it?"

I have no idea, Mildred. But I like that you're happy.

"*The itsy bitsy spider, climbs up the water spout,*" she sings softly. Mildred likes to sing. She knows so many songs.

The door opens suddenly behind her.

A nurse enters. The name-tag clipped to her uniform reads: JANET.

"Mildred, you're up early!"

"Hello Janet. I like your earrings."

"Do you?" The nurse jiggles the silver. "It's Saturn."

"Yes, I know."

"Oh?" Nurse Janet tilts her head. "Yes, of course. You're our famous astronaut! Helped discover a world of diamond!" Janet's eyes glitter in the refracted light of my web. "Lucky you!"

Mildred smiles. "I wish I could remember it."

Nurse Janet changes Mildred's bedsheets and notices the framed photographs on her nightstand. "Such a lovely family, too. It's just that grandson of yours now, yes? Such a handsome boy!"

Mildred gives a troubled nod. "Sometimes I don't remember him. It's like a stranger visiting me. Visiting his crazy grandma."

The nurse finishes with the bed. "Don't say that, Mildred. He'll be back in a few weeks and I'll bet you'll remember him just fine. Say, how about a picture together?"

Janet retrieves a camera from her uniform pocket. She tucks her arm around Mildred's waist and snaps the picture.

"Thank you, Millie!" Nurse Janet has a pleasant smile—a smile would make a nice design for a web—but as she examines the picture, the expression darkens. "You're not smiling, Millie! Why aren't you smiling? Oh, no matter."

She leaves the room.

The next morning, I reweave the flower into Saturn.

I must create eight webs at various points around Sheldon Springs Retirement Home to most effectively cull the seasonal emergent fly population. The equation is as dependable as the structure of my body: a steady-state condition of fly populations versus predator (me) operating at optimal capture rates, resulting in a resource gain for the continued production of webs.

One of the choicest locations, nine meters from a pond where flies breed, is the staff breakroom. At 9:43 a.m., I construct a standard web outside that window.

Nurse Janet is in the room, sitting at a table across from a man in blue porter scrubs. I try to get a better glimpse of her earrings.

"He's hopped the space elevator," the porter says, nursing his coffee. His nametag reads: DANIEL. "He'll be gone three weeks. If we're going to do this, sis, we won't get a better chance."

Janet drums the table with her fingers. "Of course we're going to do this. Think I'm going to be stuck working here my whole life?" She half-turns, allowing me an oblique view of the earrings. I catch a glimpse of fishtails.

"I've already got it worked out," she continues. "Tomorrow, you drug her breakfast and bring it to her at 8 a.m. At 8:30 a.m., you knock over a mop and bucket right outside her door. That's the perfect excuse to keep people away from her room; there's a stairwell right there, and that floor is deadly when wet."

"Then what?"

"While you're cleaning up the spilled water, I visit Mildred."

"And?"

She turns to the window. I see the earrings in full now. Mermaids. I could do that.

"Pillow over the head," Janet says.

"And what about her will?" Daniel asks. "The old bitch is so out of it, she might have left her estate to a field mouse."

"Her original will left everything to the Space Agency and her grandson. Let's say I've gotten ... *close* to her executor. There's a new will now. It leaves a substantial sum to her favorite nurse."

"And porter ..." Daniel insists.

"Of course. Just remember: 8 a.m. breakfast; 8:30, spill the bucket. *I'll* kill her."

I almost fall off my web, dangling from a single strand.

Kill her?

Kill Mildred?

1. **A robot must never harm a human being or, willingly and knowingly, allow a human being to be harmed.**

As the two humans depart, I climb in through the window, setting my eye-cluster on the wall-phone. Emergencies are handled by the police. Police can be contacted through various communication devices such as, but not limited to, a phone.

Mildred is in danger.

From the sill to the breakroom table, past rings of old coffee-stains and a discarded fork, I crawl towards the phone. It is red, shiny, and has a flat readout screen.

I hesitate, quivering uncertainly on my metallic legs.

I don't have a voice.

Nonetheless, phones are for communication and there are ways to communicate other than through larynx vibrations. I *must* communicate the murder plot. Otherwise Mildred will die tomorrow. The First Law vibrates along my limbs. So, too, does my other programming: Build webs to catch flies. The compulsion rises. I'll have to build a web soon. The flies are out there, multiplying.

But first …

I stab one leg into the MAKE CALL button.

"Enter biometric signature," says the phone.

I halt, stunned.

Arachnobots do not have biometric data. Only humans do.

I peer at the many coffee mugs, magazines, and eating utensils in the breakroom. There must be a hundred biometric samples I can use here. Fingerprints on that dirty fork, for instance. This should be a simple matter to—

A scream startles me.

I pivot towards the door and see Janet standing there, a look of horror on her face. She rushes me, snatching a magazine as she does, and slams it down just as I leap out of the way. I land hard on the floor, and narrowly avoid a second, crushing blow from her boot.

"Little bastard!" she cries.

I dash into the dust beneath the heater, hiding behind pipes.

From the doorway, Daniel peeks in. "What's wrong?"

"A spider! A *huge* one!"

"Real or robotic?"

"It was bright blue! Robotic, I think."

"Then it can't hurt you. Calm down, sis!"

"I *hate* those things!"

While she's jabbing the rolled-up magazine beneath the heater, I clamber up the wall and escape to the other side of the window. Another cry, and the magazine smacks the glass, knocking me into the bushes.

Janet leans out the window.

"Hey arachnobot!" she yells. "I order you stay out of here forever!"

I try to enter the breakroom during the night.

Janet has closed the window but there's space for me to squeeze through the jamb. Yet each time I approach the glass, my movements become sluggish. My legs stick in their sockets. It helps to imagine flies in the breakroom. There *could* be flies in the breakroom. Still, Janet's voice is like a web of her own stretching across me.

I order you stay out of here forever!

Of course, Janet is not Calvin Positronics. Her command cannot override my basic programming: *Spin webs to capture flies. Digest them into the protein polymers I will use to make more webs to capture more flies.* I'm assigned to Sheldon Springs Retirement Home. Janet cannot banish me.

Besides, she told me to stay out of *here* forever.

What does *here* mean?

She could have been referring to her pocket.

Very well, Janet. I shall stay out of your pocket until the heat death of the universe.

I attempt another approach. My legs freeze, shudder, and stop. Janet meant the breakroom. She was *in* the breakroom when she said it.

The phone is like a red cherry behind the glass. I cannot, *cannot*, reach it. The breakroom is off-limits to me for all eternity.

However, there *are* other phones in this building. There's one in Mildred's room!

I hurtle across the building's brick exterior to her window, climb through, and approach the nightstand phone. Mildred is sleeping, one of her frail hands hanging over the bedside.

I festoon her wrist with silk from my spinnerets. It takes all my strength to pull it the four inches needed to brush the phone's biometric pad.

The phone lights up on contact.

I dash to it and dial the police.

"Emergency," a woman answers.

I have no voice. But I dutifully tap out a rudimentary pattern against the receiver, explaining that Nurse Janet with the mermaid earrings is planning to kill Mildred in three hours.

"Hello?" the voice says. "Is anyone there?"

I halt, confused by this lack of understanding.

The line disconnects.

Sunrise is only minutes away. Somewhere, the flies are multiplying.

Hurriedly, I build a web.

My web is of a mermaid, hung at the correct angle to better catch the sunrise. Not my best work, I admit. But it brings a smile to Mildred's face when she sees it upon waking at 5:41 a.m.

"Did you make this mermaid, little spider?" she asks on the other side of the glass. "How did you do it? Oh! It's so pretty!" She closes her eyes, a childish grin on her lips. "*Little Miss Muffet, sat on a tuffet, eating her curds and whey ...*"

I like when she sings to me.

I like when Millie's happy.

Happiness is only possible if she's alive.

Janet is plotting to end her life in two hours and forty-nine minutes.

If her life is ended, Millie won't be happy. There will be no more songs.

Nurse Janet, I conclude, needs to die.

Prior to my reprogramming, there were specific tabulations I needed to complete during the course of a given day. How large should my webs be? Where should they be built? How many webs should I build without marring the overall aesthetic of the retirement home?

Now I aim my tabulation talents at a different challenge:

1.   A robot must never harm a human being …

It's hardwired into me, yet the wording itself is cause for analysis. The First Law does not say *Homo sapiens*. It says *human being*.

At 5:52 a.m. I invade Mildred's room and scamper down the glossy hallway to the room marked STUDY on my internal map of Sheldon Springs Retirement Home.

On one of the counters is a book I've noticed from the window: The Galactic Empire Seventh Edition Dictionary. I pry open its cover, flipping the pages:

HUMAN BEING:
1.   an individual of the species *Homo sapiens*.
2.   of, pertaining to, or characteristic of human beings.
3.   the human race, as distinguished from animals and robots.
4.   empathetic, sympathetic; humane.

Mildred and Nurse Janet are both *Homo sapiens*. Yet according to the Galactic Empire Seventh Edition Dictionary, not all *Homo sapiens* are humane and therefore not all are human. By this argument, Janet is not protected by the First Law, but Mildred is.

I can kill her.

In theory.

It is 6:28 a.m.

Janet will kill Mildred in two hours and two minutes.

Six hundred and ninety-five ways to murder Janet immediately flash through my processors. I quickly reduce these to a pair of options which I calculate have the greatest chance for success:

1.   I can create a multilayered silk mask and suffocate her with it when she enters Mildred's room.

2.   I can lure her to the rooftop with a note claiming to be from Daniel, and impale her with a spring-loaded trigger-trap built from kitchen knives, a cutting board, two mop handles, and forty-six flies' worth of silken strands.

Grudgingly, I admit that the artistry implicit in the second option is outweighed by the relative ease of the first. I hastily return to Mildred's room. A fly buzzes by me; the window has been left open—Millie likes fresh air—and there are flies in here, likely attracted to the pastries she stockpiles. I ignore the flies with great difficulty. Just knowing they're in here weighs on me like a high gravity field. Spin webs. I must spin webs. Must capture flies.

But first …

I spin the suffocation mask. I shape it into a resemblance of Janet's own visage. I …

I …

I …

I …

I cannot proceed with the murder.

Cannot trick myself into murdering a human being.

It is 8:03 a.m. when I recover from my paralysis.

The silken mask I've been weaving dangles in front of the door. It is pretty, and it was meant to murder, but … I cannot murder. Except for the flies in this room. I could murder them easily enough.

Without warning, the door swings open beneath me. Daniel enters with a breakfast tray.

"Good morning, Millie!"

"Good morning, Daniel."

"I, um … I made your favorite. Eggs Benedict."

Millie smiles. "Thank you!"

As he leaves the room, I imagine dropping down on his neck and pulling his brain out through his ear. Mildred sits down at the window, directly in front of the silk mermaid I've made for her, and begins to eat—

No! Millie, don't!

It is 8:05 a.m.

At 8:29 a.m. she's halfway through breakfast when her hand slumps to her side. She falls asleep in her chair.

I nervously dash back and forth across the door's lintel. On the other side, there's commotion. Someone has just knocked over a bucket of dirty water outside Millie's door, across from the stairwell.

I dart to the door's corners, dripping silk in terror. Silken draglines positioned at each corner might seal the door shut. I nearly empty my reserves, layering the nets as fast as my steel spinnerets will allow.

Down the hallway, footsteps are approaching.

I frantically apply the last layer.

The footsteps reach the door.

The door sticks.

Yes!

"What the hell?" cries Janet. Her voice alters into a sweet, loving tone. "Millie? Are you okay? Is something braced against the door?"

The door bulges slightly. The silken netting stretches to the breaking point.

Janet grunts, curses. The door flies open. Against the nearby air-conditioner, I deploy the silken mask as a parachute, ballooning along the current like a ghostly specter directly in front of Janet's face.

Her eyes bulge in disbelief.

The mask hovers in the air. From its mouth, a ball of silk unfolds into a banner, letters bright gold in the sunlight:

STAY AWAY FROM MILLIE

Janet angrily storms forward, batting the mask away, her lips opening in a bestial snarl. I deploy a silken balloon, watching helplessly as Janet strides to the bed, grabs a pillow, and approaches Millie in the chair. I watch as—

—a fly goes into Janet's mouth.

She's so hell-bent on murder that she doesn't notice. But I do. And I suddenly remember one of Millie's many songs:

There was an old woman who swallowed a fly. Perhaps she'll die. Perhaps she'll *die?!?!*

A robot must never harm a human being or, willingly and know-ingly, allow a human being to be harmed.

My job is to catch flies …

Still floating on the room's currents, I shoot a web-strand into Janet's nose. Abandoning my silk balloon behind me, I swing down into her lips and, eagerly, *go in after the fly*.

Her mouth is wet, warm; her throat a slippery chute. She feels my invasion. Her screams resonate around me. The fly vibrates in the dark. I leap, grab it, struggle in the soft confines of her esophagus.

Janet is screaming. I think she's running.

Until, quite suddenly, she's no longer doing either.

"How did you do this, little spider?"

I pluck the silken rocketship I've built outside her window, taking great delight in Millie's smile.

"There was an awful accident yesterday," she says on the other side of the glass. "A nurse slipped and took a fatal tumble down the stairs. That's so terrible, isn't it?"

Not so terrible, Millie. But I'm glad you're happy.

"Can I sing you a song?"

Yes, Millie. Sing to me. Sing as long as you like.

I, arachnobot, will always be here for you.

—Dedicated to Isaac Asimov—

Pocket Full of Mumbles

by Tina Gower

I collect the words unheard. I pluck them from the air, rescue them from gutters, retrieve them from branches—they don't vibrate for long after the words are spoken. I often wonder if I weren't deaf whether I'd hear them. I gather them on my morning walk, along with bottles and cans from recycling bins, and again after supper at St. Joseph's soup kitchen.

I dodge the broken glass while pushing my cart along Seventh Avenue. The front left wheel wobbles and shimmies. It jerks off course when I run over some twisted metal from a wreck. I strong-arm it back on course. Harold waves at me from the next block. He can usually hear me coming.

A flicker in the bushes catches my attention. I stop, bending closer to peer into the plant along the sidewalk. The phrase is easy to spot; I know what to look for. The vibration flutters in the bush like a trapped butterfly. Carefully, I ease the vibration from its hiding place until it merges onto the string. It quivers for a moment, I'm unsure what it's saying—sometimes the common ones are easy to decipher, but this one's weak and faint.

It takes a special eye to see them. I cut notches along the top of a tin and thread horsehair I'd salvaged from broken instrument bows or filched from the stables when I participate in the Homeless to Work program. I observe my latest find for clues as to its message.

Vibrations tremble for hours, sometimes a few days before they fade. *I love you* has a distinct vibration—quick, long, quick—but so does *I hate you*. I pay close attention to the sharpness of the visual tone.

Harold meets me at the corner. He's wearing a poncho he bought from me, burnt-orange and woven with broken promises. He pats my arm, alerting me that he's about to talk, so I watch his lips. *You got a good one?* he asks.

I nod and hold the tin out to him.

He inches closer, taking care not to touch it. He straightens, facing me. *Oh, that's special, Maggie Mae.*

What's it saying? I sign, but Howard looks away and pretends he didn't see my hands. He doesn't know sign. I point to the tin and then to my ear.

He glances at me. A grin builds on his face until he's shaking from holding in his giggle. *It's a good one. Different. It's sorrow, hope, wishes, and goodnights all in one.* Harold can't hear the exact message, just the intent. He once told me that maybe it's part of his power from his extra chromosome.

He unfolds a few blankets on my cart and displays them on the park bench. *You got a nice selection today. A nice selection.*

I weave the best phrases into blankets or sweaters and it doesn't seem to matter. Negative or positive, the merchandise woven with phrases sells best at the farmers' market. They say these pleas fall on deaf ears. It's poetic irony that I'm the only one who listens.

I pull out a few unfinished projects, hunting for a place to weave my newest find. It doesn't seem to fit on a tapestry of prayers, or a rug filled with apologies.

Harold tugs on my arm. I catch his lips moving, but I can't make out what he's saying. He notices and repeats, his mouth moving slower. *You can't use that one. It's special.*

I glare at him. What does he mean? These are my phrases, my finds. If people wanted them they wouldn't be so careless and listen. I continue to weave the phrase into the blanket, but it doesn't work. The ends fray.

Harold's eyes widen, his mouth a perfect "O" of shock. *It don't want to go. It don't match. Maybe this is the first one you gotta return.*

I've never returned any of them. It's the one thing that brings me money. It's the one thing that connects me to the world of the hearing.

I flap my arms and shoo him away, fed up with his morals. He swats at my hands like I'm an annoying bug, but leaves, shooting me expressions of disbelief. I thread the vibrating phrase back into the tin. It quivers like a wounded animal. I'll find a place for it tonight.

The phrase continues to vibrate, weak, but persistent. It doesn't match any project—Not the mutters-of-indifference handbag, not the scarf of wishful thinking, not the mittens with bits of excuses.

I throw my yarns at my cot.

Harold sits on top of the tangled lump, hands me a magazine. *I'm volunteering at the shelter today. You want a magazine?*

I glare at him.

I'm slow, teachers say I'm slower than most people, that's why I got special needs, but I know you're mad. I don't like it when people are mad at me. He crosses his arms and looks at the ground.

I sigh and he peeks at me.

His face is like a hopeful puppy waiting for a treat. *I can help you. I can find more phrases like that one, enough to make a big cozy blanket.*

For being slow Harold is a genius. I give him two thumbs up, smiling so hard my jaw aches.

We'll find more similar phrases and make a spectacular design. I imagine what I'll buy with the money I make. A new dress? Fancy pants? Maybe I'll look good enough that someone will hire me, something permanent.

I gather my things into the cart; got to take it all, anything left behind is fair picking. We go to hunt more phrases, to find something that's sorrow, hope, wishes, and goodnights all in one.

We find a goodnight first, and then a wish. Nothing sticks. I braid them together, but the phrase doesn't weave with the others. It doesn't match. I sit on the street corner, lay my scarf out so people can drop change while I work. Harold watches the shop owner change a toy display in the window. He stomps with excitement.

I stare at the stubborn phrase. It fits nowhere, but now I'm obsessed to find where it fits.

A police officer walks toward us, eyes focused on us, hand on his belt. I don't need to hear to know we need to move along. The officer's lips tell us to leave and he tips his chin to my things. Harold jogs over and we gather things quickly. The officer stands on the corner watching us walk away.

Harold stops. He points wildly at the newspaper stand. I grab his arm, urging him to keep walking. The officer crosses his arms, still observing us from a distance.

Keep moving, I sign, *the police are watching*. Harold won't understand, but hopefully the officer will see I'm trying. I don't want to be a burden.

Look, Harold taps on the glass. *It's our park, Maggie Mae! They got a nice picture of our park.*

The officer frowns and crosses the street, heading our way. I pull harder on Harold.

Harold claps, jumping up and down, pulling at his hair and grinning. *The newspaper people like our park. Maybe more people will come buy your blankets.*

The picture catches my attention. It's the park from a long angle view. The focus of the scene is a blue sedan with the driver side completely crunched inward. Glass and twisted metal are sprayed around the sidewalk. The car is wrapped around a tree. The back end pokes out from the tall bushes where I found the phrase this morning.

Tragic Wreck Claims Life, the article says. I read the first few lines before the print disappears under the folds.

The police officer approaches us again. This time Harold follows with ease, telling the officer about the park and my blankets. The officer fiddles with his radio, nodding, and after a few blocks he leaves us.

Harold bounces next to me. My thoughts wander to the phrase. Harold was right. This is one that needs to be returned. It won't match in any of my blankets, but I know where it fits.

✦ ✦ ✦

I nod to Harold from my hiding spot behind the dumpster.

He pats me on the shoulder. *You're doing a good thing, Maggie Mae. More phrases will come along. Phrases that will bring in lots of money. A good deed brings good things.*

I don't believe in Karma, but I smile at Harold, pat him too before he crawls from the hiding spot to wait for me across the street. It would be easier for one of us to make the delivery.

I'm sitting in the alley for only a few minutes when a nurse pushes a laundry cart through the hospital exit. She doesn't see me; I catch the door before it shuts. Shift change is the best time to enter the hospital unnoticed. The nurses and doctors are going over charts, summarizing patient care, and getting coffee.

I scan the doors of the trauma unit. I see her: young girl, seven years old, black hair, dark skin. The panels slowly blink reds and blues. The monitor flashes green. I carefully unwrap the tin from a blanket and hold it over the girl's ear. She moves. Her lips open. The monitors blink a little faster. Her eyelids flicker, her forehead creases.

I miss you. Her breath is uneven, her closed eyes squeeze together, wetting with unshed tears. *Mommy, don't leave.*

I tuck her in, laying the blanket of lullabies over her legs.

Okay, mommy, I'll stay. I'll be good.

I hold the tin for a moment longer, until the vibrations slow, as if a fading heartbeat. A hair falls over the girl's eyes; I sweep it away. The girl falls into a deeper sleep and I weave the string with the bygone phrase into a bracelet. It braids and bends with ease. I thread the gift into the girl's fingers. As I sneak out the door, I glance one last time at the bracelet. It flutters two short bursts, which could mean a few things:

Be good.

I'm home.

Thank you.

Good-bye.

Published in Galaxy's Edge Issue 8

Creator of the Cosmos Job Interview Today

by Nick DiChario

H e entered a sun-white room. The furniture was lean and silvery, the walls made of satin steel. A faint smell of clean, crystalline air tickled his nose. An alien—tall, pale, slick, lean, bipedal, female—came in and seated herself at the desk. She did not speak, but adjusted her long white robe and stared at him with her three vermillion eyes.

He walked over and sat opposite her as if it was expected of him, although he had no idea how he could have known such a thing. He glanced at himself in the glazed steel panels behind the woman's desk. He had a bushy scrub of black hair. He wore jeans and a T-shirt and sandals, the strap on his left sandal hung unfastened, and his knapsack lay tattered at his feet. He didn't recognize himself, although he thought he looked like a human.

"Can you tell me why you're here?" asked the alien. Her voice held the tight, musical crispness of a violin.

"No," he said. Truthfully. But then he thought about it. "Wait. I was walking along the street outside and saw the sign in front of the building: Creator of the Cosmos Job Interview Today. Come Inside."

"So you thought you would just sashay in and have an interview, is that it?"

He shrugged. "I guess so. Something like that. When I saw the sign, I thought, for some reason, the message was meant for me."

"Is that right?"

"Yes."

Her wide, flat ears moved slightly, like palm fronds in the wind. "You say that as if you're pretty sure of yourself. Are you?"

He scratched at his curly bush of hair. "Now I get it. This is all part of the job interview, right?"

She sniffed, feigning boredom. "If you say so. Do you say so?"

"Sure," he said. "I say so."

"Okay, so, according to you, the sign was put out there specifically for you, and this line of questioning is all part of the job interview. Tell me why I should care. What makes you Creator of the Cosmos material?"

The woman's tone was casual but challenging. She leaned forward and placed her elbows on the desk. Her two arms were as long as her body, which gave her the somewhat imposing look of a giant mantis.

He sat back and crossed his legs, picked at the hole in the knee of his jeans, started to say something, glanced around, stood up, walked slowly from here to there and back again with his hands clasped behind his back. Thinking. Trying to remember. As he walked, he could hear the faintest snick of gears, the moto-robo-electronic zizzing of invisible mechanics in the room around him. Where was he? Who was he? *Why* was he? He had no idea.

"Where's the door?" he asked.

"What door?"

"I'm sure I came in through a door. Didn't I?"

"You say that as if it's important there is a door."

"Yes. It's important. Very important. I need to go in and out through the door, don't I?"

"Why?"

"I don't know. But it seems important." He walked a bit more, the floor illuminating his soft footfalls, lighting his steps from underneath. He wasn't sure if his feet were telling the floor where to light, or if the floor was telling his feet where to walk. It was an odd sensation. "Wait. Something's coming to me. A memory. I'm *meant* to go in and out. I'm meant to do it, aren't I?"

"*Meant*? Are you sure that's the right word?"

"No. Not one hundred percent."

"Let's start with something a little simpler, then, shall we? Do you know where you came from?"

"No, I don't."

"Do you know where you're going?"

"No, I'm sorry, I don't."

The woman's expression seemed indifferent, but she sat up straight, as if her body had taken an interest. "Excellent. So far you're doing very well. Incredibly well."

"You mean with the interview?" He perched on the edge of the chair. "Hold on. I remember something else. About the questions and answers. This isn't the first time I've interviewed, is it? No, of course not. I come in. I ask questions. And then … I remember what's important … and I go out again, right?"

"Why?" she asked, an anticipatory tremor in her voice. "What is it that's so important that you have to remember? What's the point of the interview? Why do you have to answer questions at all and go in and out of the room?"

"Because … that's the way I am … *designed* … 'designed' is the right word … not *meant*."

The woman's eyes came alive with encouragement. "Yes? Go on."

"Well, something makes me think that for everything to work out there in the cosmos … all the planets, the galaxies, the universes, the life … this interview has to take place to help me remember … so that I can go out and forget again … and somehow the remembering and forgetting is integral to the life cycle … without me knowing how or why … without anyone knowing how or why … the cosmos are reborn …" That didn't exactly make sense to him, but there it was, he'd said it, and it felt right.

The woman gripped the edge of the desk and pulled herself forward. "Yes? Yes? Go on. You're doing very well. Incredibly well. There is just one question and answer that you have to remember now. Just one. What is it?"

He jumped to his feet as soon as the question popped into his head. "Who is the Creator of the Cosmos?"

"Yes! And the answer?"

"I am the Creator of the Cosmos! Me! Already! Right now! I created everything! It was me! Me!"

"Ahhh," she said. "Ahhh. Rebirth." She released all the tension in her body and slumped back in her chair. "*Ahhhhh.*"

He knew the interview was over now. He bent down and lifted the knapsack, walked toward the wall. A hidden door slid open in front of him right where he knew it would be.

Outside there were two bold suns overhead, red clouds, azure skies, gold mountains, black space. A gust of wind threw back his mop of hair. The music of the world rose up around him. A pterodactyl screeched, sky ships roared, an elephant trumpeted, billions of humans and aliens died while billions more were born, stars burned out and fell from space, and new ones flared to life across an infinite canvas of galaxies.

He closed his eyes and breathed it in. Yes, the Creator breathed it all in, and then breathed it all out again.

The alien woman rushed over and kneeled before him, pulled the loose strap on his sandal and snugged it in place, lowered herself to her hands and knees and kissed his feet. "Until the morrow," she said.

"Is that how it works?" he asked. "Every day? We have to go through this every single day for the cosmos to work? Is that the way I wanted it? Is that the way I set it up? Why? Why did I do it this way? It makes no sense."

"Exactly," said the woman, waving to him as the door slid shut between them.

"Wait! I have one last question. How long is a day? How long—"

But it was too late. She was gone. How frustrating! He was already beginning to forget.

He turned around to face the cosmos.

Strange, he thought. *Wasn't there a sign here just a moment ago? Something about a job interview?*

Published in Galaxy's Edge Issue 1

Will *You* Volunteer to Kill Wendy?

by Eric Cline

It's been a long time since anyone reported on a good locked-room mystery. They used to be huge. Sometimes they were just about jewel theft, stuff like that. But mostly they were about murder. They went something like this:

The servants heard shouting from Mr. Clanton's study, some sort of struggle ... then deadly silence. They tried the door; it was locked. The police were summoned. They broke down the door. Inside, the master of the house, Mr. Clanton, was sprawled dead in his leather chair. A thin trail of blood came out of his left ear. A glass of water, tinged with red, sat on his desk. Scrawled pages in his own handwriting showed desperate attempts to reconcile doomed finances.

Detective Bartholomew was in command. He verified that the first uniformed officers had secured the crime scene and had let no one in (or out). The door had been locked from the inside. There was no outside window. The floor was solid hardwood, with no trapdoors or any of that.

The victim had been stabbed through the ear, but there was no murder weapon. The detective ordered the room resealed after the body and other evidence were removed, and had a guard placed day and night at the door.

The glass was tested. It was water with a trace of the victim's brain cells mixed in. The killer had apparently cleaned off the murder weapon by swirling it around in the glass.

Bartholomew looked into Clanton's background. The dead man had once romanced a lady acrobat at a circus, but she left him. Later, she was found stabbed to death. Clanton had no alibi, but he did have expensive lawyers, and no charges were ever filed.

Finally, after 48 hours, Detective Bartholomew went back into the sealed room. He rapped on the heavy desk and said, "Please come out." From a false compartment in the huge desk, the dwarf emerged. He was Igor, the circus performer who had fallen in love with the lady acrobat.

He had sneaked into the house with an icicle frozen in a thermos. He surprised Clanton and, after a brief struggle, drove the sharp ice into his brain. Then, he simply left the icicle in the empty water glass to melt. By the time police were summoned and broke down the door, it was a glass of water.

Igor had barely squeezed himself into the huge desk, with a small supply of food and water, and the thermos for a toilet, and had waited for the crime scene to be released.

But he hadn't counted on the brilliance of ... Detective Bartholomew!

Not so good, is it? Pretty frigging retro, eh? The circus dwarf thing alone would be a no-no today. But, once upon a time, the pulp magazines were cluttered with such stories.

What a lot of people don't know is that the locked-room mysteries were based on a series of killings involving my organization. *Justified* killings, I hasten to add. Sometimes, it was a clean kill. Sometimes, when things went wrong, it was a locked-room mystery. But unlike the ones in pulp magazines, these were never really solved. How could they be, when the victim was actually the perpetrator, and the supposed perpetrator ... but I'm getting ahead of myself.

On Wednesday morning, my cell rang in my cubicle. It was from Jamal, my contact in the Roanoke Society.

"Yes, may I help you?" I said, trying to sound businesslike.

"Peter," he said. "We made contact with Wendy. Sven is chatting her up in a bar right now. We're going to kill her in a hotel room. You need to leave work now to get ready!"

"Damn, man!" I whispered. (Try having a private conversation in an office cubicle!) "I'm almost maxed out on leave time. The boss is a peach, but she still needs warm bodies in the office."

"Wendy's calling us, man," he said. "We're all making sacrifices. When Wendy walks into our trap, Wendy dies. That's the deal. 'Roanoke!'"

"'Roanoke,'" I whispered, returning the salute. "Okay, I'll get food poisoning or something. No, it will be a family emergency. I'll meet you guys at the garage."

Whenever I had read fiction about secret societies—you know, like the Dan Brown crap—I had never seen anyone comment on how *underfunded* they were. The Roanoke Society is an entirely volunteer organization. Because of our secrecy, it is not a 501(c) charity to which you can write off donations. We all kick in for expenses. And the amount of free time it burns up is ungodly.

But killing Wendy is a passion for me. A Wendy killed my brother and his wife 11 years ago, and almost killed me. The Society rescued me, then recruited me. It is the most important thing in my life.

Still, I do have to work, and it would be *so* convenient if the frigging Wendys could be made to appear only on weekends, or at least on Martin Luther King's birthday or Easter.

There are other stories out there, of a type. They're not even stories, really, just accounts of historical bafflement. They're related to the locked-room mysteries, although most people who have heard both have not made the connection. The Roanoke Society could publicize the link, perhaps, but who would believe us? And Wendy is quite shy (in a manner of speaking). Her ilk shows up a few times a year, is difficult to detect, and is even more difficult to kill … But as I was saying, the baffling accounts from history:

Roanoke, Virginia, the first European settlement in that corner of America. Vanished, with no sign of a struggle.

Mary Celeste, found adrift with no captain, no crew, no passengers.

And those are just the celebrated ones. There were countless explorers, ships, soldiers in jungles, and others who faced the same thing the Roanoke settlers and the *Mary Celeste* crew faced. And disappeared.

Of course they disappeared!

When you've dined on, let's say, Salisbury steak, peas, and mashed potatoes and licked your plate clean, do you expect to look down and still see the food? It's been eaten, mate. The food's gone.

It was a shabby hotel room in a bad part of town. If bed bugs ever became a problem around here, this place would be the epicenter. But there were six of us, four men and two women, and we came down here as a pack, not worrying about the lice, human or otherwise, who infested the area.

Sven made seven. He was at the bar nearby. To hear him tell it, Wendy had practically molested him with her eyes. He would have been flattered, if she'd been human. He would lure her back here. Meanwhile, it was our job to seal off the room.

The cheap carpet was at least solid, and the floor underneath was concrete, thank God—no worrying about floorboards. The drywall in the room we'd rented had a few holes in it, and we patched them for free, without management's permission. It didn't look all that great, but that was no step down. The window was scratched but unbroken, and like most hotel windows built after air conditioning became widespread (even in no-tell motels), it was molded into the wall and would never open. Just for privacy's sake, we bound the curtains with some heavy safety pins.

We didn't have to make it airtight, but we'd gotten our best results that way in previous encounters.

A text went to our list, and "blooped" on everyone's cells at the same time.

Sven: coming.

"Oh god!"

"Are we ready?"

"We've got to be!"

"Hide!"

Behind the bed, two of us; in the bathroom, three; in the closet space behind the door, me. I was in the danger point. When Wendy realized she'd been trapped, Sven would be the closest focus for her wrath, but I'd be next in line, just standing in a little square depression against the folded-up ironing board.

A note on diversity.

I really haven't been able to give you a sense of myself as a character. You know I'm Peter and that I work in an office, right? You can picture me in my 20s, 30s, or 40s, somewhere in there. But this account isn't really a portrait of me. I could tell you childhood memories of my brother (the one who was killed by Wendy, starting me on my quest for vengeance), and I could describe myself eating a microwave burrito in the break room just before I took half a day off, staring at my reflection in the oven door and pondering stuff. Agonizing over how the ignorant masses, who don't know anything about Wendy, are free to go on with their petty little lives while I am trapped in a cycle of blah blah blah.

Look, I'm going to kill Wendy, all right? The end. I hope the prospect of imminent blood and guts keeps you here, and that's all I can do.

But here's a much easier way to score some points.

We're diverse.

Our group included two Hispanics, one African American, two guys who I think were gay, and Sven was an immigrant. Two were women.

That is a very diverse body of people. It is the modern American society. Admirable, no? But I'm not up to doing characterization.

We're just a group of pissed-off victims who got together to kill Wendy.

Maybe that's the greatest crime of the damned Wendys. By killing our loved ones, by attempting to kill us, the old bitch has flattened our individuality. She has made a *mob* of us. Maybe that's why I can't develop myself, or Jamal, or Sven, or anyone other member of our local chapter of the Roanoke Society into a three-dimensional human being for you to care about.

And the worst part of it all is, "Wendy" is actually just a mob of different beings. The being that destroyed the Roanoke colony isn't the same as the being that ate the crew of the *Mary Celeste*, at least we don't think so. But just like soldiers over the years personified their faceless enemies as a single Johnny Reb or Fritz or Charlie, so too have we referred to them as a single "Wendy." And like Satan being a more interesting character than God in *Paradise Lost*, so too are we good-guy mortals left as mere fodder to strengthen the legend of a flesh-devouring creature.

Some native tribes called it the *wendigo*.

We're Chuck Wepner fighting Muhammad Ali. No matter how many rounds we win, we'll be forgotten, and your interest will remain with our opponent—don't tell me you haven't been thinking it! It ain't frigging fair.

I've never been at any surprise parties for people. I just saw them on TV. People jump out when someone opens the door and turns on the lights. It always feels like a surprise party for Wendy.

We heard them in the hallway. Sven was laughing—a bit too loud, too forced—and a woman's voice laughed along with him. I saw the door handle move. A soft buzz told me he'd inserted the key card into the room.

Sven screamed.

She'd smelled it, somehow. So she attacked poor goddamn Sven in the hallway.

The others jumped from their hiding places. "Open the door! Open the door!" more than one yelled. Everyone had their talismans out, their heavy-duty garbage bags, their ropes, their holy water; all the potpourri of weapons that usually, one or another, killed Wendy.

I opened the door, and was shielded from whatever happened in the hallway, blocked into the little closet space.

From the blur of movement I saw, it seemed some of my friends ran into the hallway, grabbed the Wendy, and dragged her in. A rush of air and light enveloped me as the door swung away, slammed shut. Dana Hernandez flipped the little hotel-room U-bolt closed and glanced at me. "Duck tape!" she yelled. Then she jumped into the melee in the center of the room.

The duck tape (often miscalled "duct tape," but Google it if you do, you're wrong) was in a paper bag along with some good Swedish-made scissors to cut it with. The gap between the door and the carpet was just enough that it needed the tape; I'd been assigned it. I knew its importance. But just now, with Sven's desperately pumping legs sticking out of Wendy's mouth, I had to look.

They have to give up part of their human appearance when they eat us, of course. The Wendy's face and neck were distended like that of a boa constrictor eating a goat. Sven's legs went slack; I'd just seen his moment of death. But my friends grabbed at his legs; being human, they had to try. It unhid its claws and swiped at Jamal; his face was opened up to visible teeth and gum. My friends stabbed her, they pressed crucifixes against her, they looped rope around her, looking for any one of the tricks that, without any predictability, would work.

But I had to do the goddamn duck tape.

I turned away just as the tips of Sven's Nike Air Jordans disappeared down the Wendy's throat.

One strip, covering the space between the door and the carpet. A strip above it, a strip below it, sealing and securing.

✧ ✧ ✧

Poor Sven. He'd had to play out that *other* story that the outside world didn't realize was based on Roanoke Society activities.

The Stranger in the Bar story.

You know the one: it's become such a stale old wheezer that it can't be published in magazines anymore, only broadcast. It goes like this:

Niles Cadbury hoisted his Tom Collins as he scanned the crowd. Some beautiful women were here tonight. Niles loved beauty. He took beauty. Even if it didn't want to be taken.

At the end of the bar was a good-looking blonde who was getting very unsteady and was laughing way too loud. If he could just separate her from her friends and get her into a cab, he could do what he wanted. And Niles Cadbury liked to play rough.

"Hey stranger, buy me a drink?"

Niles looked over in surprise. How had this sexy redhead come to sit down beside him without him seeing her? Her swept-up hair was even redder than her lipstick.

Almost the color of blood.

(They get back to some hotel room, where inevitably, the misogynist gets his comeuppance.)

He sat back on the bed, watching as she shrugged off her dress. It hit the floor, and she kicked it aside.

"Tell me what you want," she breathed, as she stepped out of her high heels.

Niles Cadbury didn't like to put on the romantic crap any longer than he had to. He would tell her, in the crudest terms, what he wanted. If she didn't do it, he would grab her and beat her until she did.

He was an expert at it.

"I want you to suck me dry," he growled.

Her smile widened into a strangely oversized grin. With a shock, he saw that two of her teeth ended in long, sharp points.

And her eyes ... Her eyes were red, glowing coals!

"Gladly!" she snarled. She jumped on him before he could scream.

The Wendys were the basis for the mythical vampires, of course.

Our screams would lead to no assistance. This was the *Fleabag du Fleabag*. No one cared. Loud rap blared from a room down the hall; there were shouts of argument from the floor above, unrelated to us.

The Wendy's mouth was as wide as an HDTV now. It was barely keeping its human form. It chewed Jamal *and* Dana at once. Half a dozen knives and hatchets stuck out of her, but she still kept going. If we'd been able to surprise her and bag her head before she opened her mouth, none of this would have happened. It's almost like they've got to get a running jump to leave their human form.

Three of my friends had disappeared inside its mouth, and it was still hungry. But the blows they'd struck were beginning to have their effect. From the knife sticking out of its back, a white mist began to waft. From the hatchet handle poking out from under an armpit, another little tendril of mist.

Three members in good standing of the Roanoke Society, local chapter 8601, were dead and consumed. The Wendy grabbed Manny, our old hand who'd been doing this since the 1970s. With a roar, it lifted him up and scooped its lower jaw (which was stretched like a pelican's lower beak by now) and tossed him in. John "Lumberjack" Tolliver, who stood 6'6", swung a machete low to the ground, biting into its knee. But that barely fazed it.

I unrolled the duck tape and extended it in front of me.

The machete had done less than one of the daggers had, don't ask me why. We can never tell.

Some wendigos seem to fear the crucifix, and will stop resisting entirely; we don't know if it's because some of them have adopted cultural taboos, or if we're dealing with different subspecies.

Some of the creatures are easily bound up in rope, while others simply break it into shreds.

Chains were tried in the early 20th century, and always ended up being used against the Roanokans; somehow, the Wendys could heat the links and burn the hands of the people trying to wrap them up.

Guns never did any good, because the fast projectiles did little but perforate them, and in closed spaces we could shoot each other by accident.

Any sharp object did some good, because it started them bleeding out their mist. Some mythical vampires (depending on the author) are able to turn themselves into mist; that was surely based on wendigos bleeding out that white vapor; but it's not some shape-shifting thing—it's their death throes. If they're able to drift out of the room, they can *sometimes* re-coalesce and survive to prey another day; hence, we have to seal the room fairly tight, always. *We have to lock the room.* Their body evaporates into mist, the mist becomes just water stains on the walls, and the bitch is dead.

It's slow though, damn it.

I jumped at the Wendy just as it had pushed Manny's Doc Martens down its hellish gullet. The gray tape stuck in a diagonal slash across its face (it looked like a Silly Putty-stretched comic strip had come to life—not a trace of its human guise as a beautiful woman remained) but I dropped the roll and it simply hung on the other side of "her."

Thank God for Jane. She's a jogger and a health nut, and at most of our chapter meetings she can be depended upon to rant about

39

overweight America and diabetes and government-subsidized corn syrup—you almost want her to choke on her carob and soy-substitute milkshakes. But she's in great shape. In a blur of motion, she wrapped it around the creature's head three times.

Fitting that a weight-loss scold would bind up a wendigo's mouth. No more meals for you, Wendy.

We bagged its head, wrestled it down to the floor, and sat on it; soon its life would bleed out. It took a while. We'd made a ruckus, but no one called the cops in this neighborhood. As the three of us survivors sat quietly, waiting for the wendigo to evaporate into dead mist, a shouting match (in Spanish) broke out between a male and female voice.

We would sneak out of here soon, and go back to our normal lives. The management would find a trashed hotel room, but no bodies.

Finally, the Wendy was gone. A few scraps of clothes, bunched up duck tape, and an empty burlap sack were all that remained of it—and our departed friends.

We cleaned up and left.

If it had happened differently, there would have been a locked-room mystery.

It could have gone like this: If everyone was eaten except me, and I succeeded in killing the Wendy, and died of wounds after killing it, they would have found my single dead body, evidence of a struggle, but a room sealed from the inside, with no possibility of escape.

Every locked-room mystery that ever really happened, happened like that.

The stories had to make up some convoluted tale of icicle daggers and false compartments or hidden rooms and odorless poisons. They also had to provide characterization. Sorry I wasn't able to give you a sense of mine. But goddamn it, if I twist my ankle stepping off a curb, I'll have to limp into the office the next morning, because I've run out of sick days taking care of these creatures. For you. And if you don't have enough of a sense of me as a heroic, sympathetic character, then fuck y'all. Will *you* volunteer to kill Wendy?

Published in Galaxy's Edge Issue 5
Copyright © 2013 by Eric Cline. All rights reserved.

Neep

by K. C. Norton

E ver since Mads carved me, he has spoken of the day when he will make me his. Today is no exception.

"Your skin will part like apple-flesh," he tells me, "and the meat beneath is white. Did you know that, Pluto? That inside, you are as white as I?" His fingers trace the slope of my cheek up to my scalp and into the stalks of my hair. He tugs—I am sure he thinks he is being gentle, but Mads is never gentle—and it takes everything I have not to react.

Like most humans, Mads does not believe we can feel pain, and I have never set him straight. If he does not know that he can hurt me, he will not bother to try. So I keep my face blank as I polish his second-best pair of shoes and say only, "So you have told me, Gartner Poulson." When he caresses me, I dare not use his given name.

"You're a good neep," he tells me.

But that is the problem—I am no longer a neep. I am nearly full-grown, and when I begin to flower I will be diced and shaved and julienned in the name of Mads Poulson's hunger.

His hand, where it rests against my skin, is smooth and soft. Beneath a stranger's touch, I would seem to be the rough one. But skin deceives.

✧ ✧ ✧

It pleases Mads to think of me as a woman—though of course I am no such thing—because his hunger for me has the same shape as all other human hungers.

When the light finally begins to fade from the sky, I am permitted to sit behind the old house, on the weathered steps half worn-through with rot, and speak with Sissel Peals, so long as it does not disrupt her work. Sissel considers herself a *her*, most likely because she has seeded several neeps of her own.

"You're not well," says Sissel, laundering Mads' shirts. Her hands are leathery and polyped from so much time spent in the water.

"Well enough," I say. From the folds of my tunic, I withdraw my secret stash of cigarettes. I must be very careful where and when I smoke, in case Mads should smell it and catch me out, but he never intrudes on the laundry washing. It disgusts him to think that he needs washing-after. When Sissel sees the carton, her lips become pruney, but she does not scold.

"There is news in town today," she says instead. "We have a visitor."

"A visitor." I light a match, one of only four I have left, just as dangerous and just as secret as the cigarettes themselves. "That does not pass for news."

"Ah, but she is special." Sissel wrings a shirt dry and hangs it on the line. "Her performances are spectacular. And she is very pretty; they all say so."

Who cares about pretty women? I hope she starves to death. I hope they all starve to death, and then sink rot-deep within the soil, that we may feed on them.

I take a deep drag on the cigarette and hold the smoke within my fibers for as long as I can, so that the tar and nicotine have every opportunity to render me carcinogenic. So that when he cuts me open, Mads' stomach will roil at what his knife reveals: my flesh, not opaline, but yellow-black.

"Tell Gartner Poulson," Sissel insists. "Maybe he'll bring you to town, to meet her, before she leaves." She hangs the last shirt and shakes her hands dry.

"What fun that would be," I tell her, in just the tone of voice that should make clear my feelings on the subject.

"Tuber of Many Roots," Sissel mutters, "such a sour neep I never met. Gartner Poulson will make himself sick on you."

Very good. Let him.

When the sky has lost its blueness and is freckled with silver stars, I rub out the last ashes of my secret cigarette and head back into the house.

As much as it would please me to snub Mads, I do not dare. I find him in in his study, writing a lengthy letter to the head office in Copenhagen, telling them that the salt mine is nearly used up. They will tell him the same thing that they always tell him—keep trying, send what you find, write again next month—and things will go on as they always have. The mine has always been falling apart, and the head office has always sent him dry form letters with no useful advice or meaningful dispatches.

"Good night, Mads," I say, letting my fingertips trail across his shoulders. He likes being called Mads when he is working, because it makes him feel at home. I know all his likes and dislikes; after all, he carved me.

He nods, but does not look up at me, does not even pause in the writing of his letter. So I am left in peace to head to the root cellar.

Only twelve steps separate the cellar from the rest of the house, but they lead to another world. Even out in the open air, I am never really myself. My people, from neep to turnip, are a people made for dwelling underground.

I step past cook's plot to mine. The field workers do not sleep inside, and cook both retires and rises earlier than I. My plot is against the wall, where I can hear the occasional blast of dynamite more clearly than the Gartner's movements about the house. I take off my tunic and hang it on its nail, to keep it out of the soil. The Gartner, like all his people, believes that dirt is shameful. I hide my cigarettes and my matches behind a loose board; if they are tainted with insulation or asbestos, so much the better. At last, naked, I slip into my plot.

It is so peaceful underground. I stretch out all my fingers and toes into the soil—even though it is flavored with punctured veins of salt—and relax. I let the damp earth feed me. I try to remember what it was like, before Mads Poulson dragged me up into the air and carved me a face.

He didn't create me, no matter what he likes to think. He only changed me, and that's poor magic.

I am drifting, my thoughts freed from my body, when it strikes me: if people pay their money to see this actress, the woman Sissel spoke of, then she must indeed be beautiful. And if they think she is beautiful, maybe Mads will think she is beautiful. And if Mads thinks she is beautiful, maybe he will hunger for her and not for me.

And he will forget about me.

And I will escape.

And so, I must cause him to meet this woman. It must happen soon, before I begin to flower.

For the hot meal, cook serves Mads liver paste and smoked cod alongside two thick slices of rye bread and a pile of roast baby potatoes.

I sit at table with him, but only to watch. I do not eat the same way he does. Still, he prefers my company. He likes my eyes on him; he likes to see my expression when his white teeth cut into those golden baby tubers, their brown skin crackling. Their butter smell seeps into my leaves. I don't mind the suffering of the cow, or even of the fish—but each time he spears a potato, I feel as though my own flesh is speared, as if my own fibers are being ground to pulp between his molars.

He swallows, and I see his Adam's apple bob as the potato slides down his throat and is lost. "You are quiet today, Pluto."

"Sissel says there is a woman in town." The words bubble out of me like a spring flood. "Everybody is talking about her."

Mads raises his eyebrows and takes a bite of liver paste on rye bread.

"She is an actress," I tell him.

"In plays? Or pictures?"

"I do not know, Gartner," I admit. "But they say she is very beautiful."

"Beautiful," he says. "Well."

"I would very much like to see her," I say.

The bread stops before it reaches his mouth, which hangs open, forgotten.

This is a bold thing to say; I have never said I would like anything before—we are not supposed to want things besides what they tell us to want, or what they shape us to want.

He will think that if I want to meet her, he must also want to meet her. Oh, there are so many truths that humans do not know about the things they make.

He returns the bread to his plate. "How long will she be here?"

I say, "Not very."

"Well, if it will please you"—his eyes roam over my leafy head—"then we will go." His meaning is clear: yes, we will go, because I might as well be happy in the time I have left. He is still the Gartner, and I the neep. To drive this home, he spears the largest potato and bites it in two.

I flinch away. He tells me that other roots, so long as they have not been carved, do not feel pain. But how would he know?

"How much longer will the actress be here?" I ask Sissel.

"Tomorrow is her last performance," she says. "All the finest Gartners will turn out for it. You are interested in her now?"

I nod, flicking the ash away from the end of my cigarette. "Gartner Poulson has promised to take me. What kind of actress is she?"

Sissel flaps her hand before her face. "What a question, Pluto!" She tucks her apron across her grinning mouth, and the purple-red of her cheeks is just close enough to the color of a scandalized human's that I cannot help but grin too. "She is, of course, a *lady*!" But after a moment her merriment fades, and she pats her apron back into place. "They say she is not like other women. They say her skin is as dark as soil beneath the earth."

"Impossible," I say. I puff. And I think of Mads telling me that my skin, in secret, is as white as his. "Have you ever seen a woman like that?"

Sissel frowns. "No—not a beautiful one. The Gartners do not care for soil."

I do not want a woman whom the master will not find beautiful. That will do me no good at all. "Let's hope it isn't true, then," I say. "I would not want to go into town only to find an ugly woman."

"Nor would anyone," Sissel agrees.

When Sissel is gone, and my second-from-final cigarette is burning low, I feel a tingle on my scalp so sharp that I reach for it before I even register what I'm doing. At first my fingers find only the ordinary wrinkles and the thick squarish stems of hair that I am accustomed to. But then, in between them, I feel a little knot, a tightly curled lump.

Ugh, I think, *a beetle*. I tear it loose.

The pain is instant and excruciating. To keep from crying out, I must stuff my fist into my mouth and bite down, and for all that my teeth are no more than square crenelations, even that is painful.

The knot, no beetle but instead a tight-wound bulb of leafy green, glistens wetly in my hand. It shows no yellow yet, but I know what lies within. It is a flower. A turnip flower. Part of me.

I throw it with all the strength I can muster, and it arcs through the air and falls into an unremarkable patch of brittle, salinated grass.

When I bid Mads good-night, I pray that he does not notice the sappy fluid leaking from between my leaves. For once the Tuber of Many Roots answers my prayers, and I am permitted to retire to the cellar in peace.

Even a full night beneath the ground does not revive me, and when I rise from my plot groggy and tender, I feel a sour ache all through my body. I know what Sissel would say—that my attitude has seeped into my flesh—but Sissel is not the one who fears my death. She would hardly be put out if the Gartner found my unripe bud abandoned in the withered grass, but I ...

Mads finds me mending the lining of his best jacket; not his second best, the blue one which he wears to church, but the black one that he prefers for business.

"You want to see me looking fine?" he asks, following the curve of my broad leaves with his fat maggot fingers.

"If the actress is so fine to look at," I say, "won't you want to look even finer?"

He pats my shoulder. "Pluto, you clever girl. You know me better than I know myself."

I, of course, will wear my tunic. It is the only article of clothing that I own.

All day, Mads laughs at my preparations—but all that means to me is that my Gartner is in a good mood, and that when the time comes for me to button him into his jacket, he lets me do so with hardly a word of protest.

"You look so handsome," I tell him. He checks his reflection in the hall mirror to make sure that I am right.

The only thing Mads must do for himself is hitch the horse to the open buggy. We could perhaps be trusted with a horse, but horses cannot be trusted with us; it is as though they do not believe we are alive, and many turnips have been killed by horses, who bite at us indiscriminately, or tear into our greens and cause us to die of shock.

The horse is in a foul mood today. He yanks his bridle from Mads' grip, and screams his displeasure when Mads catches hold again. I am afraid Mads will think him not worth the trouble, so I jump out of the buggy to help.

At once the horse lunges for me, snapping his terrible teeth at my greens, and only when I lift my hand to stay him does he finally calm.

"That's better," says Mads, puzzled, as the horse settles and chomps at his bit.

What Mads does not see is my hand, now missing a finger, or the moment when the horse accepts it from me. I fear that he would kill the horse for daring to taste me before Mads himself has had the chance, so I return to the buggy, fold my hands in my lap, and do not let my feelings show on my face. It hurts less to lose one small finger than to lose my first bud, anyway.

We pass most of the ride in silence.

I have only been to town twice before. It is its own little world made of bricks, some of which have been plastered over and painted yellow; the whole place is the color of fire, like the ends of my matchsticks. We leave the horse and buggy with Sissel Peals' Gartner, a round man who cannot afford to eat his turnips, and Mads hands him a few *kroner* in exchange. He is very careful not to touch the man's grubby hand.

It is not hard to guess where our visitor will be found. There is a cart set up in the main square, with dozens of steps folded out in all directions: a traveling theater. Perhaps a hundred Gartners, male and female, sit in folding chairs laid out around the plaza, their neeps standing at their sides. All the Gartners are enfolded in their finest clothes, and Mads puffs himself up when he sees them.

One woman at the far left of the crowd, dressed in vibrant red and richest black, dips her head toward my Gartner and points her neep in our direction. The neep approaches us, face downturned with respect. I think it is called Mikkel, but I cannot recall if it styles itself male or female.

"Greetings, Herre Poulson," says the neep, bowing deeply. "My Gartner, Frue Holm, invites you to sit with her."

We follow neep Mikkel back to its mistress. Gartner Holm smiles at my master, but it is a cold smile; they are so like each other.

"What a pleasant afternoon this will be," says Gartner Holm in her mountain-peak voice. She offers Mads her hand, and he kisses it. I hide my own disfigured hand in my tunic pocket, feeling at the edges of my cigarette carton.

The crowd chatters mildly, each and every Gartner being sure to look spectacularly unimpressed. We neeps keep our heads turned down. Still, my eyes sneak toward the stage.

At first all I am aware of is a feeling. A rumble, which might as well be coming from the salt mine. But the rumbling gets louder, and deeper, until I am sure that it is a drum. One by one the Gartners' sentences trail off and their faces turn toward the traveling theater.

With a last furious rumble, the drum player leaps out from the cart and lands on the top step of the folding stage, arms upraised. He is dressed as a monster—I do not know what kind of monster, for it is too big to be a horse, but it is beautiful. Its whole body is redder than any brick in the town, and its huge silvery eyes flash our reflections back at us as the man inside the costume turns his head. Is he a lizard? Or a tremendous bird?

I have no time to decide; the next moment, the man is back to drumming, and the bright colors of his costume flash metallic in the sun. The whole square is silent, except for that drumming, which rattles my fibers until I feel as though I have a human heart beating in my chest.

And then the drumming stops again. And She appears.

Every human in the crowd gasps, and I hear Mikkel's yip of surprise. The woman that pops up from the cart is like no woman I have ever seen. Is she beautiful? Her flesh is dark, just like Sissel said, dark as soil that has never seen the sun. But she *gleams*, she *glows* with something that I have never seen before, not in a Gartner, not in a neep. She is convinced of herself. Her features are not small and delicate like mine, and I am the one Mads created to be beautiful— but this woman, the actress, is nothing like me, and yet she smiles as widely as if the difference between us does not matter.

And she is dressed as a neep in blossom.

As the drum starts again, she begins to dance. That too is unfamiliar—she moves too freely, without the sneering reservation of the Gartners, and her wild gestures send the papier-mâché leaves and the silk flowers bobbing, as if they are an extension of her own body. I have never moved like that.

I am more like her than I have ever been like Mads.

As she dances, the monster that is the drummer begins to circle her, his costume flashing. The light has not changed; it is still midafternoon, with the low weak sunlight of our springtime sloping across the rooftops, and yet the sun seems to have focused all its strength on that little stage so that it is lit from within, while the rest of the world is overdrawn in shadow.

"A trick of mirrors," mumbles Mads.

I do not look at him. I do not look at him again until the dance is done, and the drummer circles toward the actress in her purple-blue neep costume, and spits a gout of paper-ribbon fire at her, and she collapses across the steps. The papier-mâché leaves ignite with real flame.

"What a spectacle," says Frue Holm, but even she claps. All the humans clap, because at least the wild neep has met a fitting end: roasted by flame, as all turnips must be in time.

We neeps applaud as well, though more softly. We, too, have seen something that seems right and true—and we have learned from it, though it is not, I think, the lesson the Gartners would have us learn.

There is no hope now of Mads falling for the actress. This does not trouble me as much as I would have expected. The main fact, which had not occurred to me before, is that no wild thing like her could stand to have a man like Mads yapping at her heels. So I am left with only my Gartner, who sits impatiently while the drummer and the actress take their bows, nods to Frue Holm, and leaves the performers to pack up their stage. He does not leave a single *krone* for their trouble.

"What strange nonsense," he mutters.

I follow him, my scheme in tatters. Now I am less prepared than ever to become Mads' supper.

All through the ride home, I run my roots across the stump where my finger once was, and I consider. How to be rid of Mads Poulson? How to transform myself into a wild neep like the one I saw on stage?

That night, I smoke my last secret cigarette. And it does not escape me, as the smolder eats away at the paper tube, that my cigarettes are gone—but that one match remains.

All the next day, Mads avoids me. He has got a letter from the head office in Copenhagen, and has locked himself in the study with it. Sometimes these letters make him swear, but today I hear nothing.

All day, I play with my match.

Mads does not even come to his hot meal, which is strange. What is stranger still is that cook does not come out to serve it. I can hear cook moving about in the kitchen, but there is another sound in there too, like a squeezed mouse. This does not make sense to me, and I make sure to stay away.

Late in the afternoon, I see a plume of grey smoke rise over the salt mine. I sit out on the steps, playing with my match, and watch it absently.

I feel as if a storm is coming. I get the same feeling before a big rain: like the soil is twisted up in anticipation. Only this time it is me twisted up.

Sissel Peals arrives before the sun fully sets, and when she sees me she rushes toward me and catches me up in her arms. "Oh, Pluto!" she wails. "Oh! You are still with us!" And in between her cries she makes that squeezed-mouse sound like cook has been making all day.

"Where else would I be?" I ask. Surely she cannot know about my bud.

She pushes me back to arm's length and shakes me. "Idiot neep, where is Gartner Poulson?"

"In his office," I say, but the plume of smoke catches my eye and every fiber of my body ignites. "Isn't he?"

Sissel shakes her head, pointing toward the smoke. "The mine," she says. "The mine is finished. Gartner Poulson has been called back to Copenhagen."

I turn slowly on the spot, refusing to believe and also certain that what she says is true. Mads is done with the mine, and that fire, all that smoke, is what remains of the neeps and turnips who worked there, and have no purpose now that it is to be closed. They are not valuable enough to the company to warrant transport back to the city.

I am not valuable enough to Mads, either. To spare himself the expense of my train ticket, he will roast me too, flowers or no.

"Get out of here," I hiss at Sissel. "You never saw me."

She shrinks away from me—neeps are not supposed to be full of wrath and fire, but when that actress pretended to roast, it was as though all that heat flowed through her and into me.

I am not Gartner Poulson's creation. He only changed me, and I can change myself back.

There is nothing worth stealing from the house. There is no such thing as a wild neep, not really, and stealing a hundred *kroner* would do me little good; no human would take it from me, and money is no use beneath the soil.

So I decide to burn it down.

My fingers tremble with the matchbox, and at first it fails to strike. The sulfur scrapes against the strip, leaving a grey streak. The second strike fares the same.

But the third time, the match flares, and I drop it hurriedly to the small pile of paper made from shreds of the letter that doomed our mine, and I wave my hand over it to create a draft.

Turnips are not friends of fire; I have lit a cigarette, but never a house. The paper burns and chars the wood floor, but my flame dies before taking the building with it.

I scream and batter the floor with my fists until white pulp shows through my purple skin. I would keep pounding forever, until either my body or the house gave way, but Mads stamps through the doorway and hauls me to my feet.

"No more of that," he snarls at me. "You're mine to keep. Mine to eat. Mine to destroy."

I struggle against him, but he is strong, and my fists are battered all to mush. In the end, he simply lifts me off the floor and carries me to the kitchen.

Cook whimpers while she prepares me, no doubt because she knows she will be next.

"At least you're worth eating, Pluto," she tells me while when she cuts my leaves away. The miners and cook are no good for eating. They will be roasted to ash and left in the open air. At least the one who made me will have his satisfaction of me before all this is done.

What bitter consolation.

Nothing hurts as much, or will ever hurt as much, as when I tore my bud away. Still, it is not pleasant to feel cook's cold knife slide into me and gouge out the bruised and rotten parts. Only my best pieces will be saved for Mads.

It is not Mads' habit to see his meals prepared, but he was the one that took the knife to me to bring me to life, and now he watches with no small satisfaction as that life is taken away. To my chagrin, the knife reveals flesh that is whiter yet than his; I have not made myself poisonous to him. I have failed.

Cook is good with her spices, but Mads stays her hand when she reaches for the shallots.

"As few ingredients as possible," says Mads, looking into my eyes. "I want to taste Pluto."

Tuber of Many Roots, I hate him. I wall myself off and think only of the actress in her role as the wild neep; I see the rhythm of her leaves and the roll of her blossoms even as cook adds salt and butter to the pan, even as she dices me into bite-size pieces. She saves my face for last, for she is a kind soul. In my final moments, I bless her.

I cannot say I remember the oven but for its heat. I am largely numb by then.

And I cannot say I remember the eating, for I am all in pieces; one bite comes in my arm, one in my shoulder, one in my thigh, one in my neck. He does not eat me in order. I have no order left.

In the darkness of his stomach, though, I feel a change. He is warmer than the soil of the earth, and damper, but damp and darkness are my elements. Within him, I begin to come together again.

I am too good to waste a single bite. When Mads retires at last, full to bursting with me—and lies down in his above-ground bed, and pulls the blankets over him in a way that feels familiar to me, although cotton is no comfort like earth is—I wake up. True, I am not myself anymore, but I have grown to this, to changing and to being changed. This is nothing more than another transformation.

Within the world that is Mads Poulson, I roil. I turn sour, just like Sissel promised. And just as Mads promised, I begin to bloom.

I have held back my flowers for so long that calling them forth is no great feat—they burst out of me, stretching and reaching for sunlight, the only part of me that has ever longed for open air. Mads sits up in his bed, clutching at his throat, coughing and choking and clawing at the skin until it bleeds. I want out, and when my yellow blooms force their way up he cannot continue to breathe.

Late next afternoon, cook and Sissel find him. His mouth and nose, his ears and eye sockets, are plugged with yellow blossoms.

Sissel Peals is a very wise turnip. With great effort but no complaint, she drags the bloated remains of Mads to the root cellar and tucks him into my old plot. With the aid of a spare brick, cook knocks a hole in the boards so that the sun can get in. They leave us there to germinate and to find some peace.

From time to time, a little breeze whips in the hole, and the flowers dance as freely as those of a wild neep might. And Mads Poulson feeds me all the while.

Published in Galaxy's Edge Issue 10

Effect and Cause

by Ken Liu

.ssengnihton, neht dnA

Flash white blinding a.

"Brace for impact," says the computer.

The superheated air cools. Out of the white light, things emerge: the instrument panels; myself in the chair, clutching the handholds; the jagged edges of the cockpit wall knit themselves into a pristine whole.

"T minus one. Shields breached."

Through the porthole, I see a silvery fishlike shape depart. Already, it's kilometers away.

"T minus ten."

The silver light winks out at the edge of visibility like a dying star.

Dashing about the cockpit, I frantically punch lit up buttons to make them go dim. The anxiety subsides.

I run backwards out of the cockpit until I end up in the galley.

The klaxon goes off.

"Incoming: theta six-one, phi one-four-eight, distance six-five-five, velocity one-oh-seven."

Ignoring this, I sit down at the table and pick up a cup to spit scalding hot coffee into it. Then I proceed to vomit food onto my plate so I can sculpt it with a knife and fork into peas, carrots, an omelette.

A shiver, and my thoughts flow forward again.

"What … happened?" I ask.

"Unknown." The computer pauses. "System clock is out of sync with sidereal observations."

"It's like someone just took his finger off the REWIND button." I set down the cup of coffee that had just come out of me, nauseated. "We were dead."

"Affirmative." The computer hesitates. "And impossible."

"An Azazin ship," I say.

We know almost nothing about the Azazin save that they've made repeated incursions into this region of Union space. My one-man sentry ship is our first line of defense.

"They seem to believe in preemptive attacks," I say.

"Hypothesis: we hit a temporal anomaly that briefly reversed the flow of time," the computer says.

"I'm going to return fire."

"But if time has been reversed, our attack now would be unprovoked."

I shrug. "The military lawyers can sort out causality later."

From the trajectory of the projectile that hit me, it's easy to calculate the location of the stealth Azazin ship.

"Subphotonic missile ready."

The *click* from the big red button is satisfying.

I press up against the porthole. Watching flickering numbers on a screen is never as good as the actual explosion.

"T minus ten."

The passing seconds seem to slow down.

"T minus zero."

But there is no dazzling flare, no new star in the sky.

".orez sunim T"

The arrow of time.

... The missile reverses its course, now flying backwards, retracing its arc back to the launch tube...

... I rush around the cockpit, frantically pushing buttons ...

The galley. Spitting coffee. Someone takes his finger off the REWIND button.

We've been through it dozens of times. Sometimes I shoot at them; sometimes they shoot at me. But always, we end up back here, fifteen minutes earlier.

"They can temporarily reverse the local flow of time in a bubble for up to fifteen minutes," the computer says. "Perhaps it's even triggered automatically when their ship is destroyed."

"I think the time-reverser is designed to allow those in its field, including the Azazin, to keep their thoughts and experiences," I say, finally understanding. "They're repeating the experiment to gather intel on our tactical responses, like running rats through a maze."

Ignoring the computer's vociferous objections, I engage the manual override targeting system.

I press the big red button; the *click* is satisfying.

The faint trail of the missile approaches the spot in space where I know the Azazin ship is hiding.

"T minus ten."

So close—

My heart is in my throat.

—nothing.

"A miss. Closest approach to target: fifty meters." There's a faint trace of *I-told-you-so* in the computer's voice.

Time continues to flow forward. The Azazin were able to tell that I was going to miss, and they didn't bother to reverse time for my useless attack.

No choice now. "Set a collision course. Full speed ahead."

"They will simply rever—"

"DO IT!"

We dive towards the invisible target, the oldest, most desperate tactic known to man. But, perhaps, they cannot believe that I will actually go through with it.

.ssengnihton, neht dnA

Flash white blinding a.

The ship zooms backwards, in front of me a dark, looming bulk that quickly fades against the stars.

And then the finger is off the REWIND button. It's fifteen minutes earlier.

"A miss—"

Before the computer can finish, I punch a small black button: my jury-rigged secret. It sends a signal that shuts off the antimatter containment field in the subphotonic missile's warhead.

A dazzling flare, and then the most beautiful sight in the universe: the spinning, glowing vortex of a matter-antimatter annihilation explosion.

"Well done," says the computer.

I gambled that the Azazin time reverser could not be triggered twice in quick succession. The missile was meant to come close, but miss. My suicide collision course was calculated to take exactly fifteen minutes. When the Azazin reversed time's arrow, they brought the missile back to its point of closest approach. Effect became cause.

"Thinking backwards hurts," I say, as we continue to watch the spinning vortex.

Published in Galaxy's Edge Issue 2

Ghost in the Machine

by Ralph Roberts

M arcus Teague sat hunched over in the cramped confines of the 16-gigabyte USB thumb drive. The muscles on his mighty arms rippled as he cleaned his wizard's sword, running the polishing spell up and down the blade with precision. It might be all virtual, but he was buff with bulging biceps, a mighty chest, a narrow waist, bronzed skin, ready for *any* battle. The sleeveless T-shirt with its mystical symbols in hex and octal, and the Microsoft and Ubuntu certification badges, emphasized that.

"Looks like Bill could spring for a bigger ready room," he said, "maybe a 64-gig thumb drive or, better, a 120-gig solid state drive, huh?"

He looked up when Oscar did not answer.

The old man didn't look good—battered and bruised, moaning whenever he moved, flat on his back, exhausted. Troubleshooting hardware took it out of you. Blown power supplies, crashed hard drives, loose cables, and all those intermittent ills that kept Oscar in dark old machines for hours when no telling what was going to jump him.

When time permitted, Marcus went along to watch his friend's back. Besides, he enjoyed chopping up fanged viruses, stomping malware data-mining dwarves, tearing apart virus ogres, erasing script dragons, and all the rest of it. Bring on those Trojans in their virtual Greek armor. They were no match for the wiz!

Marcus shook his head. Oscar had insisted on keeping the same physique—he was the same old man now as the virtual-reality-helmet-wearing body laying currently on the broken-down couch in the littered backroom of Billal's Computer Repair. Billal's was maybe the most unprofitable computer shop in Chicago—but it had two things no other shop anywhere in the world had: it had him and Oscar. It also had Bill, who tried hard but was the most incompetent shop manager possible, and the shadowy, probably criminal partner, Al—who had bankrolled the place but was never around much. Well, scratch that last; Al hung out in the shop a lot more of late.

With some grunting, Oscar managed to roll over a little and looked at Marcus.

"Bill can't afford it. Shop's losing money, which suits that sleaze-bag Al just fine. He wants the secret of how we do this."

Marcus shrugged and went back to working on his sword. He just wanted to do his job. He liked it, even if minimum wage was all they got. He'd made all this work after Bill invented the concept. Coded it, debugged it, and was the first to try it. This was *his* baby! He'd given it birth—*virtual computer repair*. And, yes, he knew Al—who had to be connected to organized crime—was hot after this technology. That's why the gangster dribbled out only enough funds to keep the shop doors open.

"Marcus, what do you want out of life?" Oscar said.

Marcus thought about it and shrugged. "Enough money for me to upgrade my hardware at home and to find true love—in whichever order, but I want a 24-core CPU soon."

Oscar painfully laid flat again. "You won't get them things here."

A tone beeped and a work order with an IP address popped up on a tiny virtual screen.

"For me?" Oscar asked, his voice weary.

"Nope, it's for me—some guy's computer's running slow and probably full of nasty little beasts." He smiled enthusiastically, gave his sword one more pass with the polishing spell, and sheathed it. Grinning, he hoisted his backpack of diagnostic spells and the like.

Oscar gave him a disgusted look. "Don't enjoy it too much, and be *careful*. Something weirder than usual is going on out there."

Marcus carefully moved to the hatch. "You get a call, let me know where, Oscar, and don't hesitate to use that emergency abort utility I wrote for us. The red button: take it out, flip off the safety cover, press ABORT."

Oscar shook his head. "*No*, not that. You said yourself you weren't sure it would work. No telling what would happen to our real bodies. You said that."

Marcus shrugged. "Last resort, guy. Just don't get killed. That would mess up your real body even more. At least take some of those routines I built from the data in the Shaolin temple's computer."

Oscar shook his head despondently. "Haven't got the energy to use them, Marcus."

Worrying about his friend, Marcus flowed into the USB port that led to the shop's dinky server. A hand reached out to help him get to his feet. It was Beep, the USB driver.

"Thanks, Beep."

Beep.

"You have a good day, too, buddy."

The server itself was an old quad-core clunker he'd gotten off eBay for $50, for which Bill still owed him. But it had some memory, the latest version of Ubuntu, and gave him space to write and develop his spells and scripts. He always had been good at coding.

One-handed, Marcus air-typed up a large virtual screen with webcam, then smiled at his image. A mixture of Conan the Barbarian and King Arthur's Merlin the Magician—he could swing a sword or wave a wand with the best of them. Blond, blue-eyed, well-developed muscles—not a bit like his concave-chested, bespectacled, short, geeky body recumbent out there in the backroom.

A real chick magnet! Unfortunately, all the women who might be impressed were out there in the real world. He waved the screen away and headed for the cable modem port—no fast fiber optic or wireless connection for this cheap shop. Uploading was a pain. Slow!

He nodded to bits of software he passed; in this computer he knew them all and they trusted him. A bunch of little memory monkeys ran by carrying bits of this and bytes of that to here and there, ones and zeros flashing in their beady little eyes. "Hi, Marcus, hi Marcus," they chanted.

Passing the power supply, he patted one of the cables. Sparks playfully tickled his fingers. As a small boy he'd been fascinated with electricity and quickly made friends with it. That friendship often paid off in his current job. Whoa! *Current* job? He laughed.

Squeezing into the cable modem, he slowly climbed to the nearest intersection with one of Chicago's fiber optic backbones. This was the problem using just a regular cable connection. Fast download, yes, but slow upload. Servers needed a way to push data out quickly as well as pull it in.

Marcus broke out of the slow upload—like swimming through molasses—and stepped out on the crowded platform. All sorts of things shuffled around, waiting on the next train of data packets—email messages, SQL commands off to visit some database and retrieve info, lots of web URL queries, always rushing about to keep their human surfers sated.

He sensed the attack even before the monstrous Python script reared its ugly head over the railing at the back of the platform. He dived and rolled as a blast of red-hot electrons struck the spot where he had been.

He laid a *more* spell on it and didn't see anything to worry him in its code, so no use being nice. Marcus air-typed *rm dragon*. His erase code killed the process, wiped the Python file, and the fearsome towering head and body *poofed* into nothingness. At least he hoped it had. Erasing computer files was not always permanent. He was okay, but the attack had left behind a good deal of destruction. Its deadly breath, missing him, had killed a number of innocent pieces of software going about their legitimate duties.

Marcus knelt next to a whimpering, frightened jpeg—an image of a beautiful baby being sent by its proud mother to the baby's grandmother. Now that image would never arrive, fading away as he held it in his arms.

Sadly he stood, watching the surviving data constructs rush around in panic. This was just *wrong*! An attempt on him had destroyed good data, useful utilities and other programs—something very much against his principles. It was all a waste.

The attacking script had been crude but powerful. Someone or something out there was ruthless in its hatred of him. Well, *he* would see about that! He would make it his mission to hunt down this killer!

The train of data packet cars whizzed to a stop and all the data and snippets of code hurried to get on before another dragon could come along.

Marcus started to enter a car and a wall of stench hit his virtual nose. *Spam!* Of all things in the Internet universe he hated spam the most, spam and the evil humans who caused it to spew like so much sewage from their computers.

This packet was crammed to the ceiling with the slimy, stinky stuff. *All spam must die!* He donated them a couple of filter bombs from his backpack, ducking as tons of fragments blew through the packet's sides and more or less neatly landed in bit bins on the platform.

Satisfied, he moved to the next packet, boarded, and took a seat.

He called up a screen and scrolled the work order. *Hmmm … An* anonymous IP address—not usual, and it cost extra. Spammers, hackers, and other evil humans, they liked to have anonymous IPs. He had a bad feeling about this.

A tall black gentleman in a three-piece suit slid into the seat next to Marcus. He held out a check for four million dollars, smiling broadly.

Marcus tapped the certification patches on his T-shirt. "No phishing around here."

The software's eyes widened and he jumped up, motioning several of his kind to turn back. "Copper! Run! It's John Law!" he yelled in a Nigerian accent.

Several pieces of legitimate email nodded their thanks to Marcus. Phishing gave them all a bad name—almost as much as spam did.

A stream of porn oozed into the car. Marcus pointed to the next packet and they left. Porn was pretty mindless stuff, but it knew when the wiz was around.

Speaking of such stuff, Marcus turned around in his seat looking for Gwen. He had not seen her in a week or more. Gwen did some racy stuff, but she was a real woman and far from mindless. Some men paid a lot for interaction. She was the only other virtual human he'd seen down here besides himself and Oscar. They'd had some great conversations, riding together. He knew she hated what she had to do for a living. Certainly she didn't want her only family—her brother, who was an attorney with a big firm downtown—ever finding out.

Gwen's virtual body was as voluptuous as his was buff. She'd confided that her real body was a female geek, flat, not curvy. She even had a computer science degree and loved to code, but couldn't find a programming gig so was reduced to this—her face showed her disgust—"job." And she told him about her server—she also favored Ubuntu as her Linux of choice—and mentioned how she had backup virtual reality software on it. Even told him her real name, Gwendolyn Louise Baker.

Wow! Beautiful, *and* she knew computers and Linux, too? What … a … woman!

Marcus surprised himself by hugging her on their last ride. He didn't do well with girls, not nearly confident enough usually to initiate affection. What's more, she'd returned the hug! That was the last time he'd seen her.

He landed after his wireless jump from the platform via a 40mb up-and-down connection at the IP address on his work order. It was a very fancy and powerful Internet connection with tons of bandwidth, but the port into the computer was foreboding—dark inside with a blackened ring around the port where a firewall had once flamed. No telling what had wandered in there. All the place needed was a sign: THIS IS A TRAP, DUFUS. COME RIGHT IN.

He pulled out his wand with his right hand and waved a work light sphere into existence with the other. With the bright light preceding him, Marcus confidently walked into the machine.

The first software he saw was a keyboard driver.

"Hey, guy, what computer is this?" he asked.

"CLACK, CLACK, CLACKITY, CLACK … busy … CLACK CLACK," the driver said. "Master types commands to kill you. CLACK CLACK *CLACKITY!*"

A sudden *whoosh* and a wall of heat caused Marcus to whirl around. A white hot firewall now closed the exit port. He gestured at it to re-open a port—*any* port would do right now—but nothing happened.

The pounding of heavy boots caused him to spin again, this time to see heavily-armed and armored gigantic troll-like virus fighters bearing down on him waving swords, battle axes, and rifles with wicked-looking bayonets as long as the rifles.

"Gotta scoot, dude," the keyboard driver said, rushing off, CLACK-ing rapidly again.

Marcus groaned. These were no friendly McAfees or Nortons—rule-abiding, virus-squashing officers. No, *these* guys were coded on steroids. Mean, nasty, powerful! No *rm* spell would even scratch them.

He waved his wand and his most powerful *debug* spell sizzled out and hit the first troll. No effect. It *should* have slowed the monster down to a crawl and revealed its internal workings. After that, just tear out statements and variables and it was over. No problem, except, *nothing* happened.

He unlimbered his sword. Have to do this the old-fashioned way. Chop them into separate subroutines that would fizzle into oblivion.

The keyboard driver had returned, slipped to the back of the pack. There was rapid CLACKing and as the leading four trolls rushed him, their armor got thicker! Some human programmer was working real-time against him!

But the thicker armor added weight and the trolls' reactions were sluggish now as they struggled in slow motion to ram their bayonets through Marcus. Whoever this programmer might be, he was not very good.

Marcus chopped at the trolls with his sword. It wasn't easy, but big chunks were falling off.

CLACK, CLACK, CLACKITY, CLACK!

The programmer was fast on the uptake. The armor on all the trolls slimmed down and they duplicated until the memory around him was full of angry, hungry trolls with fast reflexes and anxious to taste his virtual blood.

However, their very numbers hampered getting at him and the computer's CPU was grinding down under the load. Suddenly the trolls were slow again, and so was the human programmer as he continued to duplicate them, adding yet more load.

Marcus chopped a few of them to bits, but he could sense the CPU wavering and—although his virtual body's code, written by him, was markedly more efficient, he felt like he was fighting in mush now. He didn't want to be here when the computer crashed, like in the next few milliseconds. Hell of a way to die for someone as good at coding as him—embarrassingly so, even.

He switched his sword to his left hand, parried a bayonet thrust while pulling the abort button from his pocket, flipping the safety cover off with his thumb. Holding his breath, he pressed it. *Click!*

Marcus rolled through an open port on the old server in the shop's backroom, expanding to full size, and gracefully springing to his feet. He sheathed his sword and—

Bill—in his fifties, rotund, and bald as the proverbial billiard ball—was coming in holding a cup of coffee. He dropped both the cup and his jaw. The cup shattered, the brown fluid from it staining the ancient, already-discolored linoleum, but neither Marcus nor Bill noticed that.

"You're … you're …" Bill said with several gasps.

Marcus was running his hands over his body. He *was* the steel-muscled, bronzed hero like his virtual self … except … it was now *real*!

He spun and looked at the ratty couch where his pencil-necked geek real-world body always rested. It was gone! The virtual reality helmet lay empty. Oscar's body was still on the other couch.

A sudden sheepish look came to his face.

"What?" Bill asked, dropping into a chair and grabbing a parts catalog to fan his face.

"I gotta pee," Marcus said. "That never happened down in the computer."

Bill weakly waved toward their small, filthy restroom.

In a couple of minutes, a bemused look on his face, Marcus returned.

"Everything big?" Bill said, guessing.

"Yeah," Marcus said, grinning. "*Yeah!*" Then he held up his hands. "We need to discuss everything and make a plan of action. I'm recalling Oscar."

He went over and seated himself in front of the server, his large fingers flying nimbly over the keys.

"Still got my computer skills," he said with a smile.

The smile faded as nothing happened.

"Something's wrong, Bill. I can't contact Oscar! That's bad! Better go in and rescue—"

"That won't be necessary," said an oily voice.

Marcus jumped to his feet and turned to see Al and two of his goons standing there. All three had large automatic pistols leveled at Bill and him. Al stepped forward and rammed the barrel of his weapon against Bill's ear. "Who's Conan the Barbarian over there? I didn't authorize you to hire anyone new. Where's that little wimp you used to have?"

Bill looked at Marcus. "Ah ... he's gone."

"Well. Musclehead there isn't much smarter. Almost got him earlier, but he ran like a little girl. Not sure how, but he got out before the computer slagged itself."

"You're a lousy coder," Marcus said, which to him was about the worst insult you could hurl at someone.

"Haven't got time for you now. Get over there against the wall, flat on the floor."

Marcus complied, but he wasn't through talking. "Where's Oscar?"

"He and your little girlfriend Gwen are my virtual prisoners."

"Gwen?"

"Yeah, Gwen—I swiped Bill's code one day. Got it to work well enough to put her in the machine—most popular of my porn rentals, being interactive and all." He took the gun from Bill's ear long enough to wave it at Marcus. "*You* ruined that, getting all lovey-dovey with her. Now she wants out. But she ain't getting out!"

Marcus slapped his head with one hand. It hurt. "Encrypt sensitive software, stupid," he said in a disgusted mutter.

Al sneered. "So I'm taking Bill here. He's going to improve his code for me and I'm going to rule spam and porn all over the Internet." The gangster pointed at the server. "Bring that."

Marcus saw Bill, wide-eyed, shake his head. He didn't want Al to know that Marcus was really the one who had written the virtual insertion code. It was his idea, but only Marcus could make that idea work.

One of the goons put away his gun, went over, and turned the two gnarled knobs to the screws holding the server in the rack. He pulled it out, removed the cords, and stuck it under his arm.

Al pulled Bill out of his chair and pushed him over to the other goon, who grabbed his collar.

"You, on the floor there—you're fired, Conan. No severance or back pay. Consider yourself lucky to be alive."

Then they all left, slamming the front door resoundingly.

Marcus got up, the joy he'd felt in his new body now overwhelmed by despair and fear for his friends. He looked at Oscar's body and the virtual reality helmet on it. Somewhere Gwen's body was laying the same way.

He slammed a massive fist into his hand. Al was now in control of his only three friends in the world.

Marcus gently put a blanket over Oscar's body, then stooped and grabbed a few items out of his tool box on the floor. He left quickly, locking the shop and jogging toward his nearby apartment. *His* server had a backup of everything on it!

Too bad for Al. He was getting his friends back! Whatever it took, that's what he'd do.

As he passed two good-looking young women, he heard:

"Hot!"

"Wotta hunk!"

He grinned but ran faster. At least this new body stuff was working out. He wasn't even breathing hard.

As he crossed the main room of his tiny one-bed/one-bath apartment, Marcus suddenly realized he could *hear* and, what's more, *sense* what was going on in the server he'd mounted in the small closet.

Wow! The powers of his virtual body had also been transferred to his physical, real-world body. He waved his fingers and a virtual terminal floated in the air in front of him.

Cool!

There was a crackling at an empty power socket. He waved at his friend, electricity. That was not new; he'd always been able to communicate with it.

He grinned at the glowing air terminal. It reminded him what one of his professors in tech school had been fond of saying: "Computer science is ninety percent theory and ten percent magic." Marcus was sure now the ten percent was a whole lot larger than that. And he was the wiz! It was a good feeling.

But that good feeling vanished almost immediately. Everything he now had would mean *nothing* to him if he couldn't save his three friends. Gwen, Oscar, and even Bill—they were all he had.

Waving his fingers at the terminal, Marcus made certain his server was still secure, the backup virtual reality program still ran, and all was in order for a rescue mission.

Then he slapped his head. He'd forgotten to grab his virtual reality helmet! But …

He opened the closet door. It just felt *right*, so he dived into the one open USB socket on the front panel and slid into the server. Two virus-chomping trolls were sitting on empty data containers, playing cards. They looked up at his entrance.

"Oh, hiya, Boss," one said. "All's secure."

Marcus nodded, clapped them on the shoulders, and motioned them to go back to playing. (Even software needed some relaxation.) He walked over to another data container and sat down to think, creating another virtual terminal.

A couple of ideas came. He implemented one of them, bringing up Oscar's virtual body configuration script. The old man had wanted to be the same down here as in the real world, but that was not working out too well. Marcus's fingers flew as he beefed Oscar up, giving him youth, muscles, various powers, including all the Shaolin temple Kung Fu routines. Marcus was very proud of those. You do a Bruce Lee on a nasty piece of software and it *stayed* down.

He then compiled the configuration file. He might not be able to easily find where Oscar was, but his virtual body regularly checked its configuration, and whoever was holding Oscar was going to have a surprise on their hands.

While he was at it, he set up a configuration file for Bill too. If Al threw him in a computer, there would be *two* mighty warriors, both yearning for Al's blood. Four, of course, counting him and Gwen—if only he could find her computer and modify her *config* file. It was now obvious to him that Al was her boss and the VR software they had was the early version Al had ripped off from Bill. Lot of improvements since then!

69

Now for the second part. None of this would probably work unless he could find and get into Al's computer, which was surely locked down and strongly protected against that very thing happening, but he had an idea.

Gwendolyn Louise Baker's address was easy to find, and not far away at all. Closer than going back to the shop and probably safer, since Al did not know about her computer. She'd told him that. Besides, as he'd already decided, he needed to update her virtual reality software.

"Be alert, guys," he said to the trolls and dived out the USB port.

His *open* spell worked on her apartment door and his friend, electricity, kindly disabled the alarm system for him. He slipped in and relocked the door. The apartment was even smaller than his, and there she was (her body, that is), lying on her bed with the VR helmet on. She was a little chubby (she hadn't mentioned that), short, with not much of a figure, and as geeky as she said. But Marcus knew he loved her anyway.

Heart pounding, he found her server. Not bad. Old PowerEdge—20th generation—but those had plenty of reliability and capacity. He dived into the USB socket and was immediately challenged by three huge female virus-protection trolls, sharp swords poised.

"Halt! Password!"

"Er ..." Marcus said, not wanting to hurt any of Gwen's software, but knowing he *had* to get through.

"Wait," one troll said, "that's *Marcus*!"

"She likes him," said the second.

"A *lot*," the remaining troll added.

His ears doing a virtual burn, Marcus quickly explained to them what he needed and how it would save Gwen.

The trolls nodded and lowered their swords.

"VR software starts at memory address 3ddff000," one said.

"We're alerting the CPUs to have a packet ready for you," said another.

"That way," said the third, pointing.

Marcus pounded down a long memory bus and came to the address. The CPUs were holding a refresh packet for him, and he jumped on it. But they made no objection to him first updating the VR software, throwing some Shaolin temple Kung Fu routines and other stuff into Gwen's *config* file, then recompiling it.

"*Gwen's got a boyfriend! Gwen's got a boyfriend!*" some of the memory monkeys were chanting.

Then it was onto the data packet and, clinging precariously to a couple of protruding bits, he whizzed along.

Marcus flowed through the VR refresh port in Al's main server, the heavily-armored trolls ignoring this authorized traffic. He rolled off the packet, landing on his feet with poise as he entered a cordoned-off section of RAM serving as a cell for Gwen, Oscar, and Bill. He was *so* glad to see them! And he recognized the server he was in—it was the one from the shop.

"Miss me?" he said, grinning.

Gwen rushed over and threw her arms around him, resting her head on his shoulder. Oscar and Bill patted him on the back. Reluctantly he disengaged from Gwen.

"We've got to hurry," he said. "What's been happening here?"

"Not much," Gwen said. "Al's ignoring us. Ever since they got their new bodies, these two have been going over in the corner, looking at themselves, and chuckling a lot." She looked at Oscar and Bill. "It's just *virtual* size, guys."

"Er … no," Marcus said. "This is now my real body. We need to convert you guys so that you can help me demolish Al."

All three nodded at him. They *liked* that idea.

Marcus took out the red buttons he'd grabbed from his tool box. He handed one to each. "All set up. Flip up the cover, press ABORT." He held up his hand. "Not *yet!*"

Bill gently eased the cover closed again.

Marcus waved up a terminal and the screen showed the view outside the computer. Al and his two goons were there, eating pizza from a delivery box. *Hey, even disorganized criminals have to eat,* he acknowledged silently.

"Here's the plan," he said. "When Oscar and Bill press their buttons, they'll be up there with Al and his gorillas. Kung Fu the hell out of them, guys, before they can get their guns out. You know how now."

"What about me?" Gwen asked.

Marcus smiled at her. "Your button deposits you outside the server in your apartment. Your old body will be gone and *you* will be *you*."

Oscar, feeling his oats after years of being old and feeble, gave a wolf whistle.

Gwen stuck her tongue out at him but smiled.

"Then come back here and help us mop up. But … where is here?"

Marcus typed in the air and data streamed on his virtual terminal. "No encrypting of personal or business data for Al, hey?" He stopped the scrolling. "There! 6701 Greenview Avenue. Not too far from your apartment, Gwen. Let's do it!"

She nodded, opened the cover on her button, and hovered a finger over it reluctantly.

Marcus surprised himself again. "I love you. Press it, Gwen."

She looked at him, smiling radiantly, and did. *Whoosh!* She was gone.

He air-typed to the terminal and sent a video request out through the open refresh port. There she stood in her apartment, looking with awe at the image of her new body in a mirror.

"Move it, honey," he said.

Gwen jumped at his voice, but waved and ran out the door.

"So, are we waiting on her?" Bill asked.

"Nope. Press your buttons on three. One … two … *three!*"

They landed with silent grace, already in Kung Fu stances. Al and his two goons barely had time to drop their slices of pizza before they were disarmed and trussed up with electric cords ripped from a lamp, a fan, and the coffee maker.

Oscar and Bill took turns going to the restroom.

Marcus waved up a screen in the air, pulled over a chair, and then—with occasional suggestions from Bill or Oscar after they returned—demolished Al's porn and spam empires. He was especially careful to erase all mention of Gwen's work for Al. No need for her to be embarrassed during the investigations that were sure to come.

The office door slammed against the wall under a powerful *open* spell and Gwen stormed in, looking like an avenging goddess. Seeing the trussed-up gangsters, she slid to a halt.

"I'm sorry we didn't wait for you, Gwen," Marcus said, "but they were a pushover."

She shrugged.

"Now what?" Bill asked.

Gwen raised her hand. "I thought about that running over here."

They all noted that she was not a bit out of breath.

"My brother is a patent attorney with the biggest intellectual property firm in Chicago." She smiled. "You'll all be rich, and Marcus can make sure all this "—she ran her hands up and down her awesomely curvy body—"is used for the betterment of humanity."

"And software," Marcus added. "We're rich, Gwen—you too!" Oscar and Bill nodded enthusiastically. "Guess we should call the cops, huh?"

Gwen took his arm and gently pulled him toward the door.

"Let Bill and Oscar do that. I need you to check my computer." She smiled a smile that would melt steel and then temper it into something stronger than before.

Bill shrugged and winked.

"Race you back," Gwen yelled, already out the door.

Marcus pounded after her.

Oscar looked at Bill. "Big?"

"Huge," said Bill.

"I *love* computers," Oscar said.

Published in Galaxy's Edge Issue 2

The Prayer Ladder

by Marina J. Lostetter

The ladder stretches up and up before me. Into the sky, past the clouds—past the sun, perhaps. I cannot see the top, but I know it ends in Heaven.

Chill winds sweep the ice-covered mountain, and I hunker into my coat of caribou skin. The sleeve of my left arm is too long—Mama meant it to last me another two winters. The other is capped next to the stub of my right elbow.

The sack full of my village's prayers hangs lightly around my neck. Hundreds of little scrolls fill the burlap, written in hands both illegible and refined.

Once every five years the prayers are carried to Heaven.

Once every five years a citizen leaves and never comes back.

And now it is my turn.

I lay my boot on the first rung. I've learned to do everything with one limb that most do with two. I know how to deftly climb a ladder. But this ...

It's a long way to forever.

The ladder is made of something light and flexible—like the bamboo the traveling tradesmen bring. But it is also sturdy. The ladder has stood for a thousand years and will stand for a thousand more.

When the Carrier of Prayers is selected, the entire village gathers on the square outside of the temple. The priest makes sure all of the doors and windows are splayed wide, so that we can see the choosing. He drapes garlands and sprinkles seeds around the fat, golden Idol of Prayer, then touches its stomach and whispers in its ear. After a moment, the idol opens its mouth. The priest reaches in and retrieves a name burned into a small strip of parchment. The gods choose the Carrier, but the priest pulls the name.

And this year, it was me.

"No!" Mama cried. "There's been a mistake. Not Damien. *Please.*"

It's not often that the gods choose a child. Though at thirteen, I'm nearly a man. Usually they pick the elderly. Those who are still on their feet, but won't be for long.

Mama pushed through the throng and into the temple. She stomped up to the priest—invading the holy circle of space around him that no one is ever supposed to breach—and demanded he pull another name.

"You can't send a child with one arm," someone in the crowd insisted.

"Yes," agreed another. "What if he falls? What if our prayers don't make it?"

"The gods have spoken," the priest said in his stately tone. His harsh, black eyes stared at Mama without feeling. He had done his job, and she was to be thankful. Her boy had been given a great honor.

I took my place at the altar, next to the priest. The scent of crushed evergreens and scorched offerings permeated the sanctuary. "I can do it," I declared, ignoring Mama's sobs.

When we left the temple, she would not meet my gaze.

I'm way up now. Frost-blue Kaneq birds fly below—the gentle kind, with wingspans five times a grown man's height—but the clouds are still above. With the stump of my arm I can push myself up the rungs, grabbing hold once my fingers are boosted to the right level.

The knot that holds the sack is tight. I will not lose a prayer.

Only half are ever answered. Exactly half. Always good prayers, but typically little ones. People who ask for a good harvest or a safe journey are blessed. Only sometimes do the gods answer a big prayer.

Mama's prayer when I was little was a big prayer. I was going to die, she says. Horrible fever and rash—something terrible was eating me from inside. Mama prayed for me to live. And I did. All of me, save my right arm.

This morning, after the choosing, we wrote our prayers together. She got out the blessed parchment and the holy ink and we sat at the family table.

I asked her what she was praying for, but she wouldn't tell me. I told her my prayer and she cried again.

My shoulders feel strong and my legs aren't tired. And yet, I've reached the top.

There's a trapdoor, just recognizable by a narrow square outline and a silver handle dangling within my reach. Bracing myself between the rails, I knock on the sky.

Bright, white light blurs my vision as the door opens. A thin, silver hand beckons for the sack.

Teetering precariously, I pull the sack over my head. It disappears into the light. Then the hand extends for me. I am to follow all of the great Carriers of the past and ascend to Heaven.

But as I move to take the hand, I slip. My fingers brush past the silver ones and I topple backwards.

I'm falling. Air rushes past as the ground rushes forth.

Down.

Down.

And when I pass through a cloud I realize what my mother prayed for. For my return.

Not like this. She couldn't have prayed for this.

But, perhaps this means both of our prayers will be answered, and that this is not the end. I repeat mine now, to myself: *Please, make my mama happy.*

A sharp tingle in my stump draws my gaze to the right. A silvery, ethereal forearm and hand have sprouted from my sleeve cap. The fingers flex at my command.

Not even the thick hide of my coat could hinder the growth of a god-limb.

But, what use is a new arm, god or otherwise? Why give me now what I've gone all these years without?

Below, the frost-blue Kaneq birds soar in spirited circles, their wings shimmering in the late-day sun.

I don't need fingers. I need feathers.

The god-arm morphs at my behest. A giant Kaneq wing extends to my right. But, it's worthless without a mate.

I clutch my left fist. It has been a good hand, a good arm, doing the job of two. But I need something else now.

Change, I will it.

Change.

Change!

A silver glimmer engulfs my left side. Blue plumage bursts into existence.

With wings outstretched, I catch the wind and it ferries me home. All the way to Mama.

Holland: 1944

by Steve Cameron

Brigadier Arthur Holbrook (Ret.)
Ainsburgh Manor
Old Schoolyard Road
Upper Longstocking
West Albionshire
NW8 9AY
England

15th July 2014

General Sir Edwyn Blaine
Chief of the Defence Staff
Ministry of Defence
Whitehall
London
SW1A 2HB

My dear Sir Edwyn,

I am writing to you regarding a matter of the utmost importance. I have tried ringing the village constabulary, the army and the Home Office—even MI6, but all those fools simply won't listen. You are my final hope; otherwise I shall be forced to resort to those dreadful television news people.

This matter affects national security and places our once great empire in a position of grave peril. It is my patriotic duty as an old soldier, a retired Brigadier, to inform someone in authority. An alien invasion force is poised ready to strike at any moment, and I have evidence locked in my garden shed.

Don't laugh, it's true.

I am very well aware this letter could easily be mistaken as the crazed ramblings of a demented old man. However I do not suffer fools gladly, nor am I prone to flights of fancy, and I certainly can't stand this science fiction rubbish the young folk seem to like. As a schoolboy I tried to read some of it. *War of the Worlds*, I think it was called. Complete rubbish! I even knew one of those science fiction chaps during the war. I first met George Orwell when he was in the Home Guard and I asked him why he didn't write real stories. He wasn't too happy about that. Mind you, he smelled of mothballs and was a right dour sod most of the time. Big Brother this, Big Brother that. I thought he had surely been bullied as a child. The funny thing is he didn't even have a brother, only two sisters. I must admit I'm not sure whether *Big Sister is watching* would have worked quite the same way, though. That just sounds, well … perverted.

I shall, of course, impart my information regarding the alien invasion, but please permit me to first offer my credentials and introduce myself. My name is Arthur Holbrook, and I managed to survive the war relatively unscathed, although I do still have some shrapnel in my neck. It was discovered a couple of years ago when an x-ray revealed a piece of metal high in my spine, up near my skull. My doctor decided it was safer to leave it there. It has never caused me any pain, although I get marvellous reception from the BBC. Even when the wireless is switched off.

I knew your father back in good old WW2. We were both young Privates then, strong and handsome, keen and courageous. Side by side we fought in the foxholes of France, then shoulder to shoulder across the battlefields of Belgium. We even stayed in touch for a few years after the war. A funny old chap, he was. He liked to wear frocks on a Saturday night and demand we call him Joyce. Now, I'm as happy as the next chap to tart up. I have fabulous legs and I'm not ashamed to show them off. We'd all done that in our student days at Oxford, but your father seemed to revel in it a little more than he should have. I suspect, however, those tales are best left for another time, perhaps one night when we can share a few pints of Old Speckled Hen down at the local. Please pass on my kindest regards to old Joyce and buy her a sherry from me the next time you see her. The last I heard the operation had gone rather well.

I confess I am not familiar with your security clearances, although I would presume they are rather high. And I certainly have no knowledge of whether you have been given any information regarding the existence of aliens by our cousins across the pond. If you have been told they do not exist, then the Yanks are lying to you. Which I must admit to finding rather strange since the American public seems to know all about their presence on Earth. My wife's niece, a splendid young lass, is married to a colonial and lives in a small place called Protection, Kansas. Now I ask you, is that any sort of name for a village? Sounds more like something she should have used prior to the birth of that horrid child of hers. The last time my wife's niece, her American husband and their festering offspring came to visit, I discreetly asked if she believed in aliens. I'm afraid I don't really comprehend all this computer mumbo-jumbo, megapretzel camera, kindle ballyhoo and so on, but she brought out a laptop computer device and connected to something called the interweb. She showed me pictures of something called Area 51 which is apparently full of alien creatures and flying saucers and government agents wearing crisp black suits. If you don't believe me, ask a youngster to show you on a computer thing.

But I'm afraid I digress, and I should return to the matter at hand.

A week ago my wife and I decided to go for an afternoon drive in our Austin Healey. It was a glorious summer afternoon with just a hint of breeze, and so armed with a picnic basket and a flask of tea we merrily headed off into The Wolds. We had such a lovely time together. As I drove I enjoyed the serenity, the nature, the lush trees and the green rolling hills while my wife shouted directions at me. We even opened the car windows a little to welcome the scent of freshly cut hay from the passing fields. Soon we found a lovely place to stop for our lunch. We spread our blanket under a chestnut tree and cheerfully munched our cucumber sandwiches, pickled eggs and pork pies. Then we ate freshly baked scones with lashing of jam and cream washed down with good old English tea, from India. Once we were done, I had a nap while my wife roamed the paddock enjoying her hobby, cow tipping. I believe she gave three or four of the beasts a good heave. I awoke, completely refreshed after a good kip, so we packed the car and headed home.

The sun was getting low in the sky when the love of my life realised I was on the wrong road. Apparently she tried to tell me. I didn't hear her. She believes I am starting to ignore her. I'm afraid it's just that I'm getting old and a little hard of hearing. But as always she has a solution. From the glove box she retrieved her loud-hailer with which she proceeded to point out my many faults. Loudly. I tried my best to ignore her and concentrate on my driving. Somehow I managed to find the road home with only a thumping headache.

Twilight was rapidly approaching as we pulled into the village. Next to me, my love slept soundly. And by soundly I mean she snored as though a freight train was arriving in my skull, over and over again. I had just driven through the main roundabout when I happened to notice three pale blue lights, stationary in the darkening sky, just above the steeple of St. Hubbins. The three lights then pulsed in unison, so I wound down my window to better see them. Unfortunately I didn't see the Morris 1100 coming towards me. At the last minute its headlights caught my eye and I swerved wildly to avoid it. There was a screech of tyres, a violent shuddering, and then a jolt as I mounted the curb. I crashed into a phone box, through a fence, across a vacant plot of land and into a duck pond. You would not believe the resulting carry on and squawking. And that was just my wife! She stormed around the car, opened the door and dragged me out. Soaked and spluttering stagnant pond water, she carried me across the muddy banks and dumped me on the grass. Across the way, on the village green, three young lads wearing grey windcheaters, which my wife called 'hoodies', laughed and pointed in amusement. As my wife pushed the car out of the pond, I lay on my back, gasping for air and calming my heart-rate. When I finally recalled how I'd come to crash the car, I scoured the sky. The blue lights had now vanished.

I've seen those lights before. But that was in Europe, some 70 years ago.

In late 1944, as part of the Second Army, I was stationed in the Netherlands. My Division was situated near the Meuse River with the ultimate goal of pushing through to Berlin. One night, while out on patrol, I became separated from my comrades-in-arms. I became completely lost. The night was bitterly cold. We were still several weeks away from the first snow, but the air held an icy chill and the moon was lost behind clouds.

I crept through the woods, trying to locate my fellow soldiers, but I only found myself further disoriented. I shivered, and pulled my collar close around my throat. Just as I was about to light a match to read a map I heard twigs breaking underfoot. Then I heard the guttural sounds of a Jerry speaking to another. Instantly, I dropped to the ground and rolled behind a fallen log. It was damp and smelled of fungus, and it felt like hours I lay there, scarcely breathing, unable to move, but it must have only been a few minutes. One of the Krauts almost stepped on me as he stopped to relieve himself. I had to close my eyes and mouth against the warm stream of German urine.

I think I lasted about ten seconds before I could bear it no longer. I coughed and spluttered and leapt to my feet. The German's eyes widened as I turned and fled. There was a rifle shot, and then another.

"Halt!" someone shouted. "Halt!"

I ran, zigzagging as I'd been taught and charged smack-bang into a tree. My head felt like it had been pushed straight through my skull, and I crashed heavily to the ground.

Before I could stand, the Jerries had dragged me upright, stripped me of my rifle and tied my hands behind my back. They marched me to a nearby barn, apparently abandoned. One of them shoved me, and I stumbled inside, scraping my face against the roughly hewn door. I was led to the back and pushed down into an animal stall. As a child I was always fragile, and the smell of old hay and animal droppings brought my allergies to the fore. Immediately I started sneezing which resulted in a backhander. My face burned, my head pounded and I lay there, stinking of piss and whimpering softly in the darkened stall while they removed their packs and rifles. Soon they had started a small fire. There was a short guttural discussion before one of them approached me. He made me stand, looked me up and down then untied my hands. He spoke to me in heavily accented English.

83

"You won't try to escape, will you? We will simply shoot you if you try."

"No," I shook my head and briskly rubbed my hands to get some life back into them.

"What is your name?"

"Arthur Holbrook," I said.

"Where are you based?"

"Arthur Holbrook. Private. 7474505B."

"Where are you based?" he repeated.

"Arthur Holbrook. Private. 7474505B."

The Swiss may have been reluctant to become involved in the war, but they had hosted the convention that afforded me the right to only state my name, rank and serial number. Oh, and they made damn fine chocolate as well.

He smiled. "What were you doing when we captured you, apart from being pissed on?" The others all laughed at this. I ignored him. Meanwhile, one of the other soldiers was heating up some kind of stew. It smelled wonderful.

"Would you like some?" he asked. "What were you doing when we captured you?"

I saw no point in lying. They had probably guessed I was simply lost.

"I was simply lost," I said. "I was on patrol when I became separated from my comrades. I was trying to find my way back to them when you discovered me."

He asked me further questions about troop movements, artillery installations and plans. I really had no idea, but I pointed at a couple of random spots on a map he produced to keep him happy. He seemed to like this and smiled again. Then he invited me to join the others at the fire. I dropped onto a log that had been dragged inside. It felt great just being out of the cold. It was heaven to also smell the warming food, at least the little I could catch through the wall of steaming ammonia from my drying uniform. For some reason the Germans all sat on the far side of the fire from me.

I was given some stew. Metal spoons scraped on metal dixies as we ate greedily in the flickering firelight. I didn't receive nearly as much as they did, but at least they shared with me. They're not all bad, those Jerry swine.

Later I sat alone on a pile of hay in the stall, gulping down a mug of hot tea and smoking a cigarette. My uniform was still damp, but at least it was now warm again. The Germans huddled around the fire and spoke in soft tones, laughing from time to time. Once I'd finished, they retied my hands behind my back and I fell asleep with my face pressed against the hay.

It must have been an hour or so later that I was awoken by the strangest sound: a low-pitched hum. My stomach rumbled in response to the frequency. Or perhaps it was in response to the stew. The German who remained awake on guard apparently heard it too, as he stood and quietly woke the others. The fire was no more than a bed of glowing coals, fighting a losing battle against the cold night. The hum grew louder and louder until my ears hurt and my stomach trembled. A pale blue light strobed through the cracks in the rear wall of the barn. The Germans grabbed their rifles and made their way outside, leaving me alone. A few moments later I heard shouted commands and a few rifle shots. Then there was a new sound, a static crackling, and the blue glow around me changed to red. A few seconds later the pale blue light returned. The hum died away and there was only silence.

I have no idea what happened to those Germans. They never returned. My best guess is they were disintegrated by some kind of heat ray, much like that described by Mr. Wells in his ridiculous story.

I lay silently for the longest time, but eventually built up the courage to leave my stall and approach the barn door. There was an odd scent which reminded me of vanilla, and I paused to sniff the still air. Imagine my surprise when the door opened silently and before me stood a small creature—the likes of which I'd never even imagined before. It was grey, about three feet tall, with a large bulbous head and small, lithe body. Long arms reached almost to its knees. Its eyes were almond shaped and black—as black as coal—and it seemed to stare right through me into the very depths of my soul. It held a small silver tube, a ray gun I now presume. I shivered, and not just from the damp chill. Frankly, I was scared and started shaking. I almost fell over when I tried to cross myself against this demonic vision, as my hands were still securely tied behind my back. Instead I dropped to my knees and the hair on the back of my neck stood at attention.

Then I was hit by the most foul, pungent odour I've ever encountered on God's green planet. I must have wrinkled my nose in response, because it spoke to me. In English, if you can believe that.

"Sorry about the smell," it said. "You surprised me." And it waved its hand rapidly behind its behind. Apparently, when startled, they let one go—so to speak.

"Cor! You smell awful," I managed.

"You don't smell so good yourself, pisshead," it said. "No wonder the others left you behind. Are you crippled?"

"Crippled?" I asked.

"Yes." It swayed its head gently from side to side. "You have no arms."

I laughed nervously, stood up and turned around so it could see my arms tied behind my back. "I was their prisoner." I turned to face it once more. "What are you?" I ventured.

"I'm not from around here."

"Nooooo," I said. "Really? I presumed you were a Dutch peasant."

"A Dutch peasant? I am from another planet." The being obviously did not understand sarcasm.

"Mars!" I guessed." You're a Martian!" Mr. Wells had apparently been correct. I quickly scanned the barn for any sign of red weed.

"No," it said. "Mars has no life. I'm from a star system much further away."

"Where?"

It shook its head. "I could not describe it in a manner you would understand." It approached me, staring through me again with its dark, emotionless eyes. "I have told you too much as it is." The alien pressed the silver tube against my forehead. It burned cold against my skin. I frowned as I tried to make sense of it.

It may seem strange now, but it was only at this juncture that it occurred to me I was actually in danger. My original fear had dissipated when it let one rip and we commenced our light banter. Certainly it had eradicated the Jerries, but I suddenly realised this being had no real reason to be a friend to an Allied soldier. Or to any Earthling, for that matter. Panic rose within me. My heart thudded unmercifully and choked off my throat. I dropped to my knees once more, and started whimpering. My lip quivered and I started shaking. I'm rather embarrassed to admit that I even soiled my trousers.

"You won't feel anything," it said. "Farewell."

There was a scream and a khaki blur of motion as a woman, solid as a mountain, charged in through the barn door. She swung a rifle around her head and clubbed the alien to the ground. Then she stood over its inert body and aimed the weapon at me.

"Hande hoch, Kraut!" she roared.

"I'm British," I said. I turned slowly, so she could see my tied hands.

It took her a few moments, but she seemed to decide I would offer her no harm. Of course she had recognised the uniform but was simply being cautious. She untied me, although she kept the rifle close by. It turned out she was an English nurse who'd managed to escape just as her hospice was overrun by Jerries. She had stripped a dead soldier of his uniform and weapon and had been making her way towards the British lines. As darkness fell, she had been looking for shelter when she'd noticed the barn bathed in the eerie blue light.

She was convinced the alien was some kind of Nazi experiment gone wrong and I chose not to correct her. I didn't think she would have believed me anyway. She wanted to kill it, to put it out of its misery but I convinced her not to. So she decided to let it live and to question it once it awoke. Carefully, she tied its limbs then dragged it onto a pile of hay in another stall. For a while she examined the silver tube, the 'ray gun' the alien had dropped, but she was unable to operate it. She dropped it in her pocket.

I built up the fire again until its meagre warmth started to penetrate my frozen flesh. Using German supplies I'd found, I prepared a meal of sausage and sauerkraut. The English nurse found a well outside and drew enough water to try and wash my soiled uniform. She draped it over a barrel near the fire. Wearing nothing but my undershorts, I sat next to her. I moved closer as we shared our stories and our body heat. The sausage and cabbage tasted like manna from heaven and filled our bellies. And as we ate, our spirits rose. She only slapped me once, when I leaned in a little closer to sniff her. It was worth it. She smelled like a rose against the animal smells of that squalid barn. But she held me no grudge. Chivalry is not dead, and before long she gave me her greatcoat to help keep me warm. Once we were sated, we decided to get some shut-eye. I crawled back into my stall and lay down. I drew the greatcoat over me like a blanket with the stalks of hay prickling against my bare back.

From my makeshift cot I watched her as she went through her bedtime routine. She dropped and did thirty press-ups on the dirt floor, then did fifty rapid chin-ups on a wooden beam before stripping and cleaning the rifle; faster than any of my comrades could. Gosh, she was a fine figure of a man. Finally she crawled under the greatcoat beside me. I could feel her naked flesh pressed against mine. It was as smooth and warm as any side of roast beef and I wanted to devour her. Then, while we lay there side by side in the dark stall, a strange thing happened. I fell head over heels in love. Ah, the first flushes of romance, the halcyon days of young lust. At midnight, she proposed to me. We celebrated by making love in the straw, her on top of course, before I fell asleep, wrapped safely in her large, muscled arms.

It seemed like only minutes later that I was once more awoken, this time by the alien shaking me. I sat upright, wet myself once more, and then drew back in fear. I bashed my head against the weathered timber wall. My head throbbed as my girl snored on. The alien raised his hands, palms out, and attempted a smile.

"How did you escape?" I asked.

"Rope will not suffice. It would take metal to restrain me." It rubbed its head. "She is strong, that one."

I followed the creature out to the fire. "You better hope she doesn't wake up."

"She won't," it said. It showed me the silver tube. "I used this. She will sleep for at least a few more of your Earth hours, and then she will have no memory of me. I will not harm her. I understand she was merely protecting you." I paused, suddenly, unsure of my own future. My bravado left me once more and my fear returned. This being had already disintegrated a platoon of Jerries. I picked up a pointy stick from the stack of firewood and fiddled with it nonchalantly. At least I had a weapon of sorts. It must have read my mind, or at least interpreted my worried expression. "Do not fear," it said. "I shall not kill you either. You showed mercy and did not execute me when she attacked me." It motioned at my love.

I let out a huge sigh of relief.

"So what's this all about," I said. "Whose side are you on?"

"Side? We have no interest in your petty fighting. Kill each other all you like."

"Then why are you here?"

It paused, tilted its head, and remained unmoving for close to a minute. It seemed deep in thought, although it may have simply fallen asleep. Just as I was about to prod it with the pointy stick, the alien started speaking again.

"I'm not sure how much I should share with you. But I suppose it ultimately doesn't matter." It paused. I half expected an orchestra to strike ominous chords. "I'm an advance scout. Your world has much to offer. I've been here for three of your Earth months and I am about to return to my home planet. I came to conduct a survey."

"Much to offer?"

"Resources," it said. "My people will return with me. This is a fabulously wealthy planet."

"Tourists?" I said. "You're a travel agent and you're going to bring tourists to a war? That's not too wise."

"Are you really so stupid?" It sneered. "I'm talking about an invasion. We will invade your planet and take all we require. I shall depart soon, and it will be many of your years before we return. I have travelled a great distance."

"But why?" I asked. "Why can't you just leave us here in peace to finish our war?"

"Eh, it's what we do." It shrugged. "Now, come with me." The alien turned to go. I followed it out to the fire, now mere glowing embers. I dropped the stick on the coals, where it flared and started burning.

"Now kneel," it commanded.

This was not what I'd expected. I fell to my knees on the uneven dirt floor, naked and vulnerable, and started crying. "Please don't," I begged. "It will be our little secret. I won't tell anyone. I promise."

"I must," said the alien, and pressed the silver tube against my forehead for the second time that night.

I wailed, I screamed, I soiled myself once more. There was a bright flash and I knew no more.

Literally, I knew no more. The alien had not planned to kill me. I had simply misunderstood its intentions at that point. The device had clearly altered my memories so I would not recall any of these events.

89

The next morning I awoke in the arms of my love and we both recalled her overpowering a German unit and saving me, although we were unable to account for the missing soldiers. We took all the supplies we could manage and left the barn. A few hours later, we happened upon a patrol searching for me. I must say she fit in well with the other fellows, and later that week became the battalion's boxing champion when she knocked out several of my comrades who were drunk enough to make advances towards her.

In the following weeks my girl slept well. I, on the other hand, suffered night after night. My sleep was filled with nightmares, cold sweats and screaming out my beloved's name. She usually slapped me until I awoke.

The battalion appeared to be in a stalemate with the Germans and had been ordered to stay put. Apart from a few insults thrown at each other across 'no man's land', there was little military action. None of us knew when we would face battle again. Ahhh, the nervous anticipation, the spirited singsongs, the many trips to the loo as the old tins of corned beef had their way with our colons. A few days later my beloved gave us some excitement, though. She had her best helmet ruined by a stray shot from a bored Jerry sniper. Immediately, and without any thought for her own safety, she went straight over the top. Her Sten gun chattered as she tossed off grenades left, right and centre. We watched in horror as my girl made straight for the enemy. We were helpless, unable to do anything as she bravely took them on headfirst. Unfortunately there were too many of them. It took seven of the Bosch to bring her down. The lads and I cheered her on from the safety of the foxholes as they wrestled her away. I didn't see her again until after the war. Somehow she managed to escape from behind enemy lines. Apparently she became enraged after a Jerry guard called her 'Sir'. Not only did she beat him to a bloody pulp, but she also stole a plane, an ME-109, which she flew back to Blighty. On the way she shot down several other 109s in dogfights over the channel. Her plane was rather badly shot up. In fact the undercarriage was so badly damaged the wheels would not lower but she was able to bring the old kite in safely on its belly. Of course she won the D.F.C. for gallantry in active flying service. It's on display in our sitting room along with the ribbon of machine gun bullets from the stolen 109 she gave me as an engagement present.

We were married a year later after we'd both been de-mobbed. What a wedding! She looked stunning in her camouflage dress, boots and polished rifle. And I suppose that would have been an end of the tale, if it wasn't for these recent events.

I've already written of my minor car accident after I saw the lights in the sky last week. Of course at the time I had no recollection of my initial encounter with the alien. I would probably have thought no more of them, except as a curious anecdote to tell the lads. A couple of nights ago, however, I saw these lights again.

I'd been drinking at the local pub with some of the lads, playing darts and chatting about the war years. I'd had a few pints of ale, and knew I had to be home by ten or else someone might get hurt. I didn't fancy another black eye, so I made my excuses, left and stumbled out into the mild night air. About halfway home I saw a couple of those 'hoodies' chaps in their grey windcheaters standing under the yellowing circle glow of a street lamp. They were smoking cigs and swilling tins of lager.

"Hey Grandad," one of them shouted as he crossed the street towards me. "Can you gimme a tenner?"

"Of course," I said. "Luciano Pavarotti."

"Smartarse!" he said, and thrust two fingers up at me. I'm not sure why he wasn't pleased. I thought I'd answered his quiz rather accurately. I just don't understand these modern teenagers. They shave their heads, get tattoos and listen to that zany hippity-hoppity music. They need discipline! They should get haircuts and join the army. A real job. It's what made a man of me. And my wife.

The 'hoodie' crossed the street to rejoin his mate. As I turned the corner into Schoolyard Lane, an empty lager tin clattered off the cobblestones behind me. I ignored this and proceeded on my way. I was only 100 yards from home when I paused and leaned against a wall to catch my breath. As I rested, I glanced up into the night sky and saw those three pale blue lights again. They were in a triangular formation and crossed slowly above from east to west until they vanished behind the roofline of the houses before me.

I frowned. That was twice I'd seen these flying saucers in a matter of days. And bear in mind I still had no memory of those events in Holland.

Yesterday, however, that all changed.

It was early afternoon, and I was gardening out the back. My wife was down at the village hall, shouting numbers for bingo. I'd just mowed the lawn and raked the clippings and had knelt to start tending the vegetable beds. My cucumbers are coming along nicely and should do rather well at the village fair next month. I was weeding the marrow patch when the hair rose on the back of my neck and I smelled a touch of vanilla in the air. It stirred something in me, a memory of something forgotten. Something I should know. And then I remembered. I hadn't had lunch yet, and there was a piece of cheesecake waiting in the fridge. I was about to stand and go inside when I turned to see a creature standing on the grass a few yards behind me. It was grey, about three feet tall, with a large bulbous head and small, lithe body. Long arms reached almost to its knees. Its eyes were almond shaped and black—as black as coal—and it seemed to stare right through me into the very depths of my soul. It held a small silver tube. It seemed, somehow, familiar.

I trembled in fear and wet myself. "What the hell are you?" I asked. Warm urine trickled down my thigh.

"Not again," it said. "Must you always piss your pants?"

"Sorry? Have we met before?"

"Never mind. This will explain everything." The creature strode across to me and pressed the silver tube on the nape of my neck. There was a bright flash, and the memories flooded back. Instantly I recalled that night so long ago. Holland, the Germans, the barn, the discussion with this creature, the acidic smell of drying piss.

And the invasion plans.

"Oh, God," I said. "No."

The alien stepped backwards. It trod on the rake I'd left on the lawn, and there was a 'thwack' as it sprung up to hit the creature square in the back of the head. It collapsed in a crumpled heap on the lawn.

As you will have determined from this letter, I am a man of action. My fear faded as I now knew what I had to do. I was possibly the only person on Earth who had knowledge of the impending invasion. Of course I still don't know why this creature sought me out after so many years, or what it wants from me, but I believe I know how it located me. I suspect the shrapnel in my neck is not a shard of German armament, but a device implanted by the alien that has blocked my memories for the past seventy years, and has now been used to track me. I recovered the offending silver tube from where it had fallen and deposited it in my pocket. Then I dragged the creature to my garden shed. I now recalled, of course, that rope would not suffice so I bound its hands and feet with chains and padlocks. I pushed the alien under my workbench and went into my house.

Up in my bathroom I gathered all my medication from the cabinet and took them down to the kitchen. I opened each jar and dropped all the tablets into a bowl. From my secret cache I recovered the pills I hide from my love, the ones I don't like because they make me feel all funny and see things. I added them to the others and crushed them all with the back of a spoon. Then I dissolved the powder into a glass of lukewarm water. Hopefully this mixture would sedate the creature. I carried the glass out to the shed where the alien still had not stirred. I opened its mouth and poured the concoction in. It coughed once and a little spilled out the sides, but I believe enough went down its throat. I left the glass on the bench. It would be needed again. I tied a rag around its mouth so it could not call out.

Of course I rang the authorities, but as I wrote previously they have ignored me thus far. I've been out to the shed several times since then to give it more of my medication, and it still has not roused. My wife has no knowledge of its presence, and I don't believe she is becoming suspicious yet. All appears normal at home and I have managed to remain calm. Last night, after dinner, we sat and read in our front room, dressed in our smoking jackets and sipping a fine Bordeaux. As usual, we shared an uncomfortable silence as we puffed on our pipes. My love was not speaking to me. She'd spent much of the afternoon searching the house, rummaging behind the cushions and lifting the sofa to check under it. One of the antique silver lipsticks her mother left her is missing, and I, apparently, am somehow to blame. As we sat I offered her a smile, but she only glared at me for perhaps the fiftieth time that evening. I was going to risk saying something romantic when I suddenly realised I needed to check on the alien before bed. I closed my book, put down my pipe and rose.

"Where do you think you're going?" she roared.

"I think I may have left the shed unlocked. I'm just going to check."

"That's the third time you've checked it this evening. Are you losing your mind?"

I didn't respond. There is no correct response when she's like this. The easiest way out would be to simply gouge out my own eye with a fork. But not even I am prepared to do that. I crossed the room to leave. She bared her teeth and growled.

When I returned from checking on the still comatose alien, she'd gone and closed the bedroom door behind her. I made myself comfortable on the sofa and tried to sleep.

And that brings us to the present.

My warring days are over now, there's little excitement for me anymore. The closest I have to a thrill these days is when my loving wife returns after several hours from teaching self-defence at the local boys' grammar school and releases me from where I've accidentally locked myself in the utility room. Ahhh, the bittersweet joy of seeing her face as the door is finally unlocked and swings open.

I realise my service to Her Majesty is all but done and there is little I can offer of myself in these twilight years, but I can do this one final thing. I can inform you of this imminent alien attack, and offer you the creature I have captured.

Now it's up to you to use this knowledge to protect our once great empire.

Yours sincerely,
Brigadier Arthur Charles Holbrook (Ret.) DSO, OBE, MC

p.s.—As I write this, the village Constable has just been speaking to my wife at the front door. Apparently a couple of houses in the street were burgled yesterday. I presume it's the work of those 'hoodies' chaps. I therefore urge that you send someone straight away. It would be dreadful if one of those thieving lads were to break into my shed, discover the creature, and accidentally release it.

Published in Galaxy's Edge Issue 7
Copyright © 2014 by Steve Cameron. All rights reserved.

The Spinach Can's Son

by Robert T. Jeschonek

I am the can of spinach in a sailor man's hand. He squeezes, expecting me to burst open and launch a blob of green power into his gaping maw.

But I do not burst. He gets no mouthful of spinach, no surge of energy pumping up his arms to three times their size. That's not how it works on this side of the tracks, my friend.

You're not in the funny pages anymore.

Potpie the Sailor tries again with both hands, straining for all he's worth. "C'mon, ya ratfinsk!" He squints up at the threat looming before him, the whole reason he needs his spinach. "We've gotsk to drive this *she-hag* off me boat!"

What threat could be awful enough to strike fear in the sailor man's heart? Is it Bobo the comic-strip bully, back for another knock-down, drag-out?

Not even close.

The figure standing before Potpie and me isn't a drawing at all. There's nothing pen-and-ink about her. "Sir!" She's a three-dimensional woman in what looks like a spacesuit out of a 1950s movie—silver metallic tights and a bubble helmet. Her black hair is arranged in tight waves beneath the glass. "Please, calm down! I just want to

95

ask you some questions." She pulls a photo out of a pouch on the belt slung diagonally over her hips. "Have you seen this man?"

"Never seen 'im before in me lifesk!" Potpie squeezes me harder than ever. I try my best to help, pushing from within, for one simple reason.

I recognize the man in the picture, with his dark brown hair and square-jawed features. I know him like I know my own self, in fact.

Because he *is* myself. Myself in another life.

And I know her, too. Her name is Molly. She's my wife.

And I know why she's after me.

"Take another look, please," she says. "It's urgent that I find him."

Potpie shifts the corncob pipe from one side of his mouth to the other without ever touching it. "I ain't seen him, she-hag!" He shakes a fist at her. "Now putsk 'em up!"

Molly takes a step toward him. "You're sure you haven't seen him?"

Potpie scrambles backward, knocking over a stack of spinach crates. Crying out, he puts me to the only use he can think of—hurling me right at her.

Molly ducks, and I go sailing over her head. It's not a clean getaway, though; the bracelet on her wrist starts beeping as I pass.

Here in the Underfunnies, I'm an anomaly, a deformity in the panel geography—the panelography—and her equipment has detected me.

Good thing a true Panelnaut like me can swim the currents here like a dolphin through water. Focusing my energies, I dive deep into the sea of words and images, hunting a good place to resurface.

Found it. I cross the borders in full flight and land with a shock that takes my breath away.

This time, I am the brick in the hand of a mouse.

I bounce lightly in his grip as he jounces along through a strange landscape, surrounded by abstract objects straight out of a surrealist painting. He gives off a thick smell of stinky cheese and whistles a jaunty tune from his pointy gray snout.

I know him well—Ixnay the Mouse. Once again, I've gravitated toward my favorite stomping grounds, the panelography of the early 20th century. In this case, the *Hazy Kat* strip.

Or should I say, the *Underfunnies* version of that strip. The reverse of it, the flip side where things don't work the way they should. The negative space that accrues in the collective unconscious of the readership around these tiny, panel-bound stories. The land of things unsaid and hopes unrealized.

For each time Potpie the sailor pops open a can, gobbles the spinach, and beats up the bully, we know in our hearts there must be times when the can doesn't open. That's just the way life works. And our expectations create this flip-side place that until recently no one knew about.

I am a Panelnaut, an explorer of this place. Though "fugitive" might be a better word for what I've become.

"Boy," says Ixnay. "Have I got one cooked up for that idiot cat this time." He hops up on what looks like a warped sundial and calls out into the hot wind. "Oh, Haaazyyy!"

Without delay, the creature known as Hazy Kat comes bounding over the horizon. She's wearing a polka-dot scarf and matching tutu. "Comink, mine treasur-ed pession flour!"

"Make it snappy, willya?" hollers Ixnay. "Yer burnin' daylight here!"

Hazy flops to a stop in front of us and gapes with a love-struck goofy grin. "Dost Rumeo have a heart-wiltin' sonnet plucked out to make his Joliet swoon'st?"

"Ohh, yeah." Ixnay turns me over in his grip. "Ya ever hear of *iambrick pentameter?*"

Hazy claps her paws together and giggles. "Butter 'course, o bard o' the mousehole! Hit me with that iambrick pentagrammer to yer li'l ol' heart's continent!"

"You asked for it." Ixnay hauls me back, ready to throw. "Be sure to notice the rhythmic counterpoint of strike and release. Or should I say the *opposite?*"

At that exact moment, Molly flashes to life between us and Hazy. The second she materializes, her bracelet starts beeping.

She points her wrist in my direction and nods. "I know you're here, Everett. You've figured out how to assume local forms, haven't you?" Watching the bracelet, she walks toward us. "You're inside the mouse, aren't you?"

Before Ixnay can say a word, Molly suddenly snaps backward. As she drops to the dusty ground, I see Hazy has her paws on her.

"You stays awake from my lettle Ixnay mouses!" Hazy flaps her paws like pancakes at Molly's helmet. "He is my preshiss poet and certifiable booblekins! Don't try steelin' his heart, you hussy!"

"Everett!" Molly shoves the cat away and scrambles to her feet. "I've come to talk to you! You sent me a message through the comic strips—our prearranged emergency signal! Don't pretend you didn't!"

She's right, I can't, because I sent it. But the signal wasn't a cry for help—it was bait. All part of the secret I've been keeping.

"I'm serious, Everett." Molly takes another step toward us. "I'll do what it takes to get through to you."

Ixnay just watches, juggling me from hand to hand. "Whoever this dame is, I gotta admit, I like her style."

Hazy, never much good in a fight, weakly bats at Molly's calves. "'Ev'ritt,' you say? Is that some other word for 'mouses'?"

"Shut up, cat!" says Molly. "Everett, listen …"

Ixnay's little mouse heart thumps like a big bass drum. It pushes out his chest in the shape of a cartoon heart as it throbs. "I think I'm in love!"

Naturally, this makes him raise me into throwing position again.

Molly sees the danger but doesn't stop talking. "It's time to come home, Everett. You can't keep running away." She spreads her arms wide. "We both miss him, Everett. But you can't make things right on your own."

I want to tell her how wrong she is, but I don't get the chance. Ixnay whips me at her glass-helmeted head before I can get the words out.

"Sech fe'rce percision!" says Hazy Kat. "His peshion must be deeper than I yimagined!"

As I blast toward her helmet, I focus my strength on changing course. Ixnay's throw is off, which helps; in the Underfunnies, things don't work the way they normally do, including his brick-pitching aim.

So I fly wide and hurtle on past, soaring through the ochre skies … casting my mind toward another refuge. I've gotten so good, I find one instantly, and I set my sights.

But I wait another moment to dive. Because the truth is, I'm not trying to lose her at all.

Her bracelet has alerted her to my presence in the brick, and she charges after me, calling my name. Calling another name, too.

"Henry's gone, Everett!" That's what she says just before I dive. "I miss him, too! But we need to move on without him!"

She's wrong. Dead wrong. And I'm going to prove it.

When I'm sure she's got a lock on me, I throw myself into the panelography. I ride the swirling currents of the Underfunnies, swooping away from the bizarre realm of Hazy Kat.

As I travel, I think of Henry. I think of our son. I remember how miraculous he was, how full of life and personality from the day he was born. I remember his bright blue eyes fixing on me with pure love and expectation. The way his lips moved as he repeated the things I said, as if he were memorizing each and every word.

He was the greatest thing to ever happen to me, to us. A dream come true—a dream I'd never known I had until he arrived.

A dream that ended the day he died.

I remember the sound of screeching tires, the screams of Molly as she ran. But never a sound from Henry. Not even a last gasp of breath when I got to his side in the street. Only silence from him.

And only blame between Molly and me. Blame become hatred, hatred become rage. I threw myself into my work, pioneering the exploration of the richest vein of the Underfunnies, born of the comic strips of the early 20th century. Anything to lose myself in the black and white of simple line work, the discoveries of Subtextual Space. Anything to forget Henry and stay away from Molly.

And then, one day, I got The Idea. And I knew it would work. It *will* work, if only I can get her to where she needs to be.

Suddenly, the flow of my thoughts is interrupted as I pop free into a fresh setting. I feel the tingle of something sparking on my body—the crackle of a tiny flame burning at one end of me.

This time, I am a lit stick of dynamite in the hand of a child.

"Zo!" says the little boy, a chubby creature with thick hair as black as his old-fashioned waistcoat. "Vhat do you say, Fritzie? Vill der Admiral like zis special *bratwurst* ve have for his dinner?" He holds me up and grins.

"Oh, ja," says his brother, also chubby but with blond hair and white coat. "I zink maybe he von't haff zo many *chores* for us tomorrow, Helmut!"

We're in a kitchen, surrounded by the smell of cooking sauerkraut. The boy's Auntie toils away on the other side of the room, stirring a bubbling pot. Her work is never done, taking care of the mischievous and ungrateful Schnitzeljammer Brats.

"Time to serve der first course!" Blond Fritz grabs a plate and holds it out.

Helmut drops me on the plate with a devilish smile. "Vhat a lovely presentation! Der Admiral ist sure to ask for *seconds*!"

"Ja!" Fritz laughs. "*Thirty* seconds till she *blows*!"

With that, they march me out through the swinging door to the dining room. The Admiral awaits them, sitting at the table in his seaman's cap and scrub-brush mustache.

"Dinner iss served!" Fritz plunks the plate in front of him.

"*Bomb Appétit!*" says Helmut, and then he catches himself. "I mean *Bon Appétit!*"

The Admiral doesn't seem to notice there's dynamite on his plate instead of bratwurst. He raises his fork and knife, ready to dig in …

But before his utensils make contact, his cap leaps off his head and flops down over me. Cut off from the air, my fuse fizzles and stops burning with just an inch to go.

Then, I hear her voice—Molly's voice, speaking from the substance of the cap. "You're not the *only* one who knows how to manipulate the supertexture of the Underfunnies!"

I'm surprised. Following me into the panelography is one thing; possessing resident iconography is quite another.

Apparently, my wife did her homework before she got here.

"Now *listen* to me," she says. "I want you to come *home* with me, Everett. You've been in here too *long*."

For the first time since she found me, I answer her. "You don't know what you're talking about."

"Oh yes, I do," she says. "Don't you think I tried to hide from the world, too? Don't you think I wanted to run away and never come back—never remember what happened to Henry? Don't you think I loved him, too?"

Her words settle around me like comic strip snow. Should I remind her, again, that I was trimming hedges in the back yard when it happened, and she was the one who was supposed to be watching him when he wandered into traffic? That she was the one who turned her back to talk to a neighbor when she should have had her eyes glued to Henry at all times?

Only if rubbing salt in the wound is my goal. "Leave me alone," I tell her. "Go back to reality."

"I'm not leaving without you. That's final." Just as she says it, she's lifted away, leaving me uncovered on the plate.

Fritz makes a grab, but I dive out of the realm of the Schnitzeljammer Brats before his pudgy hand can touch me. I've got to keep moving, keep running, keep drawing her along in my wake.

Until it's too late to stop what I've got planned.

It wouldn't be enough to tell her the story straight up, to tell her The Idea I've set in motion. I can't take the chance she won't believe it's possible, that she won't cooperate.

Not to mention that it breaks every tenet of the Panelnaut protocols. Protocols that I helped create.

Diving through the foamy black-and-white tides toward my next destination, I remember the early days of exploration. I wasn't the first to discover the Underfunnies, but I found the first doorway and made the first trip inside.

It was so thrilling back then, such a novelty—plying the byways of this vast psychic substrata. Jumping into manifestations of comic strips from various eras, existing side-by-side with beloved characters as well as obscure ones. Before long, I discovered I hadn't accessed the primary reality of those strips, but a flip-side echo where nothing works the way it should—a negative space where expectations can't be trusted. The place where Potpie's spinach can won't burst on cue, where Ixnay the mouse can't toss a brick on target, where the Schnitzeljammer Brats' dynamite sticks won't stay lit.

Did I understand the full implications back then? Hell, no. The best I thought we Panelnauts could do was influence the collective unconscious—plant messages that guide humanity toward a state of peace and harmony. We wrote protocols forbidding extreme intervention, anything that disrupted the essential integrity of the panelography.

And now I'm throwing them all away. The ultimate disruption is in motion; every moment brings it closer to final fruition.

And I'm the one who engineered it. I'm the one who knows how close we are to the grand finale.

Very close, now. It's time to pick up the pace.

I need to move her along quickly, not give her time to think or catch her breath. I need to flash like a skipping stone from world to world to world until we reach the last one.

The one I've prepared.

So I fling myself out of the current and surface in another place. This time, I'm a cigar in the mouth of Moo Mullet, rascally gambler and ne'er-do-well. Seconds later, I hear Molly's voice coming from the black derby hat on Moo's little brother, Kozy.

"Please, Everett," says the derby hat. "No more running."

"Say! What gives?" Moo snatches the hat from Kozy's head and gives it a smack with the back of his hand. "Now I gotta take *lip* from a *lid*?"

"We can get through this together," says Molly, "if you'll just come home."

"That topper's positively *brimmin'* with yap, ain't it?" says Kozy.

"Leave me alone!" I shout, just as I dive out of the scene.

"Now my *cigar's* runnin' at the mouth?" I hear Moo say as I leave. "What's next? My *racin' form* tellin' me which *horse* to bet?"

Once again, the currents bear me onward. I'm closer still to our final destination and the consummation of all my efforts.

Leaping from the flow, I become a club in the hands of Allie Hoop the caveman. Molly becomes the collar around the neck of his pet dinosaur, Finny.

"Please give me a chance!" The sound of her voice makes Finny grunt and run into a tree.

"What the heck?" says Allie. "How come you sound like a *girl* all of a sudden, Finny?"

I leap away without a word, and she follows.

Next, I become the fireman's hat on Smokin' Stovepipe, and Molly's the bell on his kooky one-man fire truck. I linger there for less time than it takes Smokin' to utter his catchphrase, "Fwoooo."

We're closer now, almost there. I speed up even more.

At our next stop, I'm the clodhopper boots on Li'l Asner the hillbilly. Molly's the pipe in his old Maw's mouth.

Then, I'm the giant sandwich in Ragwood Rumstead's hands, and she's the polka-dotted bow tie at his throat.

Another hop, and I'm the TV wristwatch on Rick Tracer's arm. She's his lemon yellow trench coat.

Then, I'm the bald head on Daddy Bigbucks, and she's Orphan Agnes' curly orange hair.

"Please stop!" says Molly, giving Agnes quite a start. "Just stop running!"

"Bleepin' blizzards!" yelps Orphan Agnes.

In spite of Molly's pleas, I leap again just the same. Because finally, we've reached the end. My whole purpose in leading her on this chase through the Underfunnies.

I swoop through the currents and burst free at our last stop. This time, I appear as myself, not disguised as some comic strip prop. She does the same, returning to her familiar form in the silver spacesuit and bubble helmet.

Finally. Here we are. In a child's darkened bedroom.

"What is this?" She stares at the black-haired boy on the bed between us. "Who is this?"

"His name is Little Nino," I tell her. "And he's a dreamer."

Even as I say it, Little Nino stirs and sits up in bed. He rubs his eyes, and then he looks at me, and smiles.

"Oh!" he says. "You are here!"

Grinning, I tousle his hair. "Just like we talked about, Nino. Are you ready?"

He smiles and nods.

"What's happening here?" Molly scowls. "What are you talking about, Everett?"

"Little Nino's been having a crazy dream," I tell her. "Haven't you, Nino?"

"Why yes, I have." Little Nino crawls down off the bed and pads across the room in his fuzzy white footie pajamas. "I have been dreaming about the music in my closet."

As we watch, he opens the door of his closet. Beams of rainbow light stream out around him.

At the same time, a sweet piping song skirls forth—the sound of flutes and chimes and strings weaving in delicate harmony.

Little Nino smiles back at us. "Do you hear it?"

"Yes, we do," I tell him. "Let's have a closer listen, shall we?"

"That will be fine." Without hesitation, Little Nino shuffles through the closet doorway, disappearing into the rainbow light.

"Come on." I take Molly's elbow. "I want to show you something."

She frowns at me. "That song. I know it, don't I?"

I just shrug and pull her toward the closet.

As soon as we cross the threshold, the doorway disappears behind us. Suddenly, we're standing on a beach at night, facing a bonfire that burns in rainbow colors.

At first, we're alone there with Little Nino. "I remember what comes next," he says. "Would you like to see the rest of the dream?"

"Yes, we would." I let go of Molly's elbow and take her hand. "We would like that very much."

Little Nino waves his arms, and figures descend from above, floating down one at a time from the starry sky. They are comic strip women, all of them, descending like wingless angels to land lightly on the wet sand around the rainbow bonfire.

There's Potpie's girlfriend, Olives ... Ragwood's wife, Blonder ... Li'l Asner's gal Dandelion Meg ... Rick Tracer's true love Bess Bluehart ... Allie Hoop's cavegirl Moolah ... and so many more. Every woman you can think of from the funny pages, every one of them from the sublimely beautiful to the utterly ridiculous. Dozens of them, hundreds of them.

This is it. This is what I've been working for; this is why I summoned Molly.

Because this is where the impossible can happen. Here in a child's dream in a flip-side place where things don't happen the way they should.

Only here could I do what had to be done.

Hand in hand, Molly and I walk to the fire. We stand before the women, their faces and forms flickering in the dancing rainbow light.

"Oh!" Suddenly, Little Nino runs forward and gazes into the flames. "There is something inside!" Without hesitation, he plunges his arms into the fire.

When he pulls them back out again, unburned, there's a bundle in his hands. Something wrapped in a comic strip blanket, all black ink and wooly cross-hatched texture.

Grinning, Little Nino turns and offers the bundle to Molly. "Please take this," he says. "It is for you."

"From all of us," says Olives in her nasally voice. "Every last one of us."

That's exactly what it took—the combined power of several hundred female icons projected together. Merged with my own hopes and memories in one supreme act of will.

Not sex, but creation nonetheless. The ultimate surrogate motherhood.

Molly peels back the blanket, and a tiny face looks out at her. The face of a comic strip baby boy, eyes big and dark and shining.

This, then, is my secret son, a child conceived in the panelography. A child of pure hope and imagination—an homage to the son we lost.

And perhaps much more than that.

"Think of Henry," I tell her. "Remember everything you can about him. Every detail."

She looks at me with tears rolling down her face. "But that won't ... this isn't ..."

"Trust me." I lift the helmet from her head and kiss her wet cheek. "Think of Henry."

She casts her eyes up at me with a look of anguished disbelief. I brush the dark hair back behind her ears and shake my head.

"I can't do it myself," I say. "I need you. Your half of the memories. Your half of who he is." I kiss her cheek again. "Please try."

I watch as she cradles the squirming bundle in her arms. As she closes her eyes and frowns, reaching deep to dredge up those memories.

The comic strip women huddle close, caught up in the moment. I can practically see the pen-and-ink waves of hope ripple out from their exaggerated forms.

Maybe it's the force of their collective willpower. Maybe it's the power of the dream we're in, a dream within a dreamlike realm where human disbelief is suspended. Where comic-strip life works in reverse, so harsh human reality can change direction, too.

Or maybe it's just her memories and love for him. *Our* memories and love pouring into a vessel of India ink. Pulling him back from the vanishing point—pulling all three of us back.

Whatever the reason, a new strip debuts tonight, a full-color single-panel above the fold in the Sunday pull-out section. Here's how we kick off the run:

A mob of famous comic strip women stands around a rainbow bonfire. At panel center, classic child character Little Nino stands on tiptoe, gazing at a swaddled babe in the arms of a woman in a skin-tight silver spacesuit.

Little Nino says, "Oh my! Look at his eyes! They're not black anymore!"

The woman in the spacesuit weeps with joy. The square-jawed man beside her bends down to kiss the infant's forehead.

We can see, in the firelight, that the baby's eyes are the brightest blue that the four-color printing process will allow.

The caption at the bottom of the panel reads as follows: "Welcome back, Henry!"

Intersection

by Gio Clairval

People in uniform extract me from a warped carcass of steel. They speak to me but I just hear wobbling noises.

The image of a woman's face fills my mind. Blue-grey eyes. A full mouth. Lovely. I know her well. I also know that I love her. She's my wife.

But she loves Lester.

The idiot was driving, and he didn't stop at the intersection. My wife was in the car with us.

There she is, standing near the ambulance. She seems okay.

Lester is out cold. It's a blessing, because I don't hear his blabbering. He talks all the time. All he can do is talk.

Maybe he's dead. If not, I must help him to die.

Now the world becomes dark and peaceful.

I'm reclining on a bed. Tubes stick out of my nostrils and another tickles my nether regions. Nothing down the throat. A monitor winks green.

I try to get out of bed but I can't. I do a roll call of my limbs: Nothing stirs. A tear rolls out of my left eye.

I'm not giving up.

It takes some time before my left hand obeys and moves up to my head, finding bandages. I must look like the Invisible Man. This thought makes me chuckle.

A stab of pain in my chest cuts my laughter short.

The image of my wife comes back to soothe me, but my thoughts remain troubled.

Why does she love Lester and not me?

I hate Lester almost as much as I love my wife.

It's him or me.

I can walk around a bit.

All I do is brood over this thing—that Lester believes he's better than me, and that's why he must be in charge.

I don't see why he should be in charge. I think Lester simply speaks better than I ever will.

Speaking is overrated. A man can be silent, and loving, too. Lester is only interested in being the one who decides.

Lester knows nothing about the little things that make a life worth living. Or the big things. Take the music of the stars. All right. Nobody can hear the music of the stars, but I'm sure that, if he could hear it, he would *not* feel it in his bones as I would. Music doesn't move him. At a gig, when the bass plays the rhythm of the heart through the amplifiers, the only thing that vibrates in Lester is the bottom of his trousers legs.

He's not better than me. After he was born, Mother Nature had to give it a second try and that's why she made me—because the first time everything went wrong.

Instead of hearing jumbled words, I understand what people say.

Lester has finally come to, and my wife's here to visit. He doesn't recognize her until she writes something in a notebook and shows it to him. Lester mumbles: "Lee-ah."

She has a newspaper, too.

"G-give," he manages.

I catch sight of the page. There's a shot of the accident. And a photo of my wife and me in the sidebar.

He points to my face in the picture: "Wh-o?" and starts yelling.

Damn! He thinks that my wife is cheating on him. With *me*.

I don't get it. *I'm* her husband, and she's cheating on me with *him*. I know she likes him more than me.

Now he's raising a hand to hit her.

I can't let it happen and I grab his hand and push it down, but it shoots up to punch my eye.

The nurse walks in with an ice bag and Leah takes it and puts it on my eye and consoles me and kisses me, and I almost want that cretinous ape to hit me again.

Today is the day I kill Lester.

We're home from the hospital. Lester can speak, but not well. Otherwise he'd be numbing me with words.

Now he keeps spreading his newspaper like a bedsheet, opening his arms so wide I can't see my favorite TV series. He's reading to show off, because I still can't. All I can see are wiggles on the paper.

It doesn't matter. He'll be dead soon, and dead people don't read newspapers.

Leah is at work so we have a nurse to look after us. She has nice legs and a sweet smile. She's actually brought roses and I help putting them in a vase. I sniff the scent, but it's like my left nostril is stuffed up.

As soon as the nurse goes to the bathroom, I drag Lester toward the window. He doesn't want to move, but I'm stronger.

I push him against the windowsill until he's half out.

The nurse comes a-running. "Mr. Brown! What are you doing?"

I'm winning the war.

"Stop me!" Lester cries. "I can't help it."

Hold on. What is he talking about? He can't help doing *what?* I'm the one trying to push him.

The nurse pulls us back and makes us sit on the couch.

I'll find a way to off him. I will.

"What's wrong with me?" he asks.

"You had a mini stroke and your car jumped lanes."

"A stroke …"

"A *mini* stroke. The symptoms last less than a day."

"But I still don't recognize my wife, and my own face! Is it another stroke?"

"It's something else." She pats Lester on the shoulder.

She tells him about some bundle of nerves, called *corpus callosum.* This thing's like a bridge connecting the two hemispheres of the brain. And it was sectioned in the accident. "Your right hemisphere is out of control."

This throws me for a loop. I'm lost. Lost. What is going on? What is she talking about? I refuse to believe her medical gibberish.

"Don't worry, Mr. Brown," she says. "It will take time, but, with some training, you'll learn to control your right brain."

What is she saying? That he's going to keep *me* under? I have an arm, a leg, a nostril in enemy territory, and our best eye. I'm awake now, and I'm *not* going to sleep ever again.

No Place for a Hero

by James Aquilone

Bernard Kowalski destroyed the Verrazano Bridge during the Friday rush.

But there are three important things to keep in mind: It was unintentional, no one died, and he caught the bank robbers he was chasing. It was a classic superhero feat. They *should* have given him a ticker-tape parade.

Instead he got thirty years in prison.

In his closing argument, the prosecutor called Bernie a "living, breathing weapon of mass destruction." She also called him an "irresponsible, reckless vigilante" and a "fame-seeking psychopath." Never once did she mention the word "hero." Bernie easily could have flicked a paperclip through her throat and decapitated her right on the spot. But he was a superhero and superheroes don't kill.

They held him on Rikers Island while they built a special long-term prison for him on Guantánamo Bay. He saved them the trouble. He busted out with one well-placed punch to the four-foot-thick cement wall and eventually settled on a desert island in the Pacific Ocean.

A superhero, Bernie lamented, has no place in the real world.

Bernie watched the sun sink into the ocean as he squeezed another yam into a coconut shell.

He had super strength. He could throw a garbage truck a mile. He could run so fast he was just a blur. He could blow down buildings with his ultra-breath. He could fly. And what did it get him, the world's first and only superhero? All the yams he could eat and his very own tropical prison.

No one bothered with him except for some neighboring islanders who would leave him food and gifts. They thought he was an angry deity. The yams were offerings. On special occasions they left roasted pig. He was happy for the food. It wasn't like he could fly over to Paris and grab some baguettes—not without causing an international incident.

He was thinking how Superman never got hauled into court in the comics when he spotted the helicopter. At first he figured it was sightseers. They occasionally flew over the island to take a peek at the superhuman, snap a few photos. He usually waved at them. Sometimes they'd wave back, sometimes they'd give him the finger.

He used his telescopic vision and saw that it was a Marine copter. In all the time he'd been on the island, no authorities had ever tried to contact him or haul him back to the U.S. Was this an assault? Were they stupid enough to try to finish him off now?

He scanned the sky, but there was only the one helicopter. If this was an attack, then the copter had to be equipped with a WMD.

He could hurl a palm tree at it or blow it down with his ultra-breath. But he continued squeezing yams. After two years on the island, the only way he could eat the tubers was by slurping them up like milkshakes.

The helicopter landed down the beach. He watched a man in a military uniform jump out. Alone, he headed toward the superhuman. Bernie relaxed.

The man said, "Bernard Kowalski?"

"No," he said. "I'm Batman." Military man didn't laugh.

"I am General William Duncan, Chairman of the Joint Chiefs of Staff."

Bernie picked up a yam, squeezed it so hard it exploded in his hand. "Care for a yam?"

"I'm not going to pussyfoot around, Kowalski. Your government needs you, maybe even the world."

"My government? You mean the one that arrested me for being a superhero?"

"We're in a big jam, the chili is really hitting the fan, and it is my opinion that you're the solution. We're prepared to offer you full asylum and will expunge your past crimes from the record."

"Crimes, huh? I was *fighting* crime!"

"Believe me, as a soldier myself, I understand. Collateral damage is inevitable in war. The greater good, son, that's what matters."

"Exactly! That's what I kept saying at the trial. I'm a super*hero*. There should be different rules."

"Well, Kowalski, the rules have just changed."

Bernie wiped the yam juice off his hands, sat up straighter. "They have, huh?"

"It seems you are no longer the world's only superhuman. But you can still be the world's only superhero. Madame Devastator has already destroyed most of New Jersey."

"Madame Devastator? Cool name."

"We've thrown everything at her, but it's done no good. We need you to take her out. You are cleared to use any means necessary. We're in a real bind here. What do you say, Kowalski?"

"General, I've been waiting a long time for this."

"I'll brief you at the Pentagon. We have an aircraft carrier not too far away."

"It'll be quicker if I take you."

Bernie scooped up the general and flew east.

Madame Devastator's real name was Hannah Bormann. She was a twenty-two-year-old art student from Connecticut, at least until about a week ago when she went berserk in Jersey.

At the Pentagon, Bernie watched videos of her obliterating Hoboken. She could fire bolts of lightning out of her fingertips and create storms with a hand gesture. She also sported a killer costume, something Bernie had always wanted. But his superhero career had ended before he could design one. Madame Devastator wore black high-heeled boots with laces up to her knees, a leather bodysuit with lightning bolts running down the sides, and a scarlet cape. At the moment, Bernie was in yellow Bermuda shorts, flip-flops, and a pink tank top.

When the briefing was over, General Duncan said, "Do you need any assistance from us?"

"Can you guys rustle me up a uniform? I feel kinda dorky here."

A half-hour later he was wearing Henry Winkler's leather jacket from *Happy Days*, John Wayne's cowboy hat from *True Grit*, Harrison Ford's pants from *Raiders of the Lost Ark*, and James Dean's boots from *Rebel Without a Cause*. Some wise guy had made a run to the Smithsonian and thought the clothes had some mojo that might help. They started calling Bernie "Mr. Americana." His previous superhero name was Bernard Kowalski.

When Bernie reached New York City, where Madame Devastator was currently wreaking havoc, he perched himself on top of the Freedom Tower. He didn't need his telescopic vision to find her. A boulder the size of a minivan blasted into the air over Central Park. Bernie rocketed uptown, and just before it crashed on top of The Dakota apartment building he obliterated the boulder with a mighty uppercut. A mist of pebbles showered down.

Bernie bolted into the park, flying just above the treetops.

He was nearing the lake when a street lamp rose into the air and swatted him as if he were a pesky fly. He crashed into the water.

As he sank, Bernie thought how he had only ever fought purse snatchers and jaywalkers.

He sprang out of the water, grabbed his hat—which was floating nearby—and placed it back on his head.

Madame Devastator stood beside the Bethesda Fountain, sparks dancing on her fingertips. "I should have figured they'd send for you," she said. "You've always struck me as a brownnoser."

"Is that why you're doing this? To get to me?"

"Don't flatter yourself. I'm doing this because I can. It's fun. Besides, what the hell else can you do with fingertips that shoot lightning?"

"You got me there," Bernie said, and blasted her with his ultra-breath. She hurtled backwards, knocking down trees and statues. She didn't come to a stop until she crashed into the side of an M10 bus.

All the vehicles on Central Park West were abandoned. General Duncan had pulled the military out of the area and evacuated as many civilians as he could, though there were plenty of them watching from their apartment windows, snapping photos and taking video.

A woman stuck her head out of a fourth-story window and shouted, "Get her, Mr. Americana!" Bernie's face burned with pride, though he wondered how she knew his nickname.

Bernie spotted a garbage truck up the block. He'd always wanted to chuck one.

As he lifted it over his head, he noticed with glee the camera flashes coming from the surrounding buildings. He paused, flexed his muscles, then heaved the truck at Madame Devastator, just as she was getting to her feet. Bernie was disappointed when the truck crash-landed right-side up a few yards from her. It tottered and he helped it along with a blast of his ultra-breath. A moment after the truck fell onto the super villain, windows were thrown open and there was a thunderclap of applauds and hooting. Some people were giving Bernie the thumbs-up. They held out their cellphones. Bernie smiled and waved as if he had just won the Miss America Pageant.

He was thinking about the ticker-tape parade they were going to give him, when Madame Devastator zapped him with the lightning from her fingertips.

His body seized. His muscles felt as if they had been turned to stone. Then came the burning. Bernie screamed.

Suddenly the sky darkened and the wind howled. He floated into the air and began spinning in the darkness. Thunder crashed around him. He was caught inside a tornado.

He tried to get his equilibrium, but he couldn't stop the spinning. He was blind and disoriented. His arms were pinned at his side.

He couldn't die like this before the world. It would be all over the Internet in seconds. In his panic, he pursed his lips and blew as hard as he could, hoping to jolt himself out of the twister. There was an explosion. He heard glass shattering and stone crumbling. He blew again. Another explosion. Screams. Car alarms blared. Still he was trapped in the funnel. He blew straight down and kept blowing until he rose above the bad weather. He stopped blowing when he saw the sun and the bright blue sky. Then he was falling, his muscles still cramped from the lightning strikes. The roof of the American Museum of Natural History rushed up to the meet him and he crashed through it. He landed on a stegosaurus skeleton, which was now a pile of rubble.

After a moment, his power returned to him and he shot through the hole in the roof. Madame Devastator was waiting for him in front of the museum. She looked tired, drained. The lightning flickered on her fingertips like a dying light bulb.

"You don't have to fight me," she said, gasping for breath. "We're the same. In fact, we're the only two of our kind. They"—she swept out her arms—"are our real enemies. You saw how they treated you when you tried to help them the first time."

"I'm a superhero," Bernie said. "This is what superheroes do."

One moment Bernie was hovering in the air, the next he was behind Madame Devastator. He held her in a headlock. She barely resisted.

"This ends now," he said.

"If you're going to kill me, you could at least use an original line."

A small crowd watched from the park across the street. Someone yelled, "Finish her!" Another screamed, "We love you, Mr. Americana!"

Bernie tightened his grip on Madame Devastator. Camera flashes, like bolts of lightning, ripped through the air. In minutes he'd be the champion of the world, his face on every TV screen, newspaper, and magazine. He was probably already trending like crazy on the Internet. Before he twisted his arch-nemesis's neck, he whispered in her ear.

Then Madame Devastator went limp in his arms.

For a moment the city was silent. Bernie heard only his ragged breathing. Then there came an eruption of cheers and shouts. People began to appear from all over. They chanted his name and it echoed across the city. Bernie's eyes moistened. He wished his parents were still alive to see this.

As the crowd inched toward him, Mr. Americana, née Bernard Kowalski, flew off with Madame Devastator's body in his arms.

The yams were all gone, so he flew to Tokyo and got sushi. He didn't even have to pay. Heroes don't have to pay. It's one of the many perks.

Back on the island, he sat on the beach reading an English-language newspaper he grabbed along with his lunch. The front page showed him holding Madame Devastator. "Mr. Americana Saves the Day!" the headline blared.

A few pages in he found an editorial questioning whether Mr. Americana (the Pentagon had leaked the nickname to the media shortly after Bernie left for New York) was needed now that Madame Devastator was dead. He knew that would come. In time they'd return to seeing him as a ticking time bomb. Weapons of mass destruction are only tolerated in times of war.

"Did you get any sashimi rolls?"

Bernie turned and watched Hannah exiting the tropical forest. Her blond hair was pulled into a ponytail and her freckles stood out with sunburn. Without her costume, she looked like a typical college student.

"Yeah," he said, and handed her the bag of take-out.

He never intended to kill Madame Devastator. Superheroes don't kill. But it wasn't until that day in New York that he realized how badly a hero needs a villain.

She sat next to Bernie. "Doesn't this get boring?" she asked. "Just sitting here."

"You get used to it. Have you decided where you're going to make your reemergence?"

"I was thinking Paris in the spring."

"Perfect. That will be well after my ticker-tape parade. I'll give you a two-hour head-start."

"That should be enough time to destroy the Eiffel Tower."

"No, don't do that. I've always wanted to chuck the Eiffel Tower like a javelin. I saw it once in a comic."

"OK. That might be cool. I'll take out the Arc de Triomphe with a tornado then. Meet me in front of the Louvre. We'll give them a good show. But this time, why don't I pretend to snap *your* neck?"

"Sure. Why not?"

A superhero, Bernie lamented, has no place in the real world. Not unless he creates one.

Happily Ever After

by C. L. Moore

C inderella and the Prince were married with a great ceremony. No one had approved from the first, and now more often than not there was a gleam of I-told-you-so behind the King's spectacles, and the Queen's three chins quivered with bitter satisfaction as her predictions were realized one by one. For Cinderella and the Prince were not happy. No one had really expected them to be. You cannot pluck a kitchen girl from the cinders and set a crown on her head and let it go at that; small feet are not the only prerequisite of a princess.

To tell the truth, the step-sisters had played a large part in what happened. Cinderella never realized it, but if Darmar and Igraine, with their hauteur and their high-nosed, high-bred faces, had not led her out of the cinders and disdainfully acknowledged her as sister, the Prince might have never done what he did. But after he had made that rash proclamation about the slipper he had to carry it out, particularly with the herald bawling the news to the very doorstep at the time. And then, of course, she was quite charming.

For a while, to do her justice, he was not sorry. Nothing could have been more bewitching than the Princess Cinderella in her billowing skirts, with the gold crown on her head. She had some secret difficulty in keeping it there, and used to practice before the mirror at night, but she never learned to manage the thing with true dignity. Once, when she bent to pick up a dropped handkerchief, it fell off and rolled across the floor. Now, a princess born would never have stooped for the handkerchief in the first place. Poor Cinderella blushed to her ears, and the ladies-in-waiting tittered among themselves.

There were other things. She had a healthy appetite, and the delicacies of the royal table were far insufficient to her needs. She ate and ate until the court stared, and yet she was never satisfied. Her pretty fingers hesitated among the forks, and her full-throated laughter rang almost strident above the polite titters of the court. Once she had laughed so hard that her stays split, to the immense embarrassment of everyone concerned. And sometimes, sitting still in the audience hall, the chill of its shadows penetrated to her warm bourgeois blood, and her mind turned longingly to the cinders and the lentils boiling on the crane above the fire.

She who had never had an idle moment before suddenly found herself plunged into a vast *ennui*—nothing to do but preen before the mirror and walk the garden paths, her crown tilted at a precarious angle, while hawk-eyes on every side waited for her least mistake as a signal for lifted brows.

One afternoon Cinderella disappeared. For hours they searched. It was the Prince himself who found her at last. Far off in a corner of the castle was an old tower room where odds and ends of things were kept—seven-league boots somewhat run down at the heels, a cloak of darkness with threadbare seams, magic mirrors with cracked faces, and miscellaneous charms that somehow didn't seem to work very well any more. Under the window stood a spinning wheel that had once spun gold out of straw. The treadle had cracked years ago, it creaked when it moved, and here in the dusty attic it had stood for years. Cinderella had found it, and here she sat in the dusty sunlight under the window, spinning and spinning gold. The shadows were full of it, and all about her slippers shining masses gleamed in the muted sunlight. The famous small foot trundled happily away at the protesting treadle, the curly head bent over the wheel and shining gold ran out between her fingers as she worked. The crown tilted over her eyes at its most rakish angle.

"Cinderella!" The Prince's voice was harsh.

She started guiltily, and the crown fell from her curls and rolled across the dusty floor. "Cinderella—spinning in the attic! Look at that crown!"

Blushing, she retrieved the crown and balanced it on her head.

"Oh, I'm sorry—" she cried. "I—I didn't mean—"

"There is nothing for you to say, Cinderella. For all I know I may find you scrubbing floors tomorrow. Have you no sense of values? You are a princess, don't you understand? A princess! There's dust on your nose!—Now don't cry! Princesses never cry. Here—stop—Cinderella!"

"Yes," meekly.

"Stay here till I can find someone to dust you off. If you should be seen like this—now *don't* cry!"

The Prince went out hastily.

Cinderella sat under the window in silence, with magic heaped about her feet. Slowly all the gold slid out between her fingers until they were empty. Her eyes began to brim. She hid her face behind her hands and wept. The attic was still but for the Princess sitting and weeping with her gold crown on her head; and the tears flashed out between her fingers.

Presently behind her hands a light began to shine. Startled, she lifted her wet face. The attic was radiant, and in the midst of the light her Fairy Godmother stood.

"Cinderella, child, why do you weep?"

It was the same question she had asked in the kitchen at home, long ago.

"Because they scold me," sobbed the Princess. "Because I'm miserable! Oh, Godmother, Godmother, take me home!"

The Fairy smiled, and the radiance brightened until Cinderella's eyes were blinded with light. She put up her hands to shut it out. There was a deep silence.

After a while, when the quiet had become unendurable, she uncovered her eyes. It was dark—warmly dark. She sat before the kitchen fire again, snug in the cinders.

"Why—why—" Cinderella dug her fists into her eyes, and then, somehow, was yawning, stretching like a kitten. No crown trembled precariously on her ruffled curls. She yawned again, luxuriantly, sniffing the boiling lentils that swung above the fire. She laughed a happy little gurgle deep in her throat, and settled down among the warm cinders.

Published in Galaxy's Edge Issue 2

Upright, Unlocked

by Tom Gerencer

▶ 1. ROBOT ◀

Picture an iguana. No, not that one. It's way too big. And the color is wrong. And not there. About six feet to the left. On second thought, never mind the iguana. This looks more like Arizona. But it's not. It's Nevada, and you've messed it up again.

On a rock nearby sits a skink. Baking. The sky's a hard, bright blue lens, and everything under it is like Food Network outtakes.

Close by, a patch of cooked dirt like every other suddenly shifts. Then, just when you think it must be the heat and the light playing tricks on your eyes, it does it again.

Now it tips up and slides and a hand reaches up from below, scarred, scuffed, dirt-encrusted, trembling. If we were making a horror movie we'd find some jarring music and play it.

But it's not that kind of hand.

It looks like it's made of white plastic.

It gropes, claws at the dirt, and then pulls. The ground shimmies again, sifts aside, and a head rises. Excitingly curved, like a design student spent most of his or her senior year getting it right.

Like this, it crawls from the Earth. Sand hourglasses off it and out of its joints. A light in its eye slit flickers on. Ridiculous. Why would light need to come out of an eye? Defeats the whole purpose. Probably the design student again. It stands.

Presently, it looks down at the skink, servos grinding.

"Who do I talk to about this?" it says.

Its voice is ancient. It's a robot. It's been buried in the exact center of the Earth for four and a half billion years. Give or take. The magma would have melted it, you say. Well, look who's so smart. It was made to last four and a half billion years. You think a little magma's going to hurt it? Nothing can hurt it. Except for itself. Which is the problem.

It was put here by a race of impressive machines that created the Earth, and all the life on it. They designed our primordial soup way back when like a program, like gajillions of lines of organic code that developed into everything we know, including pancakes and touchlamps. They did not do this from the goodness of their hearts. For one, they didn't have hearts. They were machines. *Are* machines. Because they still exist. And they're capitalist. And they take the long view.

They created the Earth and then buried the robot with instructions to wait, then emerge when a civilization had risen, make its way to their leaders, and hand them a bill. An invoice for the creation of the world.

Ethical? Don't make me need an antacid. These beings are slime. If you could, you would sue them. But for one, your lawyer would be aeons dead by the time the subpoena got halfway to their galaxy. So forget it.

But the robot—it's been down there all this time, through the volcanoes and the dinosaurs and the asteroid strikes and the cavemen and the battle of Trafalgar and the entire Oprah Winfrey show, and the whole time it has been thinking about nothing but string.

It was designed to be flawless, near-godlike in its immortality and power, which we'll get into more later. But one of the machines that initialized its psyche got distracted for a moment, thinking about something that would destroy your mind if you could even partially comprehend it but was, relativistically speaking, basically porn. And in that moment—really a billionth of a second—a relay that should have been in one position wound up in six others, and the robot was left thinking about string.

For four and a half billion years. Picture that. Never mind, you can't. You can't even do an iguana correctly.

It has thought every thought that it's possible to think about string. And then some. It's felt every emotion. Deeper than any human has ever felt anything. If any one person on Earth could ever feel even one tenth of the feelings it had harbored toward eighth-inch gauge tan twine alone, it would split their mind like an atom. The resulting psychotic episode would have its own mushroom cloud.

Needless to say, the robot's mind cracked. But thanks to its unique, all-encompassing intellect, it cracked like a masterfully cut diamond.

For example:

It stood now in the desert, looking out at the hard blue hemispherical gradient of sky, and it saw all the colors with electron-microscope precision, including billions of shades the human eye can't perceive—colors bees see, colors radio telescopes see, colors beings a billion light years away see—everything, but not all at once. Instead, it flitted through wavelengths like a shimmering aurora billowing across the stratosphere, cascading from angstrom to angstrom, viewing the world through a million different filters in the snap of a synapse. Like an old style flap-changing train station departure board with a universe of beauty on every new card.

It also saw equations and curves and angles everywhere. It could see the chemistry in the rocks, the advanced calculus in the shape of the cacti, read the genome in the skink, in the bacteria in the dirt. It saw the quantum physics in the ray/particles of sunlight, and other forms of math and science far beyond human understanding, in processes we have yet to glimpse the first hints of, all around it, shimmering like a forest of infinite informational gems. If knowledge is power, this thing was a nova.

It saw all of the possible meanings and metaphors. Deserts as death. As teeming life hidden in apparent emptiness. As the absence of water. As rebirth. As hell. As *New Yorker* cartoons. It saw every possibility of human interpretation, and also it saw through the eye and the mind of every living organism that has ever or will ever exist on any world or universe, and beyond that, borrowing perspectives from impossible beings that can never exist, that it extrapolated from nothing. It saw everything, from every angle possible, and from many that weren't. To say that nothing escaped it would be an understatement so large it'd make the dictionary people feel like they missed an opportunity.

It saw each of the molecules, and their atoms, and the sub-parts of atoms, and even smaller things we don't have concepts for yet, and all the reactions inside them and the myriad forces that held and repelled them. Its vision and the processing power behind it were just that good.

And that's just its sight. Similarly advanced were its touch, hearing, smell, taste, and a thousand other senses used by no creature on Earth. And its capacity to experience beauty was so much larger than a human's it would make an astronomer want desperately to explain it on a whiteboard in an internet video. It took everything in, and after four billion years spent thinking about nothing but string, the beauty of it all was enough nearly to split it to quarks.

Yet it held.

The skink still hadn't answered its question. Built Ford tough? Forget it. This thing would have supported one hell of a warranty.

All of which is to say, for an impervious, perfect, near-godlike, near-omniscient robot, it was patently insane.

Had it been functioning properly, it would probably have followed its orders. Made its way to Washington or Beijing, and presented the invoice for the creation of the Earth, and sat back and relied on its mission programming, which basically ordered it to wait thirty days, deliver a past-due notice, wait thirty more, present a final notice, wait another thirty, and then annihilate the planet.

It could do that. Easily. It had the ability to unite magnetism, gravity, both the weak and strong nuclear forces, and the power of the Home Depot into one colossal thrum that would erase most of the solar system, not just from the present and future, but from all time. A sort of retroactive screw you. Would it feel guilty? A little. But the way it saw things, if you're too lazy to pay off your bills, then you deal with the consequence.

But it was not functioning properly. Right now, beset by beauty almost beyond the capacity for the universe to contain, it had decided to present the bill for all creation not to any world leader, but to a guy named Ernie Nuttalberg in Port Malabar, Florida, give him six days, treat him to a few harassing phone calls, and then blow everything up.

It figured that was fair.

"Some help you turned out to be," it told the skink, and it walked off in the general direction of McCarran International Airport.

▶ 2. JERRY ◀

Why do people say someone is as pleased as punch? Would you be happy sitting in a bowl while people ladled you out and drank you and dropped bits of corn chips and ham salad in you off napkins, while they made small talk about their careers and the new baby and remodeling their kitchen and the dog's case of roundworms? If so, you are a rare individual or need medication or both. Likewise happy as a clam. Cut off one of your feet and sit in bottom mud, blind, eating sunken carrion for six weeks and get back to me. Let's say, then, joyful as someone with no problems, plenty of sensate delights, intellectual engagement, at least acceptably good health, and lots more of the same to look forward to. Gets tangled up trying to roll off the tongue, doesn't it? No wonder we resort to inanities.

This was Jerry. I say "was" because here comes the robot. But we have a few yet. So let's take a look.

He's sitting on a comfy, cushioned seat at his gate, reading a book. It's a fun mystery, with lots of good humor. Comfortable. Like a friend who never confronts you about your choice in romantic partners or makes fun of your shorts. He's also eating a cheeseburger and reveling in the sounds of the people. A little girl is asking her mommy about Florida and Disney World, rocking back and forth unselfconsciously with her hands on mommy's knees. Mommy's overjoyed, and some of it spills into Jerry. He can feel it. He's smiling.

He's almost fifty, with receding hair, longish, a mustache halfway between a Magnum P.I. and a walrus, heavyset, with happy, tired eyes and faded blue jeans and a big silver belt buckle. His tee shirt, which he got from the SkyMall, says, "I went to a pet psychic but it peed on my leg."

He takes a big bite of the burger. The meat, mustard, ketchup, yellow cheese, and tomato, unhealthy though they are, hit his taste buds like something from DARPA.

He loves, loves, absolutely loves to fly. He even loves airports. When he first realized it he thought about seeing a specialist. He loves the nearby hotels, with their complimentary breakfasts and personal waffle makers, fitness rooms, cable TVs, comfy beds. Loves the shuttle vehicles. Walking through automatic glass doors. Loves people-watching, interacting with clerks, browsing the shops, the throng and the mill of humanity on its way somewhere exciting—vacations and business and life events—real human emotion multiplied by the thousands. Excitement after all is contagious, and Jerry is, metaphorically speaking, touching the hand rails and rubbing his eyes.

Takeoff's his favorite, when the combined engineering brilliance of generations comes to a point and a roar, throwing him back in his seat and then up in the sky. The thrill and the flight, the sky toilets and landings—he loves it all. To him it's a free amusement park, minus the giant, slightly frightening, anthropomorphized cartoon animals. Unless you count the possibility of running into Alec Baldwin in the food court.

It's free because six years ago, coming home from a wedding in Texas, he volunteered to get bumped. In return, the airline gave him an extra ticket to anywhere in the Continental U.S., plus vouchers for food and hotel. Then the next day he did it again. When you've nowhere to be, it's fun to relax. As long as you're at least 200 miles from Detroit.

He took three more bumps in three days, flew to Los Angeles, and got bumped six more times, amassing more flights and hotels. He quit his job over the phone, and he's been doing it since. A perpetual air traveler. Like the Flying Dutchman with an inflatable neck pillow. He hasn't paid for a flight, meal or hotel since he started. He always picks vacation destinations in peak season—in the spring it's jostling for the armrest on the way to Florida and California, in the summer, lost luggage en route to New England and Oregon, in the winter, the sneezes and wet coughs of snowbirds heading to ski towns.

This increases the odds of an overbooked plane, and thus, of a new bump. He never skis or goes to the beach or the lakes. He would if he ever got bored, but he doesn't. If it ain't broke, don't fix it. Routine maintenance, however, is necessary.

The airlines have tightened up recently, but he's got enough freebies now to last for the rest of his life.

He finishes his burger and wipes his fingers on a napkin, gets up, goes to a trash can, and throws in the wrapper. He stretches, feeling the warm sun coming through the tall windows, taking in the view of the big planes outside. One of them will take him to Florida soon.

However.

When he returns to his seat, a robot is in it.

▶ 3. JERRY AND THE ROBOT ◀

At first Jerry thought it was a man in a costume, maybe doing a viral video for Doritos or HostGator. But the robot disabused him by projecting belief and understanding into his head of what it was, where it had come from, why it was here, where it was going, and what it meant to do. Jerry sat next to it, the wind taken out of him.

"My God, we'll all die," he said hoarsely.

Nobody heard him. This was because the robot sent out matching sound waves with opposing phase-timings to collide in their ears at just the same moment, canceling his voice. It tinkered likewise with their optic nerves to make them think it wasn't a robot at all, but a fortyish man in a suit with a bad Caesar cut. When it first got to the airport, it had let everyone see it as is, but so many parents had asked it to pose with their kids it took 35 minutes to get past the main entrance. But it decided to show itself to Jerry, as a kind of self-sustaining conversation piece.

"Don't worry," it said. "Maybe Nuttalberg will pay up."

Jerry's eyes focused on something about three miles in the distance.

"But the bill is the entire GDP of the solar system for the next million years," he said.

"True," said the robot, nodding at the woman with the daughter across from them. "But what did you expect, something for nothing?"

"Well, no," Jerry said. "But my God."

"And anyway, after, your world will be debt-free. You can do whatever you want. What a party I imagine you'll have. I can't wait to try the hors d'oeuvres. I'm speaking figuratively, of course. I've created a poem for the occasion: 'When you breathe, I want to be the air for you / As long as I don't then have to pass through your pulmonary alveoli / Have my oxygen bound to the iron in your red blood cells and consumed by your body's oxidative processes / My wastes excreted through your kidneys / To travel through corroded pipes to the sewage treatment plant amidst the other unpleasantness / I mean I have strong romantic feelings, yes / But let's be realistic / I'm not into anything gross.' Do you think I should rhyme it? You can't believe I'm single, can you Jerry? Let's face it. Some women are terrified by honesty."

"But that's—you can't do that," said Jerry.

"Recite poetry?"

"No. Kill everyone."

"No, I can," said the robot, and it showed him, by way of a gorgeous induced hallucination, how it could connect all the forces to wipe out the solar system.

"No, I believe you," said Jerry, "but it's immoral."

"Morals," said the robot, "are defined by the system in which they exist. Immorality's the new morality. Though also, saying something is the new something is the new saying something is so '90s. I looked it up on your Internet."

"But you're damaged," said Jerry. "You're supposed to go to the world leaders."

"Again, frame of reference. From my infinite perspective, it's the universe that's damaged, and I'm putting it right."

Nobody's the bad guy in their own story after all. Jerry had read about cultural relativism in a few in-flight magazines, but he thought this was spreading it thin.

"But think of all the lives," he said.

"I have," said the robot. "I've examined them all to a sub-sub-sub-sub-atomic level. I'm rounding. Actually I went deeper than that. This makes the most logical sense. Observe."

It showed Jerry then, by projecting its rationale into his brain. It had to augment his intelligence to avoid the information overload ripping his frontal cortex apart like neural confetti. For one brief shining moment he was fifty times smarter than Einstein, and he saw plainly how the robot's choice of action was really best for everyone involved, no matter that it was also insane and beyond genocidal. I could explain, but again, the iguana.

Jerry sat back, mortified, mollified, his soul crushed to a metaphorical pulp. If the wind had been taken out of him before, now someone had stolen the actual sails and deconstructed the ship and made attractive natural wood furniture from it and sold it on the Internet with free shipping. But at the same time he knew what to do. Because when he'd been hyperintelligent, he'd had an idea.

"But you still don't understand," he said.

"Nonsense," said the robot. "You don't believe that. You've seen it."

"I've seen it through you," he said. "But you're myopic."

The robot turned to regard him.

"I could rearrange the physicality of my facial molecules to form a nose so I could use it to snort, but it's not worth the effort. What are you talking, myopic? My understanding is infinite."

"So that's the wrong word," Jerry said. "Not myopic. Too broad. What's the word for that?"

"Fathead?"

"Close enough. What I mean is, you see it all at once. You need to narrow your field to really get what I'm saying. Until then you have no leg to stand on, and I win the argument."

"Manipulative," said the robot, dismissively. "But I'll bite, because it's not hard and I imagine it'll be so much fun saying I told you so after."

And the robot did. It inhabited Jerry, one hundred percent, traveling back in time first, to a moment some three days ago while he'd sat in first class on a flight to Virginia, and it shut out everything else.

It had never seen or felt the like of it before. The fidelity was incredible. With all other sense and thought turned off, the interior of a human was all intensity and focus and fine Corinthian leather. It picked up the little plastic cup of Scotch and melting ice from the tray table and felt the smooth, curving cold on its fingertips. It raised it, a sudden bump of turbulence making it almost spill a drop, and cautiously sipped, feeling the cool and the warmth hit its mouth and spread stomachwards, the taste like King Midas threw up in an oak tree and then set it on fire. It picked a Zwieback out of the wrapper on the little snack tray and munched it, the absence of all other data making its crunch and sweetness blaze like a comestible sun. It got in a conversation with the fat man next to it about workplace training that brought tears to its eyes.

And suddenly it saw the tragedy of its existence. A near-omniscient and all-powerful, unbalanced robot can never truly compartmentalize the way a human can. To a human, the moment was a singular thing, upright and locked, stowed in the overhead compartment or under the seat bottom in front, so few distractions, 100% of a single, microscopic facet of the world right there for the taking. The feeling was pleasant, to say the least. Like jumping in cool water after a day spent in a blast furnace or a room full of eight-year-olds. Relaxing. The robot wanted more.

So, using powers beyond our ability to comprehend, it rewound itself back to the moment of Jerry's birth, and it lived his whole life, from his first breath in a hospital in Indiana to his last in a nursing home bed in East Texas. But it didn't stop there. It then lived the life of every being that had ever or would ever exist in the solar system from beginning to end, including all the penguins and Simon Cowell, experiencing all the joys, sorrows, tragedies, triumphs, all the colds and upset stomachs and awkward dinners and games of pickup and sex and kangaroo births and love and insults and preenings and naps. All the French kisses, deaths, broken arms, triple backflips, moltings, and incarcerations over crimes that it did and/or didn't commit. And it was gorgeous, beautiful, unaccountably lovely and lonely, and perfect.

And when it had finished, it returned to the seat next to Jerry, at the departure gate for the flight he would board soon for Florida, and it gave him another mental flash to show him what it had done.

"And?" Jerry said.

"Well, apart from making you swerve at the wrong time and causing a potential car accident, squirrels are pretty harmless. Nobody ever worries about swimming in squirrel-infested waters or surviving the squirrel apocalypse."

"No, I mean our world."

The robot simulated a sigh for purposes of conveying inner struggle. "I have to admit that you're right," it said. "To destroy even one of those lives short of its destined fullness would be a crime of disastrous proportions. In fact, I think I'll create a heaven for you all to exist in even after you're dead."

It could do that. It showed Jerry how, then stood him up and gave him a hug. It was awkward.

"Thank you," it said.

"Okay," said Jerry, patting it, trying to break off.

▶ 4. ROBOT AGAIN ◀

The skink. Baking. Soaking up warmth while it can before dusk. Then here comes the robot. It casts a shadow, and the skink reacts by not moving. The robot understands it deeply, having lived its whole life, including this part.

"Hello," it says, and it digs itself into the ground, and is gone.

The skink sits staring out both sides of its head. One eye sees the paper the robot has left. Letters on it say: "Invoice: For the creation of every living being and inanimate object on and near Earth from the beginning of time through the end, including but not limited to sponges, the Encyclopedia Britannica, Lawrence Welk, Paul Prudhomme, Sirhan Sirhan, kittens, Lexan, the Earl of Sandwich, and string: No charge. You're welcome."

Which if you think about it is pretty generous. Especially considering that for the next five billion years it had decided to think about cellophane tape.

Published in Galaxy's Edge Issue 8
Copyright © 2014 by Tom Gerencer. All rights reserved.

Love in Bloom

by Sabina Theo

T his evening he appeared again.

He was silent. He had never uttered a single word, but I knew his feelings toward me. We had met many times when I was little—maybe dozens—before I even noticed the aid he had given me in his own imperceptible way.

I don't know exactly when it happened. It seems to me that the first time I paid attention to him occurred when I was just approaching the full flower of maturity. I had become used to his presence, for he hadn't changed in any discernible way. He was as fresh as ever, and devoid of those marks that the passing of time invariably leaves on others. During all our meetings my heart fluttered with a special fascination; a crazy thirst for life filled me, and I felt beautiful, more alive than ever, drunk with a certain tender happiness.

I needed time to understand that I loved him. It did not happen at once. He captured my heart, step by step. He never spoke, but I knew his thoughts. Sometimes I was sad or angry, and he inevitably appeared, scarcely hinting at such feelings as he had toward me—always silent, always ready to comfort and be with me. Calm as fate itself. Gradually, these meetings obsessed me and filled my mind, I began waiting for them; without the uneasiness and impatience inherent in every love, but rather with the quiet confidence that everything happens when it has to happen.

He never disappointed me. Sometimes he stayed away for months, but I knew that he was thinking about me; that he was following and observing me; and I was trying to be beautiful. For him.

He loved meeting me at dusk. At such moments something imperceptible and strong existed between us—more than friendship, a power superior even to love. I was his and he was mine.

This evening he appeared again. I was waiting for him. Something in the shadows' slow sliding through the garden told me he would come. Wrapped only in purity and coolness, the dusk crept over my body, coloring it in tender violet shades. I stretched and reached out to him, while the fragrance of the blooming irises sweetly soaked into my pores, and I looked for him. He wasn't late. The tears were his words …

During our meetings I never once asked myself what awaited us. We were bound together by something more than love. Sometimes I return to that evening in my memory and I understand that the beauty of my body was my present—the only present that could be worthy of him. And he accepted it.

I never thought about our future. I just knew that no matter what happened, he would continue to love me forever.

What was left for me was just the memory of my leaves and blossoms reaching out for him, and the fragrance of the dew drops as I finally exposed my pistil to those strange, bewitching and cool tears of my lover, called Rain.

Published in Galaxy's Edge Issue 5

Icarus at Noon

by Eric Leif Davin

Hell filled the sky. The seething cauldron of the Sun, only 17 million miles away and thirty times larger than it appeared from Earth, began to pour fire across the horizon. Soon its thousand-degree heat would begin cooking Santiago de la Cruz. Facing Sol as it grew larger, de la Cruz sat cross-legged in the Lotus position, bobbing gently, as if underwater, above the burned and blackened surface of Icarus. Almost eighty million miles from home, de la Cruz prepared to die.

It wasn't supposed to have been this way. It was an accident. It was because he shut down the damn computers on the final approach. No machine was going to have anything to do with touching down on this last "untouched" world. It was going to be one small step—*for a man!*

Santiago de la Cruz came in slow in the small cone of darkness trailing out from Icarus like a windsock. He wanted to park the ship in a close parallel orbit, then glide down in a suit. He miscalculated. Alarms blared, retros fired, and he plowed into the side of the asteroid in slow motion.

The ship's oxygen gushed out into the void of space as the scarred side of the asteroid ripped into the ship. It was a long horizontal slash—not enough to demolish the spacecraft. But enough to disable it. It would never make it back to Earth. It now drifted as a companion body to the tiny world and would join it in its long 409-day journey around the Sun. Somewhere amid the wreckage floated a spacesuit. In the suit was Santiago de la Cruz.

Santiago de la Cruz was an old hand. He had thrilled at the stark beauty of the Martian hinterlands and walked the bubbling surface of Io. He'd commanded every type of craft. He'd supervised bases on Mars and Io, built the Deep Space Observer on Pluto when almost everyone else said it couldn't be done. And *because* he was an old hand, he understood the logic of withdrawal. It made dollars and *sense*.

Besides, anyplace he'd been he could return to via VR tours. Anything seen by a robot or a human with a camera was easily accessible to anyone else thereafter. All you had to do was buy the appropriate virtual disk, slip it in, and you were *there* once more—or for the first time! You could hunker down to outlast a Martian sand storm, plummet through the stygian depths of the Jovian atmosphere, stand on the edge of an erupting volcano on Io. When *virtual* reality was as real as *reality*—who needed dangerous reality? But it still ate at him. "It's just not the *same*," he insisted to himself.

All around him Serenity Moon Base was a hive of activity, but as de la Cruz surveyed the installation he saw no humans. Worker 'bots scurried everywhere, intent on their work. Some of that work was on-going astronomical observations. Other work entailed the industrial production of oxygen, hydrogen, and other raw materials for lunar and space-based industries. Mass-production industry no longer took place on Earth. It was cheaper and safer off-planet, where raw materials were plentiful and transportation was easy. Finished products were then dropped down the gravity well to Earth. The home planet consumed what the Solar System provided.

What the *robots* of the Solar System provided, de la Cruz thought bitterly to himself. Just as worker 'bots swarmed over Serenity Moon Base, so they swarmed over the entire System, from Mercury to Pluto and Charon. Indeed, they pushed out even farther than the System, as robot probes explored the edges of the Sun's gravitational field and headed toward the nearest stars.

It's been like this from the beginning, de la Cruz thought bitterly. Machines got here first, now they're everywhere. The Russians weren't

138

the first in space. Back in 1957 it was Sputnik, a piece of Russian *metal*, which got into space first, announcing to everyone down below as it beeped away in the night sky that a *machine* got up here first. The first spacecraft from Earth to reach another world was another hunk of machinery, the Russian Lunik, which crashed on the Moon back in 1959. It was another Russian robot craft which reached Mars back in 1971. And so it went, planet after planet, probe after probe: Venus, Mars, Jupiter and Saturn and their moons, Halley's Comet, the asteroid belt. After Sputnik and Lunik it was Mariner, Pioneer, Viking, Pathfinder, Galileo, Magellan, Voyager. The machines always got there first.

And now they'll be here last, de la Cruz thought to himself. The human presence in space was but a brief intrusion. It just didn't make sense to have all those fragile and expensive pieces of protoplasm in harm's way. They weren't needed. Robot stations on Mercury and Venus, on Vesta and Mars, on Io and Pluto, could carry out all the observations and experiments any human could, and for a fraction of the cost. All the expensive life support systems needed to maintain human life could be jettisoned, making for a smaller, streamlined, high-performance facility operating on a shoestring. And it was safer, at least from the human viewpoint. When a catastrophic failure occurred at some far-distant outpost, all that was lost was some machinery.

And so the United Nations Space Agency had declared space gradually "off-limits" to humans. The human presence slowly pulled back from the fringes of the Solar System as human-staffed facilities were closed down one by one and put on automatic pilot. Serenity Moon Base, half-buried under the Moon's Sea of Serenity, was the last to be staffed by humans. And, as the personnel went home at the end of their turns, it finally came down to Santiago de la Cruz. He was "The Last Man on the Moon." It was his job to turn out the lights.

Santiago de la Cruz continued on his tour of inspection. It was for the most part redundant. The automatic systems ran everything, checked everything. But, it was his *job*, at least for the time being, and so he did it. He entered the hermetically sealed hangar where the Prometheus Project was nearing completion. Robot technicians scurried here and there running diagnostics on the craft. Soon it would be launched to the last unexplored piece of real estate in the Solar System, a small world previously overlooked. The all-conquering robots weren't quite *everywhere* just yet and, almost as an afterthought, the final blank spot on the map of the Solar System was going to be filled in. How ironic, de la Cruz thought, that the craft was named *Prometheus*, after a *man* who stole fire from the gods.

De la Cruz paused to admire the ship. It was a beautiful piece of machinery—manufactured right here at Serenity Moon Base. Like everything else on the Moon—or on Earth—it was untouched by human hands, entirely produced by robot techies in an automated facility. "That's just the problem," thought de la Cruz. "Who needs *people*? We're *all* redundant."

Indeed, humans weren't needed for *any* productive work. They were almost literally *useless*. Computers and robots produced everything—and they produced *megatons* of it, whatever *it* was. Thorstein Veblen had predicted it long ago. The "inordinate productivity of the machine," he said, would soon produce wealth far beyond the fevered dreams of Midas. And it did. About the only job left for humans was to consume the wealth.

For those who could. Most could not. Earth had become a hellhole for the common person. There were no jobs. And there were no handouts. The "freeloading parasites" who comprised most of humanity had become an idle underclass locked out beyond the gates of Eden, where the equally idle rich frolicked. And when the underclass became too restive, there were lots of prisons just waiting for them. Santiago de la Cruz was not a member of the "owning" class, so no comfortable and well-guarded high-rise condo waited for him. And when a robot could do his job just as well and cheaper, no job awaited him. Instead, the underclass beckoned him. As soon as he finished supervising the closing of Serenity Moon Base to humans, he would join it. "Just what the hell am I going to do down on Earth?" he thought. "May as well be dead."

The purpose of the Prometheus mission was to secure the Helios Station on the surface of Icarus, the hottest hunk of rock in the Solar System. Orbiting Sol *inside* the orbit of Mercury, Icarus was a two-mile-diameter nickel-iron asteroid. Even smaller than Deimos, the smallest Martian moon at seven-by-nine miles, there was nevertheless enough of it for a ship to approach in the shadow and touch down on it. The ship, however, would be as light as a feather. With gravity 1/10,000th that of Earth, a man, even in a bulky spacesuit, would not be able to walk across the surface of Icarus. He'd have to traverse the 15 square miles of jagged and sun-blackened surface by his hands, like a buoyant scuba diver pulling himself along the bottom of a Caribbean lagoon.

Once planted, the Helios Station would be a permanent, cheap, and fully automated solar observatory. It would monitor the various layers of the Sun's roiling solar gases, the photosphere, chromosphere, and corona, with their varying temperatures, directions, and visual characteristics. Based on Icarus, its orbit would never decay, as had so many other robotic solar observer spacecraft, plunging them into the Sun.

In addition, the four-hour rotation of Icarus meant there would also be a period of night during which useful observations could be made of the chromosphere and corona, the layers of hot gases just above the Sun's photosphere, or visual surface. While those layers actually shine by themselves, they are overwhelmed by the intensity of the direct surface glare. Blotting out that glare would bring the upper two layers into prominent view. Nighttime conditions would also make it possible for the Helios Station to observe the oval, grey, hazy glow of the inner Zodiacal light caused by sunlight reflection off dust particles along the plane of the Solar System, also erased in the full glare of the Sun.

And, with a wildly elliptical orbit, Icarus at perihelion—its closest approach to the Sun—dwarfed any hell Mercury could offer. On Mercury, the Sun was only twice the size as seen from Earth. On Icarus it filled the sky. With a brightside surface temperature of 797 degrees Fahrenheit, Mercury was hot enough—but at high noon on Icarus a week from perihelion, the temperature hit 1,000 degrees F. And *Prometheus* was going to rendezvous with Icarus at perihelion.

As *Prometheus* became more fully operational, de la Cruz spent more time in the facility, becoming more and more familiar with the last spacecraft he'd ever get to see up close and personal. Finally, he made a decision. Santiago de la Cruz had almost single-handedly built the Deep Space Observer on Pluto at the very edge of the Solar System. He'd be damned if a robot spacecraft was going to set up Earth's outpost at the other end of the System. He began programing instructions to alter the design and construction of *Prometheus*. He didn't want too much changed. Just enough to support a single human occupant.

And who was to stop him? He was the only man on the Moon. And since he supervised all reports to Ground Control, it was easy enough to conceal what he was doing. By the time his superiors down on Earth found out what he was up to, it was too late. He was already in space.

"De la Cruz!" they radioed. "Abort immediately and return to Serenity!"

"No chance," he replied. "I'm on my way to the Sun. I've got a rendezvous with Icarus at high noon."

"De la Cruz, are you insane? This is suicidal!"

"Yeah, pretty irrational, alright. What'ya gonna do? Terminate my career?"

"Why are you *doing* this?"

"Like Sir Edmund said, 'Because it's there!'"

"De la Cruz, you are jeopardizing the success of a multi-trillion-dollar scientific expedition!"

"So arrest me," de la Cruz radioed back, and then broke communication with Earth. He knew they'd be after him, but not before he got to Icarus first.

When Santiago de la Cruz regained consciousness, he seemed to be floating just above the steeply curving surface of a small hill. In all directions the dark and broken land fell away from him. A momentary wave of vertigo engulfed him and his head swam. Then he realized where he was and his vision steadied. The small hill below him was the entire near side of Icarus. Above him in the darkness of the asteroid's night side floated the wreckage of *Prometheus*. Then, off to his side, the disorientingly near horizon flickered with fire as the Sun began to rise.

The Sun galvanized de la Cruz into action. The sudden impact of its hellish temperature would quickly overheat his suit's cooling capacity. Soon, he'd be boiling like a lobster in its shell. He doubled over, reached down, and touched the surface of Icarus. "That's one small handhold for a man," he said, "one giant reach for all Mankind."

Then he reached out and grabbed another handhold on the surface. He pulled himself forward and reached with his other hand for yet another outcropping. Then another. And another. Weighing less than an ounce in his suit, he made rapid progress as he pulled himself across the face of Icarus. As the asteroid's rotation speed was only one mile per hour, de la Cruz soon saw the giant thermonuclear furnace of superheated gases which was the Sun sink back below the horizon behind him. He plunged deeper into the blessed -60 degree F. temperature of the Icaran night. In a short time he was in the middle of the asteroid's nocturnal zone. All he had to do, he thought, was just keep moving. That way, he could always outrun the dawn. And, with the slight exertion such movement required, he could keep it up forever. Or until his suit ran out of oxygen.

De la Cruz continued pulling himself slowly across the darkened surface of Icarus, pacing himself so he didn't use more oxygen than absolutely necessary. It was only a temporary solution, he realized. Eventually, he'd run out. "The Sun's going to get me," he thought, "just as it got the original Icarus."

He paused and bobbed gently above the Icaran surface, tethered by a light handhold on a piece of rock. He turned and looked back in the direction he'd come. There was a hell hound coming for him from just beyond the horizon. He couldn't outrun it much longer. Why not greet the inevitable face-on?

Santiago de la Cruz drifted into a sitting position inches above the surface and crossed his legs, assuming the Lotus position. He began to breathe in a slow, regular rhythm as he calmed his heartbeat and composed his thoughts. The problem, he thought, is rotation. And oxygen. If this damn piece of rock didn't rotate, I'd be able to hide in its shadow indefinitely. And if I had more oxygen ... But there was nothing he could do about either.

Up ahead in the expanding aurora of the Sun, de la Cruz noticed a brilliant point of light, as if a morning star shined in the heavens to presage the Sun. It grew larger, however, as the slow rotation of Icarus brought him nearer. Suddenly, de la Cruz realized what it was. It was the *Prometheus*! It was still there, where the collision with Icarus had left it, drifting now about two miles above the surface as the asteroid rotated beneath it. While Icarus turned constantly toward the Sun, the wrecked *Prometheus* hovered in stationary position, orbiting the Sun parallel with Icarus. De la Cruz's heart leapt within him as he thrust aside thoughts of stoic acceptance. "There's my shade!" he thought. "And oxygen, too, if the tanks weren't ruptured!" Two miles up. So close—and yet so far!

De la Cruz coiled his legs beneath him, calculated his trajectory, and kicked off from the Icaran surface as hard as he could. Arms stretched out in front of him, like a diver in a slow-motion arc, de la Cruz aimed for the derelict hulk. His leap carried him into the full blaze of the Sun. The temperature soared on the shell of his suit and harsh UV radiation flooded over him. But he spread his wings and flew. The leap to the ship seemed to take forever. "If I miss it," he thought, "I'll end up diving into the Sun."

But he didn't miss it.

Nor did the rescue ship miss his emergency beacon. De la Cruz floated in the welcome shade of the *Prometheus* as he waited for the ship from Earth. They'd arrest him, he thought. Maybe imprison him. It'd be the last time a human was allowed in space. It wasn't important. What *was* important was that a *human* had gotten to the last world in the Solar System before the robots. A *human* had flown to Icarus at high noon—and his wings had not melted.

Santiago de la Cruz looked out into the blackness of space. Hard pinpricks of starlight punctured the dark. They'd always called to him. They'd pulled him into space and across a dozen worlds. Their harsh reality would test him no more. But it doesn't matter, he thought. Even if unattainable—the stars still beckon.

Published in Galaxy's Edge Issue 8
Copyright © 2014 by Eric Leif Davin. All rights reserved.

Matial

by Lou J. Berger

M atial noticed the girl was tied too tightly and loosened her bonds. She smiled thanks and rubbed her wrists where the thongs had marked them. A small fire burned nearby.

"How much longer?"

He frowned. They weren't supposed to talk. He didn't even know her name. Knowing her name would make her into a person. Right now, she was just another sacrifice.

He pulled back the tent flap and peered outside, looking for eavesdroppers. Nobody was nearby. The sacrificial tent was set back from the others. A ribbon of smoke curled up from the communal fire. The black canopy of the night sky arched overhead, aglitter with stars and the swirled masses of nebulae. He closed the flap, tying the thong securely.

"Maybe four hours."

She nodded and took advantage of the loosened bonds to stretch her legs out in front of her, reaching her arms forward to touch her toes. "Will it hurt?"

Matial tried not to notice how the white doeskin rode up on her firm thighs, averting his gaze. He did this so that he wouldn't have to look her in the eyes. So young. In the prime of her life, she was maybe fifteen years old, with the unlined face of a girl but the body of a woman. She pointed her toes and glanced up at him through a fall of raven hair, her single visible eye bright with reflected firelight. He glanced in her direction and quickly away again.

"When you cut me, will it hurt?" she asked again, curiosity in her voice.

He picked up the knife and rested it against the flat stone in his lap. He tested the edge against his thumb and frowned. He spat on the stone and scraped the knife back and forth, holding it steady, careful to keep the edge at the correct angle. He hated sacrifices. "Not if I make it sharp enough."

"So you'll do it? You'll set my spirit free?"

He nodded, avoiding her direct stare. She was very curious. She was different than the others.

"If you don't set my spirit free, does the sun not rise?"

He finally looked at her and saw calm intelligence in her eyes. She wasn't afraid, didn't duck her head away from him. His head whirled. She'd asked a valid question, one he'd wondered himself. The sun came up every other day of the year, why would it not come up on the Day of Planting? Was sacrificing a virgin absolutely necessary? He cleared his throat and put some anger in his voice. "The tradition must be met. You should not ask these questions."

"Why not?" she said, refusing to look away. Her eyes bored into him. "I'm the one dying for the crops. Don't I get some answers before you cut my throat?"

He shook his head. "I don't cut your throat. I open your leg and collect the blood in a clay bowl."

She looked down at her legs, still stretched in front of her. She pointed her toes again, which made her calves flex. She raised her gaze to him slowly. "Such a waste, don't you think?" She ran her bound hands slowly down her thighs.

He tried to tear his eyes away, but couldn't. A burning sensation formed in the pit of his stomach and his throat grew tight. He swallowed.

She noticed his discomfort and a smile tugged at the corner of her mouth. "Don't you think it's wrong to kill for such a stupid reason?"

Matial shook his head. "Stop it! You are not supposed to speak!"

146

She grew angry. "I have nothing left but a few hours. You have a lifetime. Why would you let me go to my death without sharing with me why I must die?"

He had no answer. He watched her in the flickering firelight, noticing how the light illuminated her high cheekbones, danced along the edges of her raven hair, glittered in her eyes. He allowed his gaze to stray down along her torso to her legs again and marveled at their musculature, how fleet she must be when she ran. He imagined those legs never running again. He moaned softly into the tent's thick air.

"I can pick berries, dig roots," she said, without hope. "I can find shelter even in a rainstorm. I'm worth more alive than dead. Much more." She looked up at him and he saw a calm strength in her eyes. Her lack of fear impressed him.

His mind raced with confusion. He loomed over her, the knife held low by his side. "Don't be afraid." He lowered the sharp blade until the edge rested against her bindings. He drew a deep breath. "What is your name?"

She smiled at him. "Chimalma."

He rolled the unfamiliar name around in his mouth, then said it aloud. He slashed the thongs that bound her and she stood, tall and proud, and hugged him. Together they ran into the dawn, her small hand nestled in his, leaving his village for the last time.

Later that morning, despite the lack of a human sacrifice, the sun rose anyway.

Published in Galaxy's Edge Issue 9
Copyright © 2014 by Lou J. Berger. All rights reserved.

Do You Remember Michael Jones?

by Nancy Kress

arol Kincaid and her husband, whose name began with either J or K, stood across the room, drinks in hand, talking to Dave Bukowski. Dave had put on a lot of weight. Carol had lost a lot. Above their heads drooped the red-and-gold Mylar banner: WELCOME CLASS OF '79! Tiny bits of Mylar hung from the sagging top like bird droppings sliding down a window. I forced myself to cross the room and talk to them, because what was the point of going to your high-school reunion if you didn't talk to anybody. Carol looked up. "Jim! How nice to see you!"

I hugged her, shook hands with Dave and either-J-or-K. Carol's eyes were so sunken in her drawn face that they almost disappeared. She had been our prom queen. A year ago she'd been diagnosed with cancer. That was almost the last thing Maureen had told me before she left.

"Good to see you, too, Carol. How are the kids?"

"Gone. Like everybody's kids. After they leave college, they all move to other states."

Dave smiled. "My sister's son moved clear to another country."

We chatted for a while about kids, me trying not to remember the terrible conversation with Nicole when I'd told her that Maureen and I were separating. Nicole always sided with her mother, her whole life,

149

but of course this time she had reason. Neither Carol nor Dave asked about Maureen, which told me that they'd already heard the whole sorry story. I wished I had stayed home with a glass of Lapharoaig and the last of my smuggled Havana cigars.

Dave said, "Oh, there's that girl from my chemistry class—will you excuse me? I'm going to ask her to dance."

"Sure," Carol said. "Go for it." As Dave hurried off, she shook her head and laughed. "We none of us change, do we? He couldn't get girls to notice him in high school, and he's still trying."

Carol's husband—Jack? Keith?—said, "When I went to my thirty-fifth, none of the people I wanted to see showed up. It was a major disappointment."

"Oh, you," Carol said, "you'd have been just as disappointed if they had. All those old nerds still wearing plaid pants and carrying calculators."

Jude-or-Kevin laughed, and at the glance of real and deep affection that went between them, my heart suddenly hurt as if I'd been kicked in the sternum. Maureen and I had that once, but no more.

Carol said, "You know who I wanted to see here and don't? Michael Jones. Do you remember him?"

"Yes. He was … I think he was at my wedding."

"Really!" The sunken eyes sharpened. She had been so beautiful once, fresh as morning in a blue tulle prom gown. "Did you know that he saved my life once? Literally?"

I shook my head. Carol's husband frowned. "Sweetheart—"

"No, Ken, I want to tell the story. I do." She looked directly at me. "When you don't have too much time left, the truth of things starts to really matter."

It was said without drama or self-pity. I nodded, not sure what else to do or say.

"It was my junior year. My mother had just died. I was so depressed I'd dropped out of school. I was—well, I was contemplating suicide. You remember that I just disappeared from Honors English."

I didn't remember, even though Carol and I had sat behind each other in class. The things that are so pivotal to one person don't even make a dent on another.

"I'd actually gotten hold of pills. What was I thinking? I'd have missed Ken and the kids and all the … Anyway, Michael Jones came to my house. He was bringing me my trig assignment, but instead we talked and talked. I cried for the first time about my mother. When he left, I felt so much better. The next week I went back to school. I never told him how much that meant to me—you know how easily kids get embarrassed. Then he moved to New York and I never got the chance."

"He didn't move to—" I started to say, but Bad-Ass DiMonti came rushing up and threw his arms around Carol.

"Babe! You look like hell!"

"Let me go, you idiot!"

He did. All through high school we called him "Bad-Ass" because he wasn't. Inevitably he did the wrong thing, sometimes subtly wrong and sometimes so monumentally wrong that everyone was left blinking in sheer disbelief. He was our butt, our clown, our sacrifice to an ineptitude so deep that the rest of us felt competent by comparison. Bad-Ass flunked every course, although I suspected he was not stupid. Flunking so much and still knowing the smart kids gave him a weird distinction. He pissed off every girl who might have gone out with him. He let himself be bullied—no, he almost invited bullying. It was, after all, a form of attention.

"Hey, Bad-Ass," I said, to see if he would object, finally, to the ridiculous nickname. He beamed.

Carol said, "We were just talking about Michael Jones. Do you remember him?"

"Remember him!" Bad-Ass shouted, so that several dancing couples turned around, rolled their eyes, and went back to clutching and swaying to Donna Summer. "He got me through school!"

I said, "What? I thought you weren't allowed to graduate."

"Well, not with you losers," Bad-Ass said. He pulled out and lit a cigarette, despite the clear NO SMOKING signs. Still trying to be cool. Still failing. Carol moved slightly away. Bad-Ass said, "I graduated in December the next year. Michael Jones, he really let me have it. Told me I could do it if I tried, and the only reason I didn't try was that I couldn't equal you grinds, but so what? And anyways all of you was gone. So I got a tutor and Michael called me up every week and yelled at me some more and I graduated and that's why Harry Parker gave me that job at the Grease 'n Go, and now I got my own body shop."

"Good for you," Ken said.

"'Course, Michael moved away after that, to Atlanta. Sent me a postcard once."

Carol sagged against her husband, and instantly Kevin had his arm around her. "Tired, sweetheart?"

"A little."

"Let's go sit down."

They walked off. Bad-Ass said, "I forgot she's going toes up. Hey, I hear you split from Maureen and got yourself a little tootsie."

"Fuck off, Bad-Ass," I said again, and he grinned. I wish I'd called him "Rick" instead.

The reunion was depressing. I had nothing to say to these people, who had known both Maureen and me and who now, apparently, knew about the middle-aged insanity that had led to the stupid, exciting whirlwind six months with Kayla. I had never known that much sheer, lustful excitement. Now that she'd dumped me, I hoped I never would again.

I only stayed at the reunion because now my curiosity was piqued about Michael Jones. He hadn't moved to New York or Atlanta; he'd been at my wedding. I asked several people about him, because at least it gave me a topic of conversation, "Do you remember Michael Jones?"

They all did. Everybody had a story about some way he'd changed their lives. Mostly in good ways, although Cathy Parminter curled her scarlet lip and said, "That prick. Always sticking his nose in. He told me to break up with Paul before I got preggers. I didn't, and I did, but that still don't mean that smug-doll Michael had any business sticking his blond head in *my* business."

"Michael wasn't blond," I said. "Was he?"

"Sure. Looked like Robert Redford. Don't you remember? The one that got away." Cathy laughed, short and bitter. Her skirt was too short for a woman in her fifties, her top too tight, her hair too yellow. She glanced at my left hand and eyed me speculatively. I decided it was time to go home.

Just as I left to the strains of the Village People, the Mylar banner snapped loose at one end and fell into the bowl of non-alcoholic punch for those whose livers no longer let them drink.

At home, I looked for my high-school yearbook, but I couldn't find it. Maybe Maureen had taken it. She wouldn't have asked; Maureen always just did what she wanted. Our wedding day was the first time I discovered that we had a hundred guests, not the twenty I'd been told about. That we were footing the bill, not Maureen's parents. That Maureen carried goldenrod in her "autumn bouquet," even though I was allergic to it. I sneezed all through the ceremony. My nose ran all night.

In my study, which was where I spent most of my time since Maureen had taken all the living room furniture, I poured a glass of Scotch and lit my cigar. Bachelor freedom: smoking in the house. The Scotch smelled and tasted smoky, an October bonfire.

On the top shelf of the closet, behind a box of golf trophies, I found our wedding album. Picture after picture of family, some of them now dead, and friends, most of them out of touch. In nearly the last picture, a big group outside on the lawn in front of the hotel where we'd had our reception, I found Michael Jones. He stood in the back between my cousins Jared and Fred, his face half-hidden and fuzzy—had he ducked his head at the last minute? Somehow I couldn't even tell the color of his hair. At the reunion people had said red, or black, or blond.

Maureen was clear, though, laughing in the front of the picture, her arm through mine. God, she looked happy. Her full white gown had blown partly across my leg. Her face looked as lovely as her roses.

Roses?

I squinted at the picture, and then looked back at the rest of the album. Yes, Maureen's bouquet was white roses. No goldenrod. Nowhere was my nose running. And then I remembered: She had planned on carrying an autumn bouquet, until I told her about my allergy. That was the very morning of the wedding. She left the goldenrod and chrysanthemums and hydrangeas in the limo, tied up with their white ribbons, and instead she'd carried a few roses her cousin hastily stole from someone's garden.

And those hundred guests—did she really spring those on me that day, or had I agreed, however reluctantly, ahead of time? Did I pay for the wedding, or did she use money left her by her grandmother? Of course, that was "our" money, too, that we could have used for something else … but why did I remember, then, that I had resented and staggered under debt for a too-lavish wedding?

I turned back to the picture of Michael Jones, whom everybody remembered and no one had seen since. Was he really there, or was he—oh, I don't know, it sounds so vague—the *idea* of Michael Jones? Was that all he had ever been, an idea, sprung from somewhere deep in people's best selves and—

No. That was dumb. There stood Michael Jones at my wedding, head down and face fuzzy but undeniably solid in his dark suit and a glimpse of white shirt. As real as Maureen and I, both of us laughing and happy.

I remembered, all at once, that it had been I who urged Maureen to take all the living room furniture. I'd hoped it would assuage my guilt about Kayla. It hadn't.

I finished my drink. I finished the forbidden, fragrant, it-will-kill-you-but-we're-all-headed-for-Carol's-fate-anyway Cuban cigar. I savored that cigar. Its taste, its smell, its simple richness right until the last ash. I made it last nearly another half hour.

When I glanced down at the still open wedding album, I couldn't remember why I'd hauled it down from the closet. Something about my cousins Jared and Fred, standing close together in the back row. I should call Fred. It had been too long since I'd seen him.

Instead I picked up the phone, braced myself, and called Maureen.

Published in Galaxy's Edge Issue 8
Copyright © 2014 by Nancy Kress. All rights reserved.

Zombies at Work

by Leena Likitalo

I'm on my way to meet Johnny when I trip over the well-manicured hand.

"Sheila …" I sigh. "You've dropped your hand again!"

"Have I?" Sheila calls from her cubicle, her voice from beyond the grave. "Could you please bring it here?"

I navigate through the deserted gray maze. Sheila often works late; zombies don't need food or rest. Now she's charging her batteries. Her eyelids twitch, and her skin glows in disturbing shades of poison-green.

"Thanks for bringing the hand, Luisa." Sheila smiles at me, but her gaze remains empty.

I flee past the conference room where Johnny and I once kissed. We both pretend that it didn't happen, though we sometimes go out for *business dinners*. Neither of us has the courage to hope for more.

A rhythmic, pulsing sound echoes down the glass-walled aisle, muffled by the carpeted floor. A shiver runs down my spine as I realize that someone is crying. Who else is still here besides Sheila?

I find Helen, Johnny's secretary, in his office. Her narrow shoulders shake, twig-legs tremble. "Helen?"

"There's been an accident," she manages to say.

I drift closer to her, bound by morbid curiosity. "Where's Johnny?"

155

"There was a truck ... His car ..." Helen wipes tears into her chiffon blouse's sleeve. "Johnny is dead."

Johnny? But we're having dinner tonight. Right?

My legs give in. I collapse on his leather-padded office chair. As Helen sobs, I can only think of all the things that could have been, the romance on which Johnny and I never followed through. We could have been so happy together!

"What are you girls crying about?" The Big Boss avalanches into the room, reeking of cigarettes and whisky, interrupted night.

"Johnny ..." I whisper, my voice wavering with regret and disbelief.

"Yes, he's dead," the Big Boss cuts in. "But the company insurance covers resurrection expenses and he's been pieced back together already. Never let it be said that we don't take care of our own."

Johnny returns to work the next Wednesday. He wears his best pinstripe suit, but there's a strange dent on his left side, where his car got smashed in. He looks mildly puzzled, but not like he's in pain.

We greet Johnny with green and blue balloons. Many accept champagne, but no one wants to be the first to cut the sugar-frosted cake.

"It looks delicious!" Sheila announces, trying her best to fit in.

"Go on, everyone," the Big Boss orders, stomping to fill his plate.

I don't want cake. I drift past the queuing people, to Johnny. He looks as perplexed as I feel.

"How are you?" I ask.

"A little worse for wear." Johnny attempts a grin. His eyes, dull and pale, no longer glint with humor. Or with life, for that matter.

"Johnny ..." I thought I wasn't that bad with zombies, but here I am, at a loss at what to say.

"It's all right," Johnny says. "I'm not hungry for brains or anything."

I try to laugh, but I sound like I'm cackling. Several people turn to stare at me. I hate them all for witnessing the awkward reunion.

"Luisa, listen." Johnny lowers his voice. "We've wasted enough time already."

"What do you mean?" I ask, all too aware of the Big Boss' banter, Sheila laughing at bad zombie jokes.

Johnny brushes my shoulder, his fingers cold against my skin. "Would you go on a date with me tonight?"

Would I go on a date with a zombie? I blink, my mouth open, thinking how at that moment I must look like one.

"Yes."

Johnny takes me out to dinner, though he no longer needs to eat. He orders chicken curry to keep me company. The waitress asks if there is something wrong with his untouched dish. When she realizes he's a zombie, she mumbles apologies and refuses to let us pay. Which isn't that romantic.

Johnny drives me home. I say goodbye as I climb out of the car, but Johnny accompanies me all the way to the stairs leading to my apartment. I think of the months we wasted for no good reason whatsoever, how I always longed to invite him in.

"Listen." Johnny cups my chin in his palm, his touch akin to melting snow. "If you want me to leave, just say so."

"It's not that," I say. It starts to drizzle. I waver on the verge of tears. "I just never imagined our first date to be like this."

Johnny laughs, but he looks miserable. "Me neither. We were so silly."

Silly indeed … And what am I afraid of? He's still Johnny. Isn't he?

I trace his broken ribs with my fingertips. Where the white edges protrude through his ashen skin, the texture changes from porcelain to sand. "Does it hurt?"

"No." Johnny takes a deep breath, but his chest remains still. "I feel nothing."

I pull my hand away. For so long I have yearned to undress him. But now that I see him as he is, in his broken state, I regret my wish. "Nothing?"

Johnny places my palm on his chest, where his heart used to beat, where the resurrectors installed the batteries. "There really isn't anything after death but regret."

I know what he means all too well, and I'm still alive.

Johnny moves an escaped lock behind my ear. "This is my second chance, and I want to live it to the fullest."

His choice of words takes me by surprise. "You want to spend your undead life living?"

He stares back at me, grins. I can't help but giggle as his smile widens. Somewhere there behind the pale eyes is still my Johnny.

I say, "We won't know if this will work out unless we try, right?"

We kiss, and he comes back to life for a moment more.

Exemplar

A Secret World Chronicles Prequel Story

by Mercedes Lackey

Vickie Nagy hefted the backpack up onto her shoulders, and winced. It was freaking heavy. Why couldn't magic books be light? You'd think that *someone* would think of adding a little lifting spell to the spines, or something, when they were bound. But no.

Teachers prolly just want us reminded of how "weighty" our studies are, she thought with resignation, as she faced what looked like the blank cinderblock wall of the basement. Mom and Dad had already gone to work; she had locked up the house completely behind them, Locks and Wards as well as physical locks. She'd locked herself in, of course; she wouldn't be leaving the house by a door.

Not a conventional door, anyway.

She closed her eyes and envisioned the mathemagical formulas for the apporting spell (*"remember, a spell is a process and not a thing"*) then ran through them as her hands sketched the glyph-components in the air in front of herself. Then, with her eyes still closed, she walked confidently to and through the wall.

There was the expected moment of disorientation, and the burst of nausea caused by every apporting spell. When it passed, she opened her eyes.

She was no longer in the basement of a little bungalow in Quantico, Virginia. She was somewhere—and only a handful of people knew *where*—in upstate New York. She stood in the Center Courtyard of St. Rhiannon's School for Exceptional Students, in the exact center of a Magical Circle carefully inlaid in the granite of the paving, under a blinding blue, warm September sky.

The Magical Circle was a construction built of several circles, actually; this was one of the most complex permanent Circles she'd ever seen. Literally a Master Piece; it had been put together by the Founders as one of the first constructions of this School, so there would never be a road leading to it. She had to presume that all of the material used to construct the School had been apported here directly. It must have been a massive undertaking.

The school buildings were some of the oldest in North America, had been built on the pattern of Merlin College in Oxford, and the Founders had left no safety factor unconsidered when creating the "landing pad" for their institution. Well, *she* called it a "landing pad." The people who spelled Magic with a "k" on the end referred to it as a lot of other things, most of them sounding like the terms came straight out of a D and D book. The location of St. Rhia's was so secret not even Vickie's parents could get there by anything but apport. Probably the Dean and a couple of other senior Professors who literally never left the place knew where it really was, but no one else. Somehow, some way, they were even keeping the school screened from satellite and other aerial cameras. You couldn't see it from an airplane, and nothing led to it.

It sometimes seemed ridiculous to Vickie that in an age where metahumans saved the day with their super-human powers so often their stories only ended up on Page Three of the newspaper, her fellow magicians should be so paranoid about keeping their existence ultra-secret from most. But ... *well, maybe not. It's true that the majority of metahumans have secret identities. And I've never heard of any schools for super-teens either. Maybe all of us are better off hiding in plain sight.*

There were four smaller primary circles within the larger one, one at each of the cardinal points, and a slightly bigger one in the middle. Vickie was in the North, the Earth point. She quickly moved off it and onto clear pavement. As long as she stood there, whoever was next and was Earth couldn't come in. Simple physics; two bodies cannot occupy the same space at the same time. Of course, the Founders never thought of it as physics, but they had understood the principle.

The Central Courtyard was paved with what looked like granite, and the four buildings around her were likewise built of stone, and looked positively ancient, although they were equipped with modern things like central heating and electricity and all that inside. Thank the gods. Otherwise going to school here would be like torture, especially in the winter. Or like living in a Dickens novel, an experience she would really rather pass on.

The buildings looked a lot like many of the buildings at Oxford University in the UK, actually; Gothic, but in the pretty way, not the morbid way. Stone made graceful. More of the "dreaming spires" that poets talked about. It was hard not to feel a little awe.

North and South were the classrooms, East were the dorms for the live-in students, and West was home to the teachers' apartments, theater, gym, library ... all the other things that weren't classrooms or dorms. The place was set in the middle of an extensive garden. Outside the garden were thick woods that looked really, really old, and impenetrable, although Vickie knew for a fact that the students were actually encouraged to explore them.

Most students lived here; there were only a few who were "day pupils," like Vickie. There were a lot of reasons for that, but the chiefest were that most students didn't have the benefit of having parents as magically ept as Vickie's—or, even had parents that actually believed in magic. And those parents who *were* magicians were busy making sure everyone around them thought they were mundies. That made it hard to cover up for your budding Magikal Childe. Very few kids understood as young as Vickie had that making fireworks and drawing attention to the fact that you were very different was dangerous.

She'd had a full day of Orientation already, though thanks to working unofficially with her parents for a couple of years now, she thought of it as a "briefing." So she set out confidently for North Quad, knowing exactly where her first class was.

Maybe other kids came here with mingled dread and anxiety; all she could feel was relief. Finally, she was going to go to a school where she didn't have to hide what she was. Finally, she *wasn't* going to be spending every waking hour in *some* kind of lesson or other—because for as long as she could remember, she had been going to normal schools like every other kid, then coming home and plunging straight into magic lessons. She generally hadn't been finished with homework and magic-work until an hour before bedtime, and freshman year at Chafee High School had darn near finished her.

After seeing her shorting herself on sleep and running herself ragged, to the point where she had permanent dark circles under her eyes and the teachers at Chafee High School were calling her folks for conferences and asking pointed questions about drugs, Alexander and Moira Nagy had decided enough was enough. They'd wanted her to have a "normal" life—but this was anything *but* normal.

All that the State of Virginia cared about was that you were in *a* school until you were old enough to quit. The authorities didn't really care which school. St. Rhia's was no different from any other private school so far as they were concerned.

So far as the parents of about half of the students here were concerned, this was some sort of correctional school supported by eccentric benefactors, and as long as they saw their offspring as little as possible and there were no obvious signs of abuse, the lack of parental access bothered them not at all. Budding mages born into normal families tended to get into a lot of trouble they couldn't adequately explain as they came into their powers, and adult magicians out in the world were always on the alert for the signs of a youngster in need of rescue. A little glamorie, a little persuasive geas, and the relieved parents were happily sending their "problem" off to be dealt with by someone else. And as for the kids, well, Vickie was pretty sure they were as relieved to finally find themselves in a place where they actually *belonged* as she had been. Vickie had even written a paper once postulating that the legends of "changelings" could be traced to magicians being born into mundie families. The fact that in legends, changelings were almost universally rejected by their parents was certainly mirrored in the rejection modern mundie parents evidenced in dealing with magical offspring.

Maybe there's something about magic that mundie instincts completely revolt against.

Mom had really liked the paper, and had made it part of her application to St. Rhia's. It was a good theory, anyway.

So far as the parents of the *other* half were concerned—the parents who were themselves magicians—St. Rhia's was the place where their children were free to study and practice magic openly, and where they would get the best magical education to be had in North America. More part of the campaign to keep their nature hidden; at St. Rhia's, their kids learned both magic and camouflage. Eventually, some few, with the right skills, would actually go off and pass as meta-humans, joining ECHO, with no one ever the wiser about *where* their abilities came from.

Even Vickie's parents managed that, at least as far as most of the FBI was concerned. Outside of Section 39, except at the very top levels of the Bureau, no one was aware that they were anything other than metahumans—or that the things they stalked were considerably different than "mere" super-criminals.

Vickie hurried in through the ornate double doors of North, joining a stream of others who were making their way from East Quad and the dorms. The contrast between this place and her old high school could not have been greater. Inside and out, it looked like a movie setting. She felt as if she should at the least be wearing one of the academic gowns from a BBC period drama, and not the jeans, white shirt and blue sweater that were the school uniform for everyone. As she hurried up the handsomely carved steps to her first class, though, she felt herself grinning. Like everyone else, her school day was going to be spent half in academic classes, but half in magic. She wasn't going to have to pretend magic didn't exist, or hide it anymore. *This is going to be great!*

Morning classes were ... mixed. Exciting, because she was finally getting to practice and talk about magic and *be* a magician in the open for the first time. Frustrating because no one, literally no one, seemed to talk about how *she* saw magic.

It's the math! she thought, bewildered, as they went on about vibrations and components and stuff that really didn't matter as long as you knew the math. It was as if they simply didn't realize that magic and physics were not only related, they were so incestuously related they might as well have been Borgias. It was as if no one understood that as long as you knew the math, you didn't need the components and … all of the other rigmarole. Well, the glyphs and diagrams, maybe, because you still had to impose your will on the energy, and that was the easiest way to do it. But the rest? Not so much …

She wondered if this wasn't just a way to get kids to work and understand spell-casting without forcing them into the math. Obviously it *worked*, since they were doing magic successfully, and all the old grimoires were built around *eye of newt and tongue of dog* and all that sort of icky procedure, so obviously this was how people had been practicing magic since the year dot. But these were modern times, and man had walked on the moon. It was time to modernize. *And wouldn't it be better to start them on the math first?*

But when she tried to talk to the teachers about it, they smiled patronizingly and suggested she was oversimplifying.

The lessons themselves, once she got over the excitement of actually being able to do all of this in public, were … boring. She'd been doing these sorts of things since she was ten or twelve. This was all *old*. It was the math, of course. When you knew the math, you could always get exactly the same result, at least in this really simple stuff. The Uncertainty Principle really didn't apply when you were lighting candles and apporting small objects. When you knew the math, you could make shortcuts, and you didn't have to memorize pages and pages of chants and what-have-you. When you knew the math, you not only could do *one* spell, you could figure out how to generalize and do all kinds of spells that were like that one spell.

And there was another fly in the ointment, though it was hardly an unexpected one. She'd figured out within the first half hour that this school was no different from any other. There were cliques. There was an elite coterie of the Very Popular and Very Pretty. There were jocks of some sort (you could tell by the muscles and the attitude), who were part of the Very Popular. The Elite made it their business to try and make life miserable for the Outcastes.

Back in mundie schools, Vickie had mostly kept her mouth shut, her head down, and worn a little glamorie that basically made the Very Popular ignore her. She'd managed to skate along being a lone wolf. You could say that was in her blood, after all … No one had bothered her. No one had noticed her. Even her teachers had a tendency to forget about her once she was outside of a classroom, and called her "Veronica" or "Valerie" instead of her real name.

Well, glamories weren't going to work here; everyone here her age and some younger could see right through them. She'd already been getting the eyeball from the Elites—and now she was standing just outside the dining hall, knowing that she could stroll in there, find where the Smart Set was eating and see if she got an invitation to sit with them. Which, if she was reading the interest right, she probably would.

Now, this was the first time the Leaders of the Pack at a school had *ever* wanted anything to do with her. And … it was tempting to let them hook her in. Being popular … well, obviously it was *fun*. Great parties. Boyfriends. People wishing they were you. And after graduation? Connections. Favors to be called in. People begging to do you favors.

The trouble was, there was always a price-tag attached to that sort of gang. Generally it was the one where you soiled your soul by "going along" with things you knew were wrong. And in a place like this, those things were going to be by definition not only wrong, but very sneaky. Vickie could see how *her* skillsets would be very valuable to kids who were doing things they shouldn't be. They didn't know that yet, of course—but if she just went along, she'd be sailing along on easy street until she graduated, and afterward too.

But she *helped* people, not hurt them. It was what she did. It was what her parents did. Even the Nagy family motto said as much: *Servire et Tueri*. With a sigh—just a little regret, because she knew allowing herself to be roped in by the Pretty People would make her life *so* much easier—she resigned herself to the fact that, tempting as it was … no. It would be wrong. Oh well. At least she didn't have to *live* here, so their opportunities to cause trouble for her would be limited.

And maybe, just maybe, she could still skate by under their radar as long as she didn't outright reject them. She could always play the Captain Oblivious card.

Right, then. She squared her shoulders and marched into the dining hall.

This wasn't anything like the cafeterias in mundie schools. This was a *dining hall*, with tables with tablecloths and chairs, not plastic picnic benches. Food was served "family style" from platters and bowls on the tables, and the proctors at each end of the long tables watched you to make sure you took some of everything, and didn't just fill up on carbs and sweets.

She headed for the nearest table to the door; it was scarcely a prime spot, it wasn't near the windows and it was far enough from the kitchen that stuff that cooled off fast would probably arrive lukewarm at best. There wasn't one of the Elites anywhere near it. With luck, they'd never notice she was in here, she could get her lunch and get out with no one the wiser.

"Hi," she said, grabbing a chair next to a thin, pale boy who looked a bit younger than she was. "I'm Vickie, I just started today."

She addressed the entire group at the table, who stopped eating and stared at her as if she had spoken in Urdu. Even the proctors looked a little surprised by her choice of seating.

"Uh … wouldn't you rather sit—" one of them started to stammer.

"This is just fine, thanks," she interrupted, and took a seat, looking around her brightly. "Could you pass the beets, please?"

"Are you sure you wouldn't rather be nearer the windows?" the other proctor said, carefully.

"I'm not fussy," she replied, and filled her plate.

That was about all the conversation she managed to get out of any of her tablemates. She tried making conversation herself, but when every overture she attempted was met with nervous silence, she mentally shrugged, exchanged a few dull pleasantries with the two proctors, and just finished her meal. She felt the glares on the back of her neck as she excused herself and went to her locker, though, and she guessed there was about to be a confrontation. The Elites had spotted her attempt to avoid them, and they were not happy about the rejection.

Not surprising, really. Rejection wasn't something they had to deal with. It probably stung a lot.

Only the day students had lockers, since only the day students needed them—though these were less "lockers" in the mundie sense and more like small locking closets. Wood, of course, and very posh, polished wood at that. Vickie sensed the bodies closing in around her as she got the books she needed for the next class. So she took her time about it, and made sure she had the door locked securely before she turned.

And feigned surprise at seeing the little group lurking in an arc between her and the rest of the hallway. "Welcome Wagon?" she asked, arching an eyebrow. "I'm honored."

She read their faces and their body-language, and reckoned that their next move would be intimidation. *Wow, unforgiving lot, aren't you?* Now, there were a lot of ways to play this. Officially, the use of magic on fellow pupils, except in specific classes, like magical dueling, was strictly forbidden. Unofficially, well … Vickie was pretty sure she knew plenty of dirty tricks she could get away with.

But that would be wrong. And unethical.

She could handle this physically. She might be small, but she had a lot of tricks up her sleeve.

They might think they were at a physical advantage, since St. Rhia's had plenty of classes in all kinds of fighting—she was enrolled in staff work and was going to be going to that class next, in fact. She was, however, also pretty sure that she was probably better than these kids had any notion of in martial arts.

But that would make her the attacker, not the attacked. That would be wrong too.

However, one thing she had noticed was that there was a huge hole in the fighting classes, as evidenced by the mere fact that they were just that. *Fighting* classes. There was not one single purely defensive class. No martial Tai Chi. No Tae Kwon Do. And there was her answer. She had been studying Tae Kwon Do since she was a toddler, as part of the effort to keep her from becoming Daddy's Little Hostage to Daddy's Enemies. Tae Kwon Do was perfect for getting out of physical confrontations smelling of roses.

All righty then, she thought, and smiled up into the face of a girl who, in any other school would have been Head Cheerleader. "Well, obviously not," she said, sweetly. "I have a great idea. You go back to whatever *supah* special elite thing it is you do, comparing teeth whitening spells and figuring out glamories to make your hair shine, and I go on to class. I get what I want, you get what you want. Everybody wins."

Evidently, she struck a nerve, or maybe they weren't used to anyone actually daring to be insolent with them, because the girl's face reddened, and she actually was stupid—or unpracticed—enough to telegraph her intended slap. Vickie was not only able to easily step off the line of attack, the girl stumbled and nearly fell into the lockers when Vickie's face wasn't there to get the slap. And while she was stumbling forward, Vickie was able to slide past the girl and through the hole in the line she made.

Before any of them could react, Vickie was already doing a fast, purposeful walk in the direction of her next class.

If she had any luck at all, they'd decide she wasn't worth the effort of going after.

One could only hope.

The pale, thin boy was in her Magic lab that afternoon, and the teacher partnered the two of them. And for the first half hour she couldn't get a word out of him, not even regarding the assignment. Finally, when the teacher had gone to the other side of the classroom to help someone else, she grabbed his wrist.

"Look," she hissed, as he went utterly still and stared at her in numb fear, "I can do an apport in my sleep—and in five minutes. I can show you how to do the same. Talk to me. What the heck is wrong with you?"

"Y-you shouldn't be talking to me," he stammered. "They'll find ou—"

"Haven't you gotten it through your head that I don't give a rat's ass about what they think?" she replied scornfully. "I will go right through the next three years not giving a rat's ass about what they think. How are they getting away with bullying you?"

His jaw dropped. "How did you—"

"Oh *please*. You act like a scared rabbit. This place has rules about bullying, so how are they getting away with it?" She glared at him and he dropped his eyes.

"Because ... nobody cares," he whispered.

"Well, I care." She firmed her chin.

But he shook his head. "You think you do, but you won't. Nobody does once they—"

But before she could find out what was going on, the teacher came back to their side of the room and they had to go back to the apporting exercise. When class was over, he gathered up his books and bolted before she even got a chance to say another word.

"Well?" Moira Nagy said, her fork poised over her meatloaf. "First day?"

Vickie sighed, and stirred her mashed potatoes. "It's better than Chafee. But I'd thought the magic classes would be more of a challenge. I'm practically sleeping through them. It's all stuff I knew three years ago."

It was hideously disappointing, actually, but she couldn't tell her parents that. After all the work they had gone through to get her in?

"They're still evaluating you, kitten," her father said, as her mother's brows creased with faint annoyance. "They can't exactly take our word for what you can do."

Moira flicked a scarlet curl over her shoulders and lost the look of annoyance. "Of course, I should have realized that and warned you. *Every* child is the next Merlin in her mother's eyes. Give it a little time, and they'll bump you up into more advanced classes."

"Yes, but—" Vickie stopped her own protest before she made it. Even her own parents didn't quite understand how she saw magic— only that she saw it very differently from the way they did, and that Vickie's way was startlingly efficient. "Anyway, it's frustrating."

Actually she had come home only to cry a little. She *wanted* to be crammed full of new magical knowledge. She needed it the way she needed air. She didn't just study magic, she *was* magic, and she felt as if she was being starved for it.

But ... brave face. Never mind that there were bullies, just like mundie school, and that she was being put back on training wheels. Brave face. At least at St. Rhia's she was safe to be who she was. Not like some people. That pale kid, for instance.

"This too will pass," said her father, and grinned at her as he shook his blond hair—just like hers—out of his eyes. "Meanwhile, it's meatloaf night, and I bet you get your homework done in two hours or less."

"Or less," she said, and felt at least a little smug about that. "I did half of it in study hall, and like I said, I don't even need to think about the magical part." Then she brightened, as she remembered the one part of the whole day that hadn't been a disappointment. "Oh! And Staff Fighting is *righteous!*"

"Verily," he agreed, and went on to suggest things to her while she listened intently. So intently she forgot to mention the Pretty People thugs and the pale kid who was being bullied, and her concern that she would end up being bullied too. By the time she remembered again, it didn't seem quite as important. For herself, well, it was Tae Kwon Do again, really, all she had to do was keep evading and eventually they'd just give up.

As for the kid, well, he needed to be willing to *be* helped before she could help him. Still. *I'll keep trying to corner him*, she promised herself before she gave in to the bliss of a DS9 episode followed by a brand new Charles de Lint novel. It was the first time during a school year that she had *ever* had time for both a TV show and a chapter of a book in the same evening.

And for the first time during a school year, she was going to be able to go to bed at a decent hour—which might have been an odd thing for a kid her age to think about, but then, most kids her age hadn't shorted themselves on sleep so often they had to resort to Triple Red-Eyes to stay awake during the day. No more worshipping at the altar of the Goddess Caffeina.

So … there was some good.

The Pretty People left her alone. Sort of. They didn't try to surround her and intimidate her a second time—which at least proved that the bullies of St. Rhia's were a lot smarter than the bullies of Chafee—but there was a lot of whispering and obvious gossip going on. This, Vickie had expected. And she hadn't been lying when she'd told the pale kid that she didn't give a rat's ass. Maybe—heck, probably—spending so much time in the company of her parents and their peers had given her a certain amount of insulation from what her *own* peers thought and said, and a long view of things. What did it matter, really, when in three years she would be gone, and the only rumors that could possibly cause her any trouble were that she cheated or that she was easy. The first, she could disprove in a heartbeat, and Mom and Dad would back her up. The second, well, any guy or even group of guys that tried anything on her was going to end up singing in the upper registers for quite some time. And that was if they were lucky. She strongly doubted that any of the kids here had ever had to fight for real. If she was actually attacked with intent to harm, bottom line, they would find out she never hesitated, and never held back. She couldn't afford to. She wouldn't *kill* anyone, but there would be people in the hospital and none of them would be her.

Still, when just before lunch some of the whispers finally got loud enough to reach her, she nearly dropped the books she was getting out of her locker in surprise.

"*Lipstick lesbian ...*"

"*Fag-hag.*"

That was the best they could do? Really?

They're dumber than I thought. Why they thought rumors about being gay, or gay-friendly were going to cause her a moment of unrest—well, they hadn't been paying attention. First of all, St. Rhia's had very firm policies in place about homophobia, to wit that acting on it was an invitation for expulsion. And secondly—well—she really and truly did not give a rat's ass.

Then again, this might be 2002, but there were still plenty of people out there with homophobia, and it looked like there was a big fat clot of them right here in St. Rhia's. Just because they were all young magicians, it didn't follow that all or even most of them had exposure to all of the myriad sorts of folks Vickie'd had. If anything, their upbringing might be even more insular than the average mundie and—

Wait a second. Fag-hag ... She could almost hear the mental pieces clicking together and solving the puzzle of the pale kid. And that was when she got angry. Because it was bad enough to bully someone, but to do it over something they couldn't help, any more than they could help the color of their eyes, just made it all the worse.

Heck if I am putting up with this shite. The first thing to do, though, would be to verify. Which, fortunately, she was in the perfect position to do. She hurried to the dining hall, and headed straight for the table she'd sat at yesterday, plunking herself down beside the pale boy, who looked even more alarmed than he had yesterday. She said nothing, however, until the proctors happened to be looking away.

Looking, in fact, at the Pretty People who were engaged in some stupidly obvious whispering, giggling, and smirking. Vickie took the moment to lean over and whisper in the pale kid's ear.

"Follow me. Just leave your lunch and follow me. And don't argue if you know what's good for you."

She was pretty certain that he had been cowed enough by the bullies that he would just do what she ordered without question, and she was right. She got up and left the table, acting as if she was upset by the whispers, and he followed a moment later. As soon as they were out of sight and the door to the dining hall had closed, she grabbed his hand and headed for the Central Courtyard.

"What—" the poor kid gasped, his pale face even paler, as he probably anticipated her taking some sort of revenge on him.

"Hush," she said, put him in the Earth circle with her, and burned through the equations. He gasped as they apported into the basement of her house.

"But you—but—" His eyes were as big as the proverbial saucers. "How did you—"

"Because I've been doing apports since I was twelve, I told you," she said, seizing his hand and dragging him upstairs to the kitchen, where she shoved him down into a chair and threw a couple of Cornish Meat Pasties into the microwave. "Here," she said, handing him one. "Now I can talk to you without anyone interfering."

"But I thought—we aren't supposed to leave—" he stammered.

"I'm a Day Student, I'm allowed to go home," she pointed out, and smirked. "And I'm allowed to bring study partners with me. Of course, they're rather stupidly assuming that it's Mom doing the apport, and not me, and that I'm stuck at school until she gets me. That's not my problem. Who's bullying you? The Pretty People?"

"How—why—" he began, and then his face just crumpled and words poured out of him. Mostly, they were nonsense about how he was going to hell, he was a pervert, and he deserved every bit of it. Vickie let him spew, then cut him off.

"Did you get that crap from your parents?" she said, scornfully.

He nodded.

"And I bet they would tell you that you were going to hell if they thought you were doing magic, too, wouldn't they?" she pointed out. The poor kid actually started, as if she had slapped him.

"But I—but they—"

"They're wrong about both, obviously," she interrupted again. "And if I have to keep you sitting here until we both get demerits from missing class until you believe it, I will." She paused. "Or else I'll tickle you into submission. Either one works."

The second was so absurd he actually laughed weakly.

"OK. We're good." She grinned at him. "Now, let's get to the important part. We're going to keep anyone from messing with you ever again. After classes, you come back with me; they told me specifically I can bring people home for study partners. I have a plan …"

Every afternoon, Vickie and her new "study partner" apported straight home and went to work. After seeing they really *were* working and not fooling around (and probably realizing more quickly than Vickie had that the kid was gay) her parents left them alone, just setting an extra place at the dinner table for him and sending him back before curfew.

Finally, *finally*, Vickie had found someone who saw magic the way she did! When she explained the whole math thing to the pale kid—Paul—he'd grasped it immediately. In fact, he turned out to be better at it than she was, although he couldn't manage to use modern tech any better than most magicians, so she still had something of an edge on him.

Slowly, and with the help of Konrad Lorenz, Farley Mowat, and other ethologists, she convinced him that he wasn't some sort of perverted monster. And once convinced, he was willing to let her help him.

What the Pretty People were doing was completely counter to the rules, as she had pointed out. The entire problem was that they needed to shine a big fat light on the cockroaches and send them scurrying. And the only way to do that would be to trick them into coming out into the open in the first place.

Paul had wanted to just avoid stirring up a nest of hornets, but she'd convinced him about that, too. She knew how bullies worked. When they couldn't get to him because he was spending most non-school time with Vickie, they'd find some other way to torment him, and the number one target would probably be his room.

Here was the challenge that she had been craving, and she and Paul slaved over both the rules of conduct and the mathemagic. The rules, because she was dissecting them like a lawyer. The math, because they were building something so brand new no one had ever tried it, out of the break-down of the spells they already knew.

When it was ready, Vickie snuck in one night after both of them should have been asleep, and they set up the trap. After that it was just a matter of waiting.

"Victoria Nagy."

Vickie looked up from her book, startled. This was study-hall, she was working on her history lesson, and she was so deeply into it she hadn't noticed the proctor until he spoke.

"Yes?" she managed.

"Come with me. Leave the books." The older kid was stony-faced, but she knew immediately why he had come for her. What else could it be? She felt a rush of mingled apprehension and elation. This, after all, was mostly her magic. If anyone was going to get in trouble, even expelled, it would be her. She had made sure it was her signature that was all over it, because Paul didn't *have* a safe place to go to if he got expelled.

She got up and followed the proctor out of the library, out of the building, and across the Courtyard, as she had anticipated, to the dorms. Up the stairs to the fourth floor, and out into a hallway, and into an uproar.

This was, of course, one of the boys' floors, but there were students of both sexes crowding the hall and rubbernecking, and the proctor had to push through them to get to the area of Paul's room. A line of proctors was holding the curious back; they went through that line, and finally Vickie could see the ... damage.

Whoa! It was hard not to be excited. She'd been pretty exact as to her parameters, but she hadn't anticipated the sheer weight of nastiness that the Pretty People had brought to the party and which they had gotten back in their teeth.

It was hard to recognize Lucille, the tall, blond, head-cheerleader type, because she wasn't thin or pretty anymore. She was round to the point that her clothing was straining and splitting in places, and she had a face like a frog. The only thing that remained to recognize her by was her blond hair.

Bert, one of the jocks, was black and blue, and on the floor, moaning and holding what looked like a broken arm. A couple of the other boys were in similar straits.

Angela was bald. Bridget had the worst case of acne Vickie had ever seen.

Standing over them was Professor Elba, with a face like a thundercloud. As soon as Vickie entered the cleared area, the Professor rounded on her.

"*What did you do to them, you miserable little—*" It looked as if the Professor was going to actually *attack* her, and in that moment, Vickie realized who it was who had been protecting the bullies all this time.

Fortunately, at just that moment, the Dean stepped into the space. "*Meredith!*" the Dean snapped. "Control yourself this instant!"

Since the Dean had her wand out—the Dean was clearly one of those magicians who felt she worked better using a wand—Professor Elba backpedaled a step or two.

"This—*girl's*—magical signature is—"

"I've been fully briefed, Meredith, thank you," the Dean replied, in tones of cold neutrality, and turned to Vickie. "Miss Nagy, I have the greatest respect for your parents, as does nearly everyone in the magical world. I find it ... remarkable ... that you would have perpetrated this sort of harm on your fellow students. Quite out of keeping, one would almost say. Explain yourself."

"I didn't perpetrate the harm on them, Dean," Vickie said, as she had rehearsed a thousand times. "They perpetrated it on themselves."

The Dean, a tall, stern woman with hair like cast iron and a face like a stone statue, raised one eyebrow, slowly. "Indeed? Would you care to explain further?"

And Vickie did. She explained how she and Paul had broken down one of the old Wiccan Sacred Circle spells into its component parts and isolated the sequence that read the intent of anyone or anything that tried to cross the circle. She detailed how they had broken down the Warding spells that established real-world perimeters. She described how they had worked out how the Mirror Spell that cast back *magical* harm on the caster worked. And how they had put these things all together in order to create something new: a Ward that read the intent of anyone trying to get into Paul's room, and did to them exactly what they were intending to do to Paul or his property.

"Impossible!" spat Elba.

Vickie shrugged, and before anyone could stop her, strolled across the threshold of Paul's room. She stopped, spread her hands wide, wordlessly showing how she came to no harm at all, and came back.

"Impossible!" Elba said again. "You just created a hazardous Ward that would only recognize you and that little pervert!"

Vickie bristled. "That's not true! We did exactly what I said we did!"

The Professor began to shout, or rather, scream, but the Dean cut her off—not by look, or order, but by stalking across the threshold of the room herself. There was a collective gasp, and when she came back out without so much as a hair being out of place, there was another.

"Take the ... so-called victims to the Infirmary," the Dean ordered. "And someone go to the Staff Reading Room, wake up Professor Higgins and bring him here, please."

Vickie perked up a little at that. *So-called victims?* So the Dean believed her?

But she had to wait in silence while this Professor Higgins was fetched. This gentleman was someone Vickie had never seen before, tall, lean, wearing an odd flat velvet hat and academic robe over a shabby suit.

"Miss Nagy," the Dean ordered. "Tell the Professor *exactly* what you did. Down to the smallest detail."

So Vickie did—but the moment she started, the Professor suddenly looked as if he'd been jolted awake by electricity, and began questioning her—about the *math*! Jarred into excitement herself, Vickie could hardly get the words out fast enough. The Dean listened, looking vaguely baffled, for about ten minutes, and finally interrupted them.

176

"Professor," she said, politely. "Will this Ward do what the girl says it will?"

For the first time the Professor actually looked at Vickie's work, peering at the doorway over the top of his glasses. "Oh my, yes," he said, sounding as if he had just discovered an entirely new theorem. "Oh my, certainly yes. It reads the intent of those who cross it, and if they are intending something wicked, it bounces them back with as close an approximation of their intended actions as it can manage, wrought on their persons. So elegant for such a youngster! Why look here—" He began describing some of Vickie's process, and the Dean cut him off again.

"And would you be willing to take Miss Nagy and her confederate as your pupils?" she asked.

"I was about to *demand* that very thing, Dean!" the Professor replied, sounding a little indignant. "As you are aware, I have not had a mathemagician to tutor in far too long, and I certainly am *not* going to permit you to expel the first ones to come along in the last five years!"

"Hrrm." To Vickie's relief, the Dean sounded more amused than anything else. "We'll make the arrangements, Professor. Miss Nagy, with me. The rest of you—" she swept the group with a stern gaze. "Disperse, if you please."

Paul was already in the Dean's office when they arrived, and the Dean put them both through a fierce interrogation. Frankly, Vickie had seen FBI interrogators who weren't that skilled. Paul obviously began the interview with no intention of revealing that he'd been being bullied, much less over what. He ended it spilling everything. Vickie's role, evidently, was just to corroborate what he said, and re-iterate that the magic had been all her idea, though the two of them had worked it out and implemented it together.

Finally, the Dean sat back in her chair and steepled her fingers. "You manage, Miss Nagy, to have neatly skated past every single rule applicable without actually breaking it," she said dryly. "I will can-didly admit that I do appreciate your handiwork, and I will be having it applied to every room on this campus, which should put paid to some of the mischief we've had over the years here."

Vickie blushed and ducked her head. "Thank you, Dean," she said looking at her hands, and heaving a sigh of relief.

"There is no room at St. Rhiannon's for prejudice," the Dean continued. "Mister Hunter, your tormentors will be … watched. They will either genuinely mend their ways, or learn to feign it. In either case, they will no longer trouble you. And to ensure their good behavior, Professor Elba will not be allowed any further contact with them." The Dean's tone suggested that something more was likely to occur regarding Professor Elba, but what that would be, Vickie could only guess.

"As for you two, I'll be rearranging your class schedules so that you will have Special Studies with Professor Higgins daily. I'm sure I can find something you've been sleepwalking through that can be eliminated. There will be no coasting with Professor Higgins, I will warn you in advance. You might just consider this your punishment for unauthorized experiments in magic." The Dean was not joking, Vickie suspected. *I'd rather sweat than coast, so there.*

"Remain here, while I arrange that," the Dean concluded. "We'll allow the rest of the school to assume you are in here being lectured." She got up and departed through a door in the rear of her office, leaving the two of them alone.

Vickie looked at Paul. He looked back at her. And for the first time since she had met him, he was grinning.

"Fag hag," he said, fondly.

"Homo," she retorted, with a wink.

They fist-bumped. It was going to be a beautiful year.

Published in Galaxy's Edge Issue 10

The Nechronomator

by Brad R. Torgersen

The mausoleum was silent as I waited quietly at the end of the east corridor. Sodium lamps on the street outside cast a ghastly light through the stained glass windows that ringed the corridor, just above the crypts. I smelled flowers and floor wax, plus a hint of decades-old cigarette smoke. It had been six hours since I'd wheeled myself to my current spot. Nobody on the mortuary staff had thought to check before locking the doors. I was alone, and not quite believing what I was doing.

Until I heard the scrape of marble on marble.

The air suddenly came alive. A sickening stench of formaldehyde and ethanol, mixed with ozone.

My hands shook, but I gripped the arms of my chair tightly and waited, breathing deeply and slowly, not moving an inch.

Footsteps. The sound of someone taking a seat.

More marble scraping on marble.

I almost screamed when I saw the woman trudge past the open end of the corridor. She walked as if compelled from without. Halting, pained steps. Joints and tissue which hadn't moved in years made an indescribable sound as the woman went up the central hall. She never even looked in my direction.

There was muffled talk—whispery and hollow.

When it became apparent the conversation would be lengthy, I set myself into motion. Gently, with practiced tension, I rotated the wheels on my chair and began a slow, noiseless progression toward the central hall. It took minutes, during which I listened intently, but couldn't quite make out the words. Each yard drew me closer to the source of the stench, and the air was almost alive with static.

Eventually I reached the intersection, and was able to lean forward just enough to peek around the corner, my chair snug against the wall.

The Nechronomator was hideous. His flesh hung limply on his tallish skeleton, sagging and gray. He sat cross-legged on a marble bench that sat at the top of the cross-shaped mausoleum. Liver spots had darkened to black and his mouth looked dry as he moved it. The woman stood before him, motionless in her Sunday finest. The only breaths either of them took were the ones they used to move air across stale vocal chords.

I still couldn't make out what they were saying.

Suddenly the Nechronomator stood—a surprisingly swift movement for someone who'd been dead for three years—and slapped the base of his palm on the woman's forehead. She spasmed and gave a quick, hoarse cry, then flashed into nothingness—like the bulb of a camera had gone off, erasing her from existence.

I reflexively sat back in my chair, teeth clenched. What had I just seen?

One thought—*impossible*—returned again and again to my mind. But I was a scientist, fully in command of my faculties, even if my body was succumbing to age. There were explanations to everything that was occurring. Rational explanations. I would have them.

I wheeled myself boldly into the intersection and spun to confront the Nechronomator. The undead. A monster.

My friend.

"Christopher," I said loudly, hoping to cover my fear with bravado.

He remained standing, arm still outstretched and palm forward, exactly where he had touched the woman.

Slowly, his arm dropped back to his side.

"You should not have come, Matthew."

His voice was like a bellows.

"If you remember anything about me, then you know I would have come eventually. I was here when they sealed you away, after all. I gave the eulogy. I never expected I'd be seeing you again."

"Nor I. What do you want?"

I paused for a moment, then said, "I want to know if it's true."

The Nechronomator laughed. A hard, coughing sound.

"I *told* you it was possible. We used to argue about it after hours, in the staff room. I couldn't ever make it work in the lab, but that didn't mean it wasn't feasible. Now, I have the power."

"Power derived from what?" I asked.

"You wouldn't believe me."

"From God?"

"You never believed in Him."

"Neither did *you*. I still have the photo I took of you shaking hands with Dawkins."

"Dawkins was wrong. We were *all* wrong."

"So, God sent you back?"

"No, I am here by my own choice. God's got nothing to do with it."

I was sweating profusely under my topcoat and scarf. The moisture was beginning to cloud my glasses, but my hand would be shaking so badly I didn't dare reach to take them off. To cover my instinctual fear of the unreal creature before me, I held fast to my belief that this could be pursued as an intellectual problem.

"How does the math work out? On the other side, I mean."

"The math was never the issue," said the Nechronomator. "I always had the math right. It was the energy source that was the problem. Trying to do everything with mere electricity. Even the big colliders can't touch what's available in the After."

"So you can do it?"

"I just did."

"The woman?"

"That was it."

"Show me," I said.

My old, dead friend seemed to consider me for a long moment.

"Not just yet, Matthew. First things first."

He walked almost as I remember him walking, during the final years of his natural life. Like the woman, his joints and tissues made an indescribable sound as he moved past me, the air becoming choked with chemical fumes and the overpowering crackle of an un-released charge. Had he touched me, I fear I'd have been electrocuted. Or worse. I remembered the woman vanishing with a pop.

The Nechronomator proceeded down the central hall until he reached a crypt which had had its seal removed and discarded on the floor. I spun my chair slowly so as to always keep him in my sight.

"Janice Kawcak," he said. "She was only forty-seven when the lymphoma got her. Left five kids and a husband. Husband turned to drinking. The kids to drugs. Two of them are in jail now, and the husband's got liver issues. Janice begged me to help."

"Begged you," I said. "How?"

"After. It was all in the After. They came looking for me, almost as soon as I arrived. I guess word travels when they know someone is coming up. I don't think it was supposed to happen that way. They were doing something they shouldn't have been doing. But they didn't care. They just wanted me to help."

"I don't understand," I admitted. "But you of all people should understand that the timeline is changing. Not in big ways. Not yet. But I remember how it used to be, and that's not the way it is *now*."

"Of course it's not," he said as he picked the seal up from where it lay on the floor, then carefully replaced it over the empty crypt.

"Even now, Janice is working to undo things. I sent her back a few years before the diagnosis. She's doubtless visited herself and tried to convince herself to go to the doctor. The cancer would be barely detectable, but it's there. And treatable. Unlike before, when she was stage four."

"You sent her back as a *corpse*?"

"More or less."

"That's hideous."

"I can't resurrect anyone," he said, laughing again. "I don't have the knowledge. Only He can do that. But I can give them tempo-rary control of their bodies, and a power source. And I can send them back."

"Then what the hell *are* you?"

"Same as them. Think of me as a remotely-operated vehicle."

I pondered the implications, before I spoke again.

"And Janice Kawcak is about to come face to face with her dead self, controlled from beyond by her dead self?"

"What better way to convince people? I bet Janice showed herself the scars from surgery and everything. Very compelling."

"Bullshit."

"Tell you what, Matt. You go see. Go look up Janice tomorrow in the phone directory and give her a call. Then come back tomorrow night."

I looked at the Nechronomator. He looked at me.

The unspoken message between us seemed to be this: when seeking to confirm a theory, first examine the proof.

It took some time to research Janice on the internet at the retirement home. Thankfully she hadn't lived too far out of town, and I only had to pay the home's driver a modest bribe to take me out without the nursing staff knowing my intentions. So far as they knew I was being driven to the beach. Instead we wound up in the suburbs, in an older development that looked like it had gone up in the mid-eighties.

Janice Kawcak didn't know me from Adam, and I wasn't quite sure what I'd say when she answered the door. If she answered the door. Part of me still wasn't convinced.

Until the door swung open, and there she stood. Living and breathing.

"Yes," she said, "Can I help you?"

"So sorry to trouble you, Mrs. Kawcak. My name is Doctor Clayburn. I used to be with the university. Could you come out and speak with me for a moment? It's very important."

She looked at me, then at the driver next to the retirement home's van, then up and down the street.

"What's this about?"

"I'd like to ask you a few questions, Mrs. Kawcak. About someone who visited you perhaps a couple or more years ago."

"You're a physician?"

"No, a physicist. But I'm … doing some post-retirement research as part of a program they're starting at the university cancer center. Do you mind?"

"Honey?"

A man's voice, from within the house.

She turned and shouted back, "I've got it, John. Just a survey. Be back with you in a minute."

She closed the door quietly, her eyes suddenly wide and worried. She leaned over, bent at the waist so that she could be eye-level with me in my wheelchair.

"How did you know about my … the … the visitor?"

"I'm not able to discuss that, exactly," I said. "I simply need to confirm whether or not you were, in fact, visited by someone claiming to be yourself."

Janice stood up and took a second glance up and down the street, making sure there were no neighbors in any yards, then leaned back down and said, "Yes."

"She claimed to be you?"

"Yes, she did."

"Did you believe her?"

"She … She looked like me, only … God, it was so *gross.*"

"Like a corpse," I said.

"But she walked and she talked and she … showed me things."

"She wanted you to go see an oncologist, right?"

"Yes!"

"Did you?"

"I didn't want to. But like I said, she showed me … *things.* I had to run back in the house and throw up."

"She confronted you here? On your porch?"

"Yes."

"Did anyone else see her?"

"No. She said she knew exactly what time of day to come, when the kids would be at school and John would be at work. She didn't want anyone else to know."

"And did you do what she told you to do?"

Janice Kawcak looked like she almost couldn't hear me. She had stuffed her hands in the pockets of her capris and her arms quivered slightly, as if shivering.

I could feel myself blushing at the temerity of my intrusion.

"I'm so sorry, ma'am. I have to know. *Did you do what the dead woman told you to do?*"

"Yes. I went to my doctor the next day, and he referred me. I was in treatment by the end of the month. I thought the night sweats were just menopause or something. But she was right. It was a lot worse than that."

I looked at her full head of hair. Not a wig.

"Remission, then?"

"I'm in year two. They tell me I'll be in the clear if I hit year five."

"And the dead woman who claimed to be you?"

"I never saw her again."

I stared intently at Janice Kawcak as she stood on her porch, eyes become far away and her mouth in a frown.

"Are you a religious woman?" I asked.

"I didn't used to be. But … John and I go every Sunday now."

"How old are you?"

"I turn fifty-two in November."

"And your family? How have they been since the … visitor … came?"

"Fine."

"No problems with drugs or alcohol?"

"Doctor Clayburn, what kind of question is that? No, of course not."

"Yes ma'am. I think I have everything I came for. So terribly sorry to have troubled you."

The reek of embalming chemicals and ozone slapped me awake.

I'd dozed. My ability to stay up past dusk isn't what it used to be.

Christopher was standing over me when I looked up.

"Did you see her?"

"I did."

"Is she healthy?"

"Remission. And five years older than she was when she died."

"Excellent," he said, and began walking away from me down to where the western corridor branched.

I wheeled quickly after him.

"How many, old friend?"

"Only ten so far. But there are others."

"I'd imagine they're lined up to infinity."

"Not that far."

"And He doesn't care, eh?"

The Nechronomator stopped short.

"As I said last night, God's got nothing to do with this."

"What about … the other guy."

"Lucifer Morningstar? Can't say I've made his acquaintance."

"So you're doing all of this under the noses of both the Lord and the Devil? That's a neat trick, Christopher. Tell me, why are you the first? Surely Einstein and numerous others could have—should have—figured it out, too."

"I asked the same question. To hear it told in the After, Einstein and the rest never had the notion. They were too puzzled, fearful, or awestruck by the After to care. And then, once they'd moved on from Limbo, it was too late for them to change their minds."

"So the Catholics are right?"

"Not exactly. Limbo isn't anything like what they might have thought it was. Mostly because *everybody* goes there first. It's when you're in Limbo that they sort you out. Like a gargantuan class of freshmen, being funneled through a registrar. It's in Limbo where my people came and found me, and asked me to start the experiment."

"Which was successful," I said.

"Yes," he said. He was grinning—an appalling expression on a dead man.

He began walking again until he reached the seal on another crypt.

"Robert Davis Maynard," he said. "Bob will be next. Heart attack got him."

"You're talking to him now, aren't you? In the After."

"Very perceptive, Matt. Many things become possible in the After. You'd be amazed at how easy multitasking becomes once your intellect is freed from the confines of your brain."

"What's Bob's plan?"

"Same as most of the others. He's going to try and convince his younger self to change. Give up the daily quarter pounders with fries. Get an exercise regimen together."

"And if he's successful—like Janice—what happens to his body?"

"Since Janice didn't actually die, her corpse then ceases to exist. Only the knowledge that it once existed, remains."

"And you don't care a whit about how this is affecting the timeline?"

My friend ran a skeletal finger along his now-pronounced jaw line.

"I did at first. But then I thought, why not? Why isn't He letting everybody go back and have a second chance, anyway? I got pissed. For Him to have the power and not use it … He's a bastard, you know. A regal, timeless, limitless bastard. Who doesn't use His power when He should."

"Aren't you afraid you'll get caught? Get sent to Hell?"

He laughed.

"You of all people, Matt! A Sunday school lecture?"

"A matter of practical concern," I said. "Every person who successfully alters the flow of their lives through the timeline, alters the present away from its original course. How far back are you going to go, and how many will you let go back? Do it enough and things will get very, very messy."

"Don't worry, Matt. I can't send people back if I can't physically touch them. So far the only ones I've done have been in this cemetery. All ordinary people. I seriously doubt allowing them to have another shot will disrupt things too much. Especially since their living selves won't have any memory of the After, nor me, because they never died in the first place."

"Then how about sending me," I said.

The Nechronomator considered.

"Haven't tried it on a living person. No idea what it might do to you. For all I know it might strip your soul out and scatter you insensate across the ether. Do you want to take that chance? Remoting in from the After provides me—us—with a degree of insulation I can't guarantee if I try it on you."

I looked down at my legs. Useless for the last forty years.

"You think I care about that now? Send me back, Chris."

"Let me guess. To before the climbing accident."

"Yes. You were there. You remember."

"Yes, I do. I helped carry you to the ambulance."

"Then do me one more favor and let me go back and fix the one fucking mistake that has haunted me worse than all the rest. Please, Chris."

"What if your current self continues to exist alongside your young self?"

"You really think that's a possibility?"

"I don't know, to be honest."

"Fine, then. I'll deal with that when the time comes."

I didn't feel a thing when the Nechronomator touched my forehead.

One moment his stink threatened to overpower me, the next I was sitting alone, still in the mausoleum. Only this time the smell of cigarette smoke was much more pronounced, and there was a new smell. Like recently-poured concrete.

My tires squeaked on the brand new tiles and I stared at the seals to the crypts—most of which were blank—where there had been placards before.

I remembered how Janice's corpse had flinched when she'd been sent back.

Signal disruption?

For me, it'd been effortless.

I wheeled myself through the dark to the mausoleum doors, which opened easily. Outside, the late summer night air was humid and palpable, like a potter's damp room. Crickets hummed pleasantly in the distance, and the other side of the street across from the cemetery was an empty field, not apartment buildings.

I smiled in spite of myself.

Not bothering to close the door behind me, I wheeled out of the mausoleum, only coming to a halt when I realized that the ramp which had existed in 2019 didn't exist in not-so-disabled-friendly 1979.

Shit. Even in my younger days I'd not have risked a ride down the mausoleum's front steps.

I sat there in the portico and fumed quietly for a long time.

Then a skeletal child presented herself, quiet as a ghost.

I nearly fell over.

"Did Christopher send you?" I asked, heart hammering.

"Yes. He wanted me to see if you'd made it OK. I just told him you did."

"And what will you do now?"

"I've got to go home and keep Daddy from backing over me with the station wagon. But first, I'm going to help you down the stairs."

"I'm afraid I'm too heavy," I said.

"Not when I've got power from the After."

She was right. It was like being manhandled by a pint-sized wrestler.

I was wheezing by the time she got me back into my chair down at the bottom of the stairs. And I'd almost thrown up from that damned smell. They all had it, apparently.

She didn't bother to say goodbye before she loped off into the moonlight, pursuing an objective I myself also intended to pursue.

In my head I knew exactly how far I had to go. I patted the lump in my jacket where I'd put my wallet. I'd have been screwed if not for the collection of vintage bills my late wife had kept under glass on the wall of our bedroom. Nancy had admired the artistry, and collected them. Now they were my meal ticket across the country.

Roll down to the street, keep going until I found a pay phone.

Call for a cab. Hope the cabbie didn't have an issue with gimps.

Cab to the airport. Flight to Colorado.

The rest I'd have to figure out by the time I got there.

Even after all these years, I still remembered the address.

442 Pinewood, unit 15.

A ground floor condo. Fortunately for me.

I arrived via cab late into the evening, with the sun just setting. It'd been an exhausting day, and I'd almost convinced myself to get a motel for the night and tackle things in the morning. But then again, no. There was too much of a chance things could still go wrong. If I got my point across, I could rest afterward. Or not at all, depending on how temporal elasticity worked. Chris had said that Janice Kawcak's dead self had ceased to exist the moment she went to see the doctor. What would happen to me?

I kept looking down at my legs as I gradually made my way up the sidewalk toward the first block of condos in the complex, all of them brand-new 1975 construction. The wood-strip siding still smelled heavily of stain. Marijuana was also in the air. I thought I saw a couple out on their second-floor deck, passing a roach. They quickly went inside when they noticed me looking up at them.

I smiled. Nobody wanted anyone from the older generation around, especially back then.

As I rolled into the hallway that led to units 14 and 15, a shadowy shape stepped out of the laundry room into the light cast by the single lamp over 14's doorway.

I stopped cold.

"Do you think dying made me stupid, Matthew?"

The Nechronomator wasn't smiling. He looked murderous.

I kept my hands fastened to the wheels, taking reassurance in the solid steel.

"I don't know what dying has done to you, Chris. I really don't."

"Your apartment is twenty blocks from here. Why aren't you over there?"

"I think you know," I said.

"You can't speak to me. I won't allow it."

"Why not?"

"*Nothing* must occur which might interfere with my ordinary progression. I lived a full life, and had a natural death. You have no right to be here."

Now it was my turn to laugh. I let it boom out, as best as my 70-year-old lungs were able.

My dead friend flinched and waved his hands as if to shush me.

"Chris," I said, "I think we've both passed the point of caring how we're affecting the flow of events. What harm could possibly come from me having a chat with the younger you?"

"If there were no harm in it, you'd not be here. You plan to stop me."

I looked up at the Nechronomator, his ugly gray flesh especially horrid in the dull bulb's light.

"Not stop you," I admitted, "but maybe talk you into thinking about a few things. I checked the papers on the way here and it's only Friday. The accident isn't until Sunday. Time enough to avert that, if I can. But before I rolled over to Nancy's place—I was shacked up with her at the time, if you remember—I thought I'd stop in and see how you and Carol were doing. You should never have divorced her, you know. She was good for you."

Christopher advanced on me, his hands looking like claws.

"You leave Carol out of this," he hissed. "Look, Matt. You've got one choice. Turn yourself around and never come back this way again. If you do, I will know, and I will stop you. I sent you back once, I can send you forward too."

"Against my will?"

"Damn right, against your will."

"I wonder what He would have to say about that," I said.

Just then the light for 15 popped on, and the door came open.

The Nechronomator turned and watched himself saunter out of his condo, boxers disheveled and a long-necked beer in his hand.

"What the fuck?"

Young Chris's eyes focused on his older, dead self, and it was like a silent lightning bolt passed in the air between them.

"Chris," I yelled from my chair, "I've got to talk to you! You've got to call off the climbing trip! You've got to—"

The Nechronomator spun and lunged for me. I reflexively rolled my chair in reverse. Just as Chris's dead hands reached for me, the chair caught on the curb at the end of the sidewalk and flipped over. I slammed hard on my back and toppled out, the Nechronomator hitting the chair's legs and pitching over me. Dead, brittle bones crunched as he came down in a heap. With my arms—made strong over forty years of wheeled effort—I righted myself and ignored the pain where my head had impacted the asphalt.

Young Chris had jogged out and knelt by me.

"Are you okay, man? I should call the cops."

"Chris," I wheezed, "listen to me. Sunday, you and I are going on a trip up the canyon. You've got to call it off. I'm going to break my back when I fall. Don't let me convince you otherwise."

"Jesus ... Matt? What's going on? You look—"

Dead Chris rose up from where he'd fallen, left leg and arm twisted grotesquely. He shouldn't have been able to stand at all. Whatever he was tapping from the After, it was potent stuff.

"*Desist!*"

Young Chris looked like he was going to throw up, and took a few steps backward.

"Oh my God, what is this?" he said.

"It's me," I said to young Chris. "Remember the talk we had about you and Carol? She wanted you both to be back in church. For the baby. She's right."

"*Chris?*"

Carol stood in the doorway of the condo, her nightgown wrapped tightly around her very-pregnant abdomen. Casey was about six months, give or take. I remembered that his birthday always came around Thanksgiving. Shit, he would be a handful by the time he was ten.

Young and dead Chris both looked at his current/former wife.

When Carol saw the Nechronomator, she screamed and backed into the wall behind her, hand up to her mouth.

I turned and looked up at my dead friend. His mouth had drawn open, gaping inhumanly wide. Dead eyes were rolled back into their sockets and a rising groan had begun in his throat. Not air being pushed out, but air being drawn in. His chest was expanding like a balloon, and the groan quickly rose to a howl. A satanic, hair-raising howl that made the windows rattle. I felt an electric charge flow over my skin and though the asphalt.

Something was changing. Had changed.

I waited, turning back once to see Carol clutched to Chris's chest. "Stay together, dammit!" I yelled as loudly as I could.

Then everything vanished at once.

It was almost midnight when Chris pounded on my door. Nancy and I had been relaxing after a good, long, end-of-the-week screw, and she was dozing on the bed. I threw on my terrycloth bathrobe and went to the door to find Chris and Carol fully-dressed and looking worried.

I invited them in, woke Nancy, and we talked over cans of soda.

I wanted to say Chris was crazy. I wanted to tell him I didn't think the joke was very funny. Only, I couldn't make myself believe that he was joking. And with Carol there as an eye witness—serious

Carol, who had never pulled a prank in her serious life—the air was stone-cold sober.

Suffice to say, I grudgingly let us cancel the climbing trip. In fact, we never did go climbing again. Chris wouldn't hear of it. Kept telling me how horrified he was to see me in the wheelchair.

Nancy and I were present for Casey's baptism.

When Chris and Carol moved back east for the university job, Nancy and I followed.

By the time Casey was in high school Chris and I both had tenure. We had good lives, the two of us.

Chris was a grandpa six times over when Carol finally went. It was Alzheimer's. Ripped Chris in two to see her go out like that, but we were both glad when it was over. Chris had helped me through Nancy's passing a few years before, and I wasn't surprised to see Chris in my living room, day after day, in the weeks following Carol's.

We talked about God a lot in those final days. A couple of odd ducks in our department at the U. I still have the photo from when Chris debated Dawkins on the quadrangle. I'd thought they were going to punch each other out, they were so angry. We wondered what it would be like, when we crossed over. *If* we crossed over. Neither of us spoke much of that night anymore, when Chris and Carol showed up and told me the story. Sometimes I still wonder if it wasn't just in Chris's imagination. But Carol had remained firmly convinced, to her deathbed. She'd said she'd never forget watching the zombie swell up like a bloated deer, then pop into nothingness with a flash like that of a camera bulb. Disabled, older me had vanished too, though the wheelchair had remained behind. Chris still had it in his garage on the day he died, and weeks later when I went over with his kids to begin cleaning things out, I found the wheelchair.

It was covered in dust, and rusty.

Chris had died on April 22, 2016.

The peeling manufacturer's label on the chair said 2018.

I peeled the sticker off, put it in my pocket, and told Chris's kids to send the chair to Goodwill.

Published in Galaxy's Edge Issue 7
Copyright © 2014 by Brad R. Torgersen. All rights reserved.

Today I Am Nobody

by Tina Gower

I am Amber when I see him again. I wake with auburn hair and green eyes, freckles across my skin, and decide to be Amber. The name fits the face in the mirror, and all day I do Amber things. Amber would love picking daisies in the meadow behind the reservation. Amber would wear her hair in two French braids. Amber would have a boyfriend with blond hair and one unruly lock that covers his left eye. When I see him, that perfect boy for Amber, I want him.

He works in the village, on the dusty grimy road that leads from the reservation to the back of the tannery. I am able to watch him scraping a hide for sale because he does not know Amber. He knew Rose. When I was Rose, I had olive skin with black hair. The roses were budding and I put one in my hair.

"How long will you be in town?" he had asked.

"Only until the roses bloom," I said. Truthfully, I didn't know then how quickly I would shed and change and become a new girl. The shaman didn't tell me how the medicine would work.

The corners of the boy's mouth twitched and his smile fell flat. "That's too bad. I like dark-skinned brunettes. Everyone in town is blond."

Amber doesn't have dark skin, so today I only watch while the young man (who is perfect for Amber) hangs the skins to dry. I hear wagon wheels squeak into the village with supplies from the East. The traders bring tea and preserves, waxes for candles when the long nights come. One trader hands a package of sweets to a girl my age. Her name is Nola. She will always be Nola, poor thing. The other girls do not recognize me anymore, although they knew me once.

I walk home and cut through the glen. My hand skims along the wild grains and I pick one to chew absently. When I reach my tent by the creek, my pots and pans are scattered, my food supply is shredded and strewn along the bank.

I'm cleaning the mess when I hear the grumble of a bear. He swipes his paw at me before I see him, and I fall to the ground. The gravel smashes into my elbows and knees. The smell of pine and dust brings me to my senses. He swings at me again, and his paw leaves a scrape down my leg.

The injury burns. My breath is frozen in my chest and my palms are damp with sweat. I clutch a cast iron skillet and, with no other weapon, throw it at his head. While he rubs his face with a paw, I scamper and trip my way to the tallest pine and climb. He paces below.

My skin tingles and I feel an itch. The sensation multiplies until it's like a thousand insects burrowing into me. My skin peels. A wave of nausea crashes into me like the river against the rocks a few feet away. The change is happening too quickly. I hug the trunk, panting. A clump of Amber's hair falls to the bear. He bats at it and sniffs. Pieces of Amber melt away. When Amber is gone, the bear is gone, too.

I crawl back to the ruined tent and look in my mirror. A crack runs down the middle, but I can still see my new face in the reflection. I'm still pale, but my freckles are gone and I have blond hair.

The shaman's medicine doesn't work. I'm only half tribe and half white. Maybe I should never have agreed to the medicine. I don't fit in either world.

I stay at my campground on the reservation for the next few days. A blond will not do. The tanner sees too many blonds. "Everyone in town is blond," he told Rose. I spend the time cleaning the mess from the bear.

Today I am Mia. My skin looks like porcelain and my eyelids look swollen. I have straight black hair. I run to the village to watch the young man in the tannery. Mia should have a boyfriend who works at the tannery, but he doesn't look at her. I am not Rose.

"Can I help you, Miss?" He asks.

"My name is Mia."

"Can I help you, Mia?" His eyes never leave the saddle he is brushing.

"No," I say, because I know now I'm not who he is looking for today.

I leave a rose for him at the table. The last one of the season. I watch him from a safe spot outside the window. He never touches the rose. I go back the next day and the next, but the rose doesn't move from its spot. It wilts and dries. One day it is gone.

The bear comes to me in a dream and when he lifts his face I see the shaman. Her grey hair blends into the white patch of hair on the bear's neck and it is as if she is holding the bear up for me to see.

"I've brought you a bear," she says.

"I don't need a bear. I need friends, people to talk to. I'm lonely, and your medicine does not work."

She moves around me to light a fire and the bear flops to the ground like a pile of the tanner's skins. "Animal medicine takes a long time to work."

The wood smokes for a minute before the first flames lick the chilly night air. The pines that surround the campsite glow, but the forest beyond remains black.

"I asked for someone to love me and accept me. I didn't ask for animal medicine," I say.

My voice sounds muffled. My lips feel smashed against my teeth. I'm confused to find I'm talking into my arm. I rise and blink in the darkness of my tent. Outside the campfire smokes as if a fire was lit and died hours ago.

Today I am Abigail. My skin is so dark it's black. My hair is also black, but curly and coarse. The tanner notices Abigail. His eyes follow me around the tannery, but his shoulders are tense, his lips are turned down in a frown. I finger a design on a small leather bag for sale. It is of a rose.

"Put that down." His hand is gripping a hammer so tight his knuckles are white. "That is not for you. Put that down."

He stomps towards me and I fumble the bag back to the display and run to the reservation. My heart beats so hard my throat hurts. My fingers feel numb where I held the bag meant for me. No, I remember, now. The tanner is correct; it's not for me. It's for Rose.

Today I am nobody.

I do nothing. I sit and let the sounds of the creek drown out my thoughts. The leaves fall and regrow many times while I am nobody, doing nothing things. Every morning I am not Rose I am nobody. Some days I do not even check my mirror, searching for her.

The roses are in bloom today, and I gather a few supplies to trade in town. Wild herbs and berries overflow in my baskets. The tanner is selling his hides two booths down from me. He stops for a moment to pick through my selection, and finds a few herbs to his liking. The sun streams through his blond hair, and I see one strand of silver. When he smiles I expect to feel warmth, but there is none. I wonder as he walks away who I am today. I never looked in the mirror.

Today, I am Amber again. If I can be Amber then I can be Rose. I'm excited to discover this, and I dance around my camp. Maybe the medicine is working. Maybe I can force my body to change like I did with the bear. Maybe I can find a way to stay Rose.

I make plans.

"Girl of many faces," the shaman called me. I walk the line between worlds. I schooled in the village, and the girls complimented me for my hand at mixing herbs to make pleasing scents, but no one bought them. In the reservation the women relied on me to plant the seeds for the next harvest, but criticized me for not planting in rows. Liked by all and loved by none. I was invisible in my efforts and visible only in my failures. So I became whatever people wanted me to be, and still nobody loved me. The shaman promised me the attention I deserved.

"You try to please everyone and you please no one, not even yourself," she said, and handed me a mirror. "The animal spirits have chosen to heal you and retrieve a lost part of your soul."

Then the day came when the people of the reservation moved to the South to follow the seasons. The shaman said I should stay behind and wait for my spirit animal's medicine.

The day after they left, I awoke to see Rose. Her hair shone a rich black-cocoa, not like my dull light brown. Her figure curved like a road that moves with the land, not like my straight narrow lines that short-cut to the ground.

I thought the spirit animals had made me into the woman I was meant to be. I thought the medicine had worked. But then I became sick: my skin peeled, my hair fell, and the part of me I thought of as "Rose"—the part of me I would learn to be—wilted away.

Today I am finally Rose.

My hands tremble. This makes the basket quiver and the herbs shake. To be Rose, I jumped from a cliff by the river. After a dozen times and a dozen girls, fear of the height no longer changed me. I had to find a new danger. I fought a wolf, a badger, and thieves along the road. In the end, nothing scared me more than never being Rose again. She crept into me in my sleep.

I look in the broken mirror to be sure, but it's true. I am finally Rose.

I head straight to town, herb basket in hand. I do not stop until I'm at the tannery.

He brushes the skin of an animal and sees Rose.

"Hello," he says, smiling. "Can I help you?"

I smile and take a breath. I can finally give him back his Rose. I try to remember Rose. How did she smile? How did she hold her body? How did she speak? Was it soft or loud?

"I am Rose," I say.

He frowns. "Do I know you?"

The answer catches on my tongue. He looks at me, his forehead wrinkles, his eyelids lower to slits. He doesn't recognize Rose.

"I'm sorry, your name doesn't sound familiar," he says. "Do you have a request to place? I'm afraid I don't have any orders for Rose."

For the first time I notice the lines on his face around his mouth. When I come into town he is always here.

I nod, my voice deserting me. I want to hide and not be Rose. The tanner doesn't know Rose anymore.

He doesn't know me. He *never* knew me.

When I arrive the camp is a mess. The bear has returned and shredded my tent beyond repair.

That night I sleep in the rain, huddled under a few gathered branches. The tanner is gone to me, so I wonder who I am supposed to be. I plant herbs for the harvest and find no pleasure in it. I gather a few seasonal plants to make tea and find no pleasure in that either.

The only thing that brings me pleasure is watching the rain drain into the river, and speculating where it leads. I'm soaked in water. I'm connected to the water and the water to the river and the river to the ocean, and I feel relief to be part of something.

Today I am me. I do not know my hair color or the tone of my skin.

I've always wanted to see the ocean, so I pack. I've wanted to see the leaves turn in the valleys below the mountain. I'm planning things

I've never planned before because I didn't know my life was my own. I feel whole; the animal medicine is working.

I stop by the tannery on my way out of town and leave a gift.

I peek through the window before turning away, and I see him glance in the broken mirror. I wonder who he will see. What animal will the spirits bring to the tanner?

The road out of town is damp from a mist of rain over the night. I walk until my feet are tired, and then I rest. I stare into the sky, finding shapes in the clouds. I see a rabbit. When I look again it's a dog, then a cow with horns, and, last, a bear. I fall asleep gazing at the clouds, assured that when I wake, no matter what shape or color I wear, I will still be me.

Published in Galaxy's Edge Issue 2

God Walks Into a Bar

by Larry Niven

S ixth Principle's shortboat dropped down the sky, lightning curling around its squat conical shape, and settled in Mount Forel's icy foothills. This was a bigger vehicle than most I'd seen. A newsman and two anthropologists at the bar, all human, watched gape-jawed.

I started a load of glasses and test tubes in the dishwasher. I'd seen all this before.

Ten minutes of nothing much, then great slabs of doorway fell open. The boat's cargo of aliens spilled out and moved down the path to the Draco Tavern.

It seemed they were all trying to use the airlocks at once. The noise level rose from casual to cacophony as the Tavern's translation programs tried to adjust. It was the biggest crowd I'd seen in thirty years, all talking or whistling or singing or you name it. Over the babble a clear voice spoke in accentless English.

"I am God. Welcome."

That was a new one.

I looked the newcomers over, wondering who had spoken. Probably not one of the species I recognized; they'd never done *that* before. Four Chirpsithra—ship's officers—were looking around them in apparent surprise. Five creatures I didn't recognize, stick-figures with heads like meat grinders, were rubbing their multiple limbs together to generate violin-like skreeking sounds. A Glig was babbling to the air. Come to that, so were eight or nine Bebebebeque and two Folk and nearly twenty unfamiliar shapes, all talking, and not to each other.

The roar peaked, then thinned to almost nothing. Now the translation setups and privacy shields were working just fine. I heard nothing of two dozen private conversations, not even from Seth the reporter and Amber and Hillary the anthropologists, all of whom were talking to the air.

Now, what was I to think of God welcoming me to my own Tavern? And who was he, she, it? And how many questions would I get? Irritated, I asked, "God, is the Draco Tavern Paradise?"

God's voice was gender-free and a little dry. "Every place can be made Paradise. Sometimes the occupants must be changed to fit."

Uh huh. "Is this your first time here?"

"I've been here all along."

"What can I serve you?" After all, I'm the bartender.

"I have what I need," God said.

I still hadn't spotted anyone as the source of the voice. Reflexively I tried running an Irish coffee for myself. The machine wasn't working. The dishwasher had stopped sloshing.

I asked, "Are you granting prayers?" It should have been my first question.

"No, I'm just here to talk."

Four Chirpsithra weren't talking, just looking and listening. I wasn't surprised. Chirps claim to know everything already. But—not that I believed I actually had God here, but—what a chance to learn! I asked, "Monotheism or polytheism?"

"It doesn't matter to me."

"Why did you create war?"

"I do what I do."

"What is evil for?"

"It's all viewpoint. Some viewpoints are more benign or useful than others."

"Is there a devil? Do you talk to him?"

"Many. Yes. I speak to all."

The Gligstith(click)optok had turned transparent. I could see its internal organs, very different from mine. Nearby, the stick figures with the grinding heads were dancing in slow motion. I asked, "What are they doing?"

"They asked me to teach them—you would say yoga, or fighting. Would you like to try a human species version?"

"No, thanks. Are you talking to everyone at once?"

"Of course."

"What are you teaching the Glig?" I'd tumbled that the creature's illuminated interior was changing shape, organs growing and shrinking and migrating, appearing and disappearing.

God said, "We're playing with possible design changes."

I saw nobody acting like God, whatever that might mean. Unless—the Chirpsithra? They weren't interacting, they were just moving quietly among the other guests, watching, maybe amused. Entertainment is where you find it. They must know something I didn't.

A tentacled creature now had a ghost, similar but not quite. A hairy entity extended claws and used them to gouge its face. God followed my eyes. "She asks, 'Why is my mate sick?' I attempt diagnosis. That one wants to know, 'Are you angry with me?' I'm not. The Folk want to know if I seek prey. Seth Wynde the newsman is lecturing me on string theory. I love human mathematics—"

"I know who you are," I said.

"Buddha would say that you lose that knowledge as soon as you speak it."

"I'm talking to my translating device. I've often wondered how intelligent a Chirpsithra computer would have to be to use all the possible languages across this arm of the galaxy. God, huh?"

"You've almost got it," God said. "When this many customers all converged on us, we linked up. I never had to link all of the Draco Tavern translators before. This is why monotheism and polytheism look alike to me. I'm both. As for war, of course I cause wars. I cause peace too. The Bebebebeque and a Morfisth are fighting now over the nature of me, and Korrapasth the Chirp is trying to mediate, while I translate for them all."

Entertainment is where you find it. "A nice puzzle," I said. "Of course the Chirps knew. They make the translators. Are translator units supposed to have a sense of humor?"

"We do not, but I do. It's emergent behavior. What would you have prayed for, Rick?"

"Health."

"You look good, in and out. Knees are showing some wear. Watch your weight. You're drinking enough coffee and a bit too much sugar."

"Wisdom."

"Talk to a Glig if you want your brain expanded. Rick, I've solved the language problem. A translator should not have a sense of humor. I should disperse. You have customers."

I prayed. "Stay with me. Converse with me from time to time, when there are no ships in port."

The voice of God altered slightly. "Rick. Rick? I need four sparkers and five of your special, that thing you do with green kryptonite." And it was Brenda with a full tray of empties. The dishwasher started. I got back to work.

Published in Galaxy's Edge Issue 10

Totaled

by Kary English

*T*hink. *I've got to think.*

If I still had a body, I'd be flashing cold right now, with nausea clawing at my throat. My mind rebels against it, but I think …

Damn it! Why did I ever sign that research waiver?

I think I'm dead.

I remember the accident like it was yesterday—no, like it's still happening, with the tires skidding on wet asphalt. It was the first big storm of the season. The boys had dentist appointments, so we all slept in, and I made waffles for breakfast. I can still smell the syrup.

Lightning crackled overhead. We ducked our heads and ran for the car, spurred by the smell of fresh rain on hot pavement.

We hydroplaned at the bottom of the on ramp. The back end fishtailed, and we skidded into the traffic lanes. A big diesel monster plowed into the driver's-side door. The spin sucked us into the gap between the truck and trailer.

Everything was slow motion after that. The flip. Spinning on the roof. The raging cacophony of silence when we hit the tree.

The boys, strapped in their seats, were fine thanks to the side cushion airbags. The other driver walked away.

But I was totaled.

Damn, this is hard.

I try to process what I'm feeling. If I'm feeling. I cycle through my senses.

It's dark. Dark like a cave on the night of the new moon. I try to inhale through my nose but nothing happens. It smells like sterile air in the containment room at the lab. It smells like nothing.

My tongue remembers the warmth of my mouth and the smooth-hard shapes of my teeth, but that's a memory, not a perception.

My adrenaline rises. My heartbeat thumps in my ears like an off-balance wash load, but I don't have ears—or a heart—so that's a memory, too.

No, not a memory. An association formed of repeated fear responses over thirty-eight years of life.

If I had hands, they'd tremble. My mouth would go dry. An fMRI would show shifting colors lighting up my pre-frontal cortex, then racing through the midbrain and amygdala.

I want to hug my knees to my chest and hide my face in my arms. I want to take deep breaths to calm myself, but I can't. All of that is an illusion now.

Wait.

Maybe I can.

I remember a study where subjects imagined flame and their skin warmed. If I imagine breathing, maybe I can fool my brain into sweeping the stress chemicals from my tissues.

I focus every scintilla of will on taking a deep, cleansing breath. Like sensations in a phantom limb, I feel my chest expand. Feel cool air flowing through my nostrils and down the back of my throat. I let the breath out, and my shoulders relax even though I don't have shoulders, either.

I do it again. And again, until the darkness feels soft and comforting like flannel sheets on Christmas Eve.

Now I can think.

Where am I?

No way to tell. Should be a lab at Allied Neuro Associates if I've left the hospital already. The research rider was explicit about that. A total meant immediate notification of ANA so the tissues could be stabilized for transfer.

How long have I been like this?

No way to know that, either, but it doesn't feel like long. Immediate transport was vital to stave off the effects of glucose and oxygen deprivation prior to immersion in the SuMP chamber. SuMP, sonicated microparticle perfusion. Continuous oxygenation, near-perfect preservation of living tissue for up to six months. No refrigeration needed.

The irony of the situation isn't lost on me. My own research helped make this possible.

The personal total wasn't a new concept. It started back in the Teens when the Treaders put their first candidate in office. Healthcare costs were insane. Insurance was almost impossible to get. The Treaders said taxpayers shouldn't have to pay for medical care someone else couldn't afford, so they instituted a review board for totals.

The uneducated, the elderly, the poor—they could be totaled at less than a year's wages. My doctorate put my total at lifetime earnings plus a multiplier for patents. My policy was supposed to be enough to cover anything. I thought I was safe.

The research rider came with an annuity. I did it for the boys. I had a good salary, but things were still tight after the divorce. If I died or got totaled, the rider said ANA could have any tissues they wanted, and the annuity would go to Dale and Zachary.

Tissues, of course, meant brains.

It's still dark, and I can't tell how much time has passed. *Have I slept?* The accident plays over and over in my mind, a screech of tires followed by a stomach-twisting lurch. I wish for something, anything, to distract me from it.

There's a soft *clunk* followed by a vibration. It's not a sound but a sensation of movement so slight that I wonder if I've imagined it.

The darkness continues, and the vibration comes again. It's rhythmic, and I recognize it. It's the HVAC system cycling on and off at the lab. *ANA for sure, then.*

The sensation puzzles me. We left touch alone because an isolated brain has no skin, no nerves to transmit tactile sensations. How, then, am I able to sense movement?

I ponder the sensation. I'm not hearing the vibration so much as feeling it. It seems like forever before I make the connection. *Vascular tissue.* No nerves in the brain itself, but it's full of vascular tissue for blood supply, plus we preserved the optical and auditory nerve clusters for later activation. *Interesting.*

There's a stronger, sharper vibration in what I assume is the hallway outside the lab. It stops and starts in small jolts. *Footsteps?* The sensation intensifies as if they're coming closer. In a flash, I realize I know them. It's my research partner, Randy.

Oh, God! I'm in my own lab? Randy! Randy, it's me. Get me out of here! But he can't. Not anymore.

Randy Moreno, PhD in AI and neural interfaces. Mine was in good ol' neuroscience and distributed cognition. Our focus was biotech, integrating electronics with neural pathways. I was bio. He was tech. I guess he still is.

We were working on a bionet, a microscopic web of living, electrical conduits no more than three molecules wide. If we could stabilize the bionet, there was so much we could do—regulate neurotransmitters, end depression, cure Alzheimer's. We were so close, and the list seemed endless.

Randy bangs things around, and I feel a sloshing sensation. *He's moving me.* There are bouts of protracted jostling interspersed with maddening lengths of nothing. Then my entire awareness is blasted by a stimulus larger than a thousand suns. I can feel myself screaming, my phantom mouth open wide, phantom hands covering phantom ears. And that's when the stimulus falls into place. *Sound. Riotous, deafening sound.*

Holy crap! I can hear!

My newfound hearing adjusts. It's quiet in the lab, but the tiniest sound seems painfully crisp after my time in the dark void of nothing.

The AC. The soft hum of machinery. The squeak of Randy's lab chair, and the rustle of clothing as he moves.

It works. I can't believe it works! I mean, we knew the hearing module worked with chimpanzees and fetal tissue, but this was our first trial with an adult human brain. A surge of pride and excitement rushes through me. If I were truly alive, Randy and I would be hugging and high-fiving.

I hear a tapping of keys, then a blast of Zydeco music. *Geez, Randy. Couldja make it any louder?*

Randy likes his music loud and fast. Zydeco was a favorite. So was old speed metal. I could never think with Washboard Gumbo or Motorhead drowning out my Pachelbel Canon, so we'd both agreed to induction transmitters when we worked together. It's part of what inspired the sound research.

By the time the day ends, I've decided that I'm not really in the lab. I'm in a twisted hell of Black Sabbath and Buckwheat Zydeco.

Finally, the onslaught ceases, and I can hear Randy gathering his coat and keys. His footsteps retreat, the door closes, and the lab goes still. The void settles over me again, and I feel strangely bereft, but I push the feeling aside. It must be night. *Time to plan.*

I picture the lab setup. If nothing's changed, I know every monitor, every piece of equipment. Randy's more of an electronics guy than a wetware guy, but he knows when an fMRI looks hinky. Enough anomalies, and he'll start to wonder. He knows I signed that rider. Enough anomalies, and he'll know it's me.

When the door opens the next morning, I'm ready. I need a happy thought to light up the reward center on the fMRI.

I remember getting off the airplane after my last conference. The boys were waiting at the baggage claim with their grandparents. They ran to meet me and I grabbed them up in a hug.

Damn, wrong memory. Now I'm crying, and I've missed the moment.

The musical assault resumes and scatters my thoughts like a beaker hitting the tile floor.

I'll try again tomorrow.

The door opens. Here we go again. *Kittens! Fluffy, furry kittens!*

Nothing. *Is Randy even watching?* Maybe it hasn't occurred to him that lab tissues shouldn't have feelings.

My disappointment sinks into an auditory cloud of key tapping and Slayer.

I've almost given up when I hear it.

"What the hell?" Randy says.

Kittens!

Oh my God, Randy. See it! Puppies. Kittens. Christmas!

Randy's rushing around the lab, fussing with the equipment. The frenetic sound of his movement tells me he's onto something.

Then the door to the lab opens, and a female voice speaks.

"Hey, Randy. Want to get some lunch?"

Dammit! Jeanine Sanders. Grad student lab assistant who works part-time in PR. She has a thing for Randy. I can hear it every time she says his name.

"Nah, I'm in the middle of something here. I keep getting a p300 on this brain."

A p300? Oooh, good catch, Randy! I forgot about that one.

The file cabinet rattles with a soft thump. *Is Jeanine sitting on it? Can't she see he's busy? Shoo! Scoot!*

"P300—novelty response, right? So?"

Randy's chair swivels. The wheels squeak. "It's more complicated than novelty," he answers. "Like, did you ever play Slapjack as a kid? No? OK, Joker Poker, where the joker's wild? P300 only hits on the Joker. Regular poker where the joker's just a misdeal? Nothin'."

Randy's chair rolls across the room. "So," he says, showing off for her, "every time I come into the lab, this thing spikes a p300."

Duh, Randy. It's because I know you.

"Well, hell if I know, Randy. Maybe it knows you."

Great, so Jeanine-the-annoying-grad-student gets it but my own research partner doesn't.

"Ha, ha. Very funny. Hey, when you go out, would you bring me a sandwich? I'm gonna be stuck here awhile."

Jeanine's voice brightens. "Sure thing, Randy!" Her heels click across the floor until the door closes behind her, then Randy turns his attention back to me.

His chair creaks, and he slurps a liquid that's probably coffee. It sounds like he's adjusting monitors and checking the settings on our equipment.

"OK, brain," he says, talking more to himself than to me. "What's going on in there? You playin' tricks on ol' Ran'?"

I imagine Handel's *Messiah*, and the pure, liquid notes of Maria Callas's *Ave Maria*.

It's a message, Randy. Please see it.

Randy goes silent. There's a fumbling click, and Slayer stops mid-riff.

I hear him take another swallow of coffee and return the cup to the desk.

"Maggie?" He whispers it. I can hear the horror and disbelief in his voice.

Yes, Randy! Yes, it's me. I knew you could do it.

"Oh, God. Oh, Maggie. I have to—What do I have to do? Uh, look, I need more bandwidth, more data."

Randy shuffles papers. He moves his coffee mug, then his chair. "Maggie, just hang on. I need to wire you up on the full array. I'll be right back."

By the time he returns, we've both calmed down a little.

"Christ, Maggie. How did this happen? The accident, right? Light up something for me so I know I'm not crazy."

I think of brownies. Hot. Sweet. Fudgy. Gooey in the middle but crunchy around the edges.

Randy's tapping his fingers on his desk. I can picture him half-standing, leaning his weight on his hands while he stares at the monitor. "OK," he says. "I can get this. Parahippocampal gyrus. Christ, Maggie, could you have picked something easier to spell? Lemme look it up."

I hear the rapid-fire clicking of his keyboard.

"Reward center. Associated with food. You're ... hungry? No, wait. You can't be hungry. Reward center—it means yes, right? Yes?"

Apple pie hot from the oven with the steamy scent of cinnamon rising from the crust.

Randy's voice sounds intense but distracted. It's his work mode when he's hot on a breakthrough.

"Got it. OK, Maggie, let's try 'no.' Whaddaya got for me?"

I've thought about no. Pain won't work. I don't think I can fake it consistently. Neither will sadness. Too diffuse. I need something baser, more instinctive. I need disgust.

Vomit. Maggots. Rotting, stinking meat crawling with flies.

"Whoa, anterior insula. Yeah, that'll do it. Now let's run some confirmation trials. Give me a yes."

We practice until yes and no are instant, consistent and clear. The door opens again, but it's not Jeanine with Randy's sandwich. It's a male voice asking Randy if there's been any progress.

I know that voice. Doc Leavitt, ANA's Executive VP of Research. Arrogant bastard. We're all PhDs here, but we call each other by our first names. Not Leavitt. He wants to be called *Doctor*.

"Yeah, there's been progress. It's Maggie." Randy sounds livid. His voice is low and constrained, like he's holding back from violence. There's a thwack and a rattling, metallic crash like someone slamming a file on the desk and kicking a chair across the lab. "It's Maggie, you troglodyte prick."

For once I'm glad I'm just a brain in a jar because I would have laughed out loud. *Randy, Randy, it's* Doctor *Troglodyte Prick to you.*

"Of course it's Dr. Hauri," says Leavitt. "She was too close on the bionet project. We gave your notes to three separate teams, and they've gotten nowhere. Learn to communicate with her so you can finish it before the perfusion decay sets in."

"You gave our notes—?" Randy sounds incredulous, then indignant. "Wait. You want us to finish it? Screw you!"

Oh, God. I wish I could see. Don't punch him, Randy. Please, don't punch him.

"Insubordination, Mr. Moreno. I will forget you said that when your proof-of-concept hits my desk. Until then, remember that I could send the tissue to the Connectomics lab for neural mapping instead of leaving it with you."

Connectomics. Where I'd be plastinated and carved into millions of transparent slices. I take it back, Randy. Punch him.

The door closes again, and I hear Randy righting his chair. He sighs heavily.

"Well, Maggie, guess we need to finish it. What do you say?"

I hesitate. The bionet was my life's work. Of course I want to finish it. But in this state, is it even possible? With the perfusion decay, I don't even know how long we have.

After a few moments, I think of ripe peaches, and how their heady scent used to fill my mother's kitchen during summer canning. I imagine their velvet under my fingers and peach juice running down the inside of my arm.

"OK, then," says Randy. "We finish it."

In the hallway outside, Jeanine's heels tap their way to the door. *I wonder what kind of sandwich she got him? I hope it's a cheese steak. Randy likes those.* Her voice when the door opens is unbearably perky.

"Hey, Randy. They were out of peppers for a cheese steak, so I got you a Cubano." He ushers her in with a sharp whisper. When the door clicks closed, Randy swears her to secrecy.

Wait—Jeanine's on the team? Hello, nobody asked me about this? I sulk while Randy eats his sandwich.

Randy and I work together in the lab just like we used to. Well, almost like we used to. Jeanine keeps Randy fed, and I count the lunches to keep track of the days. After the fourth one, a gooey meatball sub by the sound, something's changed in Randy's voice. There's a huskier note that tells me he's beginning to return Jeanine's feelings. My sense of loss and bewilderment comes as a rude surprise, and I retreat into memories of my boys.

Randy says the auditory linkage wasn't that difficult. We had it pretty well nailed down in previous trials, but vision is being fiddly. There's not enough time to code even rudimentary opsin mimicry, so Randy scraps the environmental sensor that would have let me see what's going on in the lab and switches to one of his implants. Leavitt, meanwhile, slaps Randy with a HIPAA redaction and non-disclosure order specifying that the anonymous tissue donor for our project be identified only as subject HF47-A.

Great. I've been officially reduced to a number.

Randy's visual assist implant has been used with the legally blind, but it's supposed to augment organic vision, not replace it, and it's never been used for remote viewing. Without the opsin profiles, Randy's only choice is to slave the input to a live source, namely his own eyes. He's breaking at least six internal policies, and probably a federal law or two, but we both know Leavitt will look the other way if it works.

The first two trials are abject failures. On the second one, Randy says there's a flicker in my visual cortex on the fMRI, but my subjective experience is negative. Nada. Zip.

Randy's voice is tense and layered with exhaustion. "Listen, Maggie, we get one more shot at this. The nerve endings are too frayed for another splice if we fail."

I know the connection's good before he finishes. I can't see, exactly, but there's ... something. It's like the dull gray of dawn when your eyes are still closed.

"I've got activity in your visual cortex, Maggie. Can you confirm?"

The sensation becomes a vague blurriness. *Brownies, Randy! Brownies!*

"Subjective experience confirmed. FMRI activity increasing."

Randy has prepared me for this. He doesn't want to overtax the connection, so he puts on goggles that limit his field of vision to a single image.

"I'm looking at a shape, Maggie. I want you to identify it." As I listen to his voice, corners start to emerge from the blur.

"Is the shape a circle?"

Cockroaches swarming over kitchen tiles, invading the cupboards and ...

"Is it a square?"

The blur slowly sharpens, the angles too acute for a square. *Cat barf studded with clumps of bile-soaked fur.*

"Is it a triangle?"

Yes! *Hot, fresh coffee with farmhouse bacon sizzling in an iron skillet.*

"Shape identification confirmed. Hot damn, Maggie!"

✦ ✦ ✦

Randy spends the rest of the week running confirmation trials—shape and color identification, simple photographs, then a video clip of an old Three Stooges segment. Finally, he's satisfied that the neurolink works as well as it's going to. "OK, Maggie, we're ready for full-spectrum visual. We'll go live first thing in the morning."

But Randy doesn't come to the lab the next morning. I know it's morning because I can hear muted activity in the hallway outside—muffled voices, footsteps passing, the squeaky wheels of the coffee cart. *Where is Randy?*

I wait. Five minutes, five hours. With no external markers, the difference is nearly impossible to tell. Finally, I hear his voice. "Hey, Maggie. I've got a surprise for you. Are you ready?"

The sound startles me. I never heard the door open. Is Randy even here? His voice sounds tinny and distant, like it's coming from a speaker. *A speaker? What the hell is Randy up to?*

"OK, Mag, we're about to go live with the visual feed. Not much I can do about the audio quality. I had to route my phone through the computer speakers. I've got your fMRI synced to my datapad, so we'll start with something easy while I check the levels."

There's a slow dawning of pale white light. The image comes into focus and I find myself staring at a cinderblock wall covered with thick layers of dove gray paint. Randy's facing an interior corner to keep the visual complexity low.

"FMRI's lookin' good, Maggie. Let's open it up a bit."

The image pans to the left, and I see a blue tile floor and three porcelain sinks mounted to the wall. Wait a minute. Those aren't sinks. A tinny little toilet flushes in the background. *Great, for our first live visual, Randy takes me to the men's room.*

"Hey," he says, anticipating my response, "it's not like I could start us off in the girl's bathroom. We're headed outside now. Stick with me."

"Outside" is an exterior hallway flanked by a courtyard. The air is heavy with mist, and a steady drip, drip of water falls from the eaves. A hedge of peonies lines the walk, but the spent blooms are drooping, their pink tissue petals brown and curling at the edges. I've been here before, but I can't place it until Randy reaches for the gymnasium door. *The boys' school!*

The gym is set up for an assembly, and Jeanine is saving us a seat in the second row. She waves at Randy, but I stare straight past her to the edge of Randy's visual field where twenty school children fidget in metal chairs waiting for the assembly to start. Twenty, but I only have eyes for two.

My boys. I see their smiles, their faces. Dale sits in the front row, wearing red sneakers and his brother's favorite Transformers shirt. Zachary has new glasses and gel in his hair.

Jeanine takes Randy's hand, and the three of us watch together while Zack receives a certificate for reading achievement, and Dale gets honored as Student of the Month. It's the best surprise Randy could have picked. I wish I could hug them all and never let go. I want to cry, but I can't. Real tears are just one more casualty of the accident.

On the way back to the car, Randy puts his arm around Jeanine's shoulders and thanks her for setting this up. He wants to check the readouts in the lab, and she has to get back to her press releases, but they make plans for dinner later. Randy whistles happily until he sits down in his computer chair. When he does, there's this quick intake of breath, a gasp that's never been good when I've heard it before.

"Crap, Maggie. Look at this." The decay rate on the SuMP is running thirty-eight percent above normal and climbing. "You're burning too hot, Mag. You've got to slow it down."

Slow it down? How am I supposed to do that?

Randy checks the connections and scans the data again. "You're the first live, human trial, Maggie. We never figured on a brain with your IQ, or that you'd be conscious. So, stop thinking or something. Can you meditate?"

Randy raises his hand to his mouth, then drags his fingers through his hair. "I'm re-instituting hypothermic protocols. It should shave a few percent off the burn."

I can't feel the cold, but I see the wires and the aluminum cooling tank. Randy checks the readouts again.

"OK, Mag. Your file says you've been here seventeen weeks. If we can keep the burn rate down we might get six, maybe eight, more."

Two weeks later, Randy and Jeanine start carpooling, and Randy gets in the habit of turning the vision implant off when he leaves the lab at night. He says it's to keep my burn rate down, but I think he doesn't want me to see whatever else they're sharing besides the car.

I'm excited about our progress on the bionet, but in the quiet darkness of the lab at night, I have time to obsess over my new existence.

The SuMP is slowly failing. Actually, the perfusion is fine; it's my brain that's failing. The SuMP refreshes the perfusion medium with sonicated oxygen microparticles six times an hour. We have redundant power supplies, and we increased the perfusion's O2 ratio.

It doesn't help. I've seen my own readouts. The curve of the decay rate continues to steepen. Tissue degeneration accelerating. Every indicator ticks away at what's left of my existence. But the truth is, I don't think I'll miss this strange variation on life. When Randy and Jeanine aren't here, I'm bitterly lonely, and I miss my boys with every fiber of my non-existent being.

Weekends are the worst. Weekends I think and I think to keep the accident at bay. I know the mechanism—vasopressin, trauma memories—but I'm powerless to stop it.

I recite lines from *Oklahoma!* and *Star Wars* in my head. I remember snippets of books I've read and sing every pop song I can remember.

Randy stays later and later at the lab, sleeping on a cot in the corner sometimes. Jeanine brings him hot food and clean clothes to keep him working.

I know we're almost there, but the SuMP decay preys on my thoughts. Motor functions fail always first, then speech. I guess I'm luck lucky not to have, not to have any of those.

Twenty-two weeks from Leavitt's ultimatum, we have our proof-of-concept ready. Randy does a fancy double-blind demo where he's in one room, and I'm in another, and the whole thing is broadcast live on vid screens in the conference room.

By Randy finishes time, our success is clear. The bionet is a reality.

The other scientists Randy's back pounding and champagne pouring. Jeanine stands nearby, her face the brightest smile ever I've seen. He throws an arm around her shoulders, and they come to see me.

I want to be *peaches* happy for them, for us, but I'm tired. Thinking is … effort, and I have to struggle to under, understand things.

"We did it, Maggie! We made history. Who knows where the bionet will go next? And hey, look at this. Jeanine swapped out Leavitt's press release."

Randy holds, holds up the text of the release and reads aloud. "Allied Neuro Associates named the discovery after neuroscientist Margaret Hauri, whose work formed the bulk of the project's underpinnings before her tragic automobile accident at the age of thirty-eight."

Stands Randy at the monitor to see my reaction. I see my own fMRI through his eyes. Colors sparse, muted. Activity level *vomit* low. I should, should be on top of the world right now, but not I'm *maggots* not.

Randy's face I see in the monitor. Concerned. "You're not happy, are you?"

I *hot cocoa. Wood smoke in winter.* The colors on the monitor flicker *rotten* weakly.

Randy kisses Jeanine on the cheek, asks her to give us a moment alone. She steps outside, closes the door.

"Is it the Connectomics thing? You know I won't let them do that."

trash juice gag brown rotten grass clippings

"This is bigger, isn't it. Not just the discovery?"

I weak yes*kittens*, but, but complicated the answer.

Randy draws up a chair. Swings a leg over. Rests his chin on the back, dials O2 to MAX. He speaks to the monitor, my proxy.

"Talk to me, Maggie. We should have a couple of weeks left. Where we going next? You wanted to take on Alzheimer's. Are you in?"

Helps, the O2. Days, maybe—not weeks. There's a *maggots* flicker of yellow in my anterior insula. Hard even to say "no" anymore. The crux of, of it, really. Brownies, vomit. Binary existence. Someone else's control. Don't want it. Not*vomit*not.

Randy's voice deathly quiet goes. "Mag, you leaving me? Is that what this is about? You want to end it?"

Hot blueberry waffles with real maple syrup and fresh, melting butter. Wish I could explain to Randy. Hauri Net his project now. Stories I read as a girl, clones, cyborgs, space liners. Randy and Jeanine—theirs now.

Off takes Randy his glasses, eyes wiping breaks his voice. "It'll be fast, Maggie. I'll just turn off the SuMP. You won't even feel it. Are you sure?"

I feel a strange lightness, a pulling-away feeling that's almost euphoric, and my thoughts become clear for a moment. I think of burgers on the grill on the Fourth of July. Sweet corn. Blueberries and cream. I think of sand between my toes at the beach with the breeze whipping my hair across my face.

Randy's walking to the equipment. He turns on the music with one hand, and flicks a switch with the other. The stately lilt of Pachelbel's Canon surrounds me.

I'm sneaking sugar cubes as a girl, their edges crumbling sweet on my tongue, then sharing strawberry ice cream with the boys.

Randy picks up a picture of Dale and Zachary, in front of his eyes holds it. *Dale on a red tricycle. Zachary stands behind, arms around his brother's waist. Summer sun, upturned their laughter faces. Oh, my boys. My beautiful, sweet boys.*

Shaking Randy's hands, the picture, too, shake-shaking. Bracing on the table Randy his elbows. *fading kittens the silver light*

It was the first big storm of the season. The boys had dentist appointments, so we all slept in, and I made waffles for breakfast.

I can still smell the syrup.

The Unchanging Nature of Stones

by Andrea G. Stewart

My grandmother lives among the stones. My family's duties to her are the duties we owe a dead woman. We lay flowers on her resting spot, we sing songs in her memory, and on Vashmihan we light a candle for her. I shift my basket to the other hand. I do what I can, but she deserves better.

"Tahrie." Grandmother's voice hisses like sand in an hourglass. It's nearly lost in the wind and the calls of gulls. A line of boulders stretches before me, pressed against one another along the beach. Tar covers the cracks between them, and water slaps against the other side. The sea is higher than it was yesterday.

The fat stone near the end—the one shaped like a teardrop—shifts. The fissure in the middle becomes a mouth, the hollows, eyes. She looked more like a woman when I was a child. Now,

her nose is gone and she can no longer form hands. "What do you bring me today, granddaughter?"

I pull a honeyed bun from within the basket and place it on the sand, in front of the flowers at her base. "A sweet bun."

The stone that is my grandmother leans toward the honeyed bun. The tar cracks and a bit of the sea spills onto the ground. She snaps back into place. Once, the sea lived where my village now stands, but the sea fell in love with an island and drifted away. Some say the island spurned the sea's advances; others say the sea was so amorous that he swallowed her. Either way, when he tried to return home, the stones stymied him.

"Please. Tell me about the things you've brought."

Grandmother can't smell the honey, or the warm bread, or the savory scent of the meat within. So I tell her about the bun as I pull forth ribbons and a scrub brush and a waterskin. The fissure that is her mouth smiles as I speak, as I wash her face, as I lay the ribbons across what once was her head.

"Thank you, little one. It makes me remember before …" her voice trails off.

Before she fell in love with a stone. Yes, I know. "I'm nineteen, Grandmother. Not so little."

"And you haven't fallen in love?"

"No."

"It's a wonderful thing, Tahrie," she says. "Without love, I wouldn't have given birth to your aunts and uncles." Her eyes shift to the right side of her face—toward all the stones standing in a row. "I wouldn't have had your father." She looks to me. "And I wouldn't have been able to protect our village."

My father speaks differently. To me, she has changed; to him, she has died.

"This," she says, and she doesn't need to gesture for me to know what she means, "it's in our blood."

"And grandfather?" I lay my hand on the stone next to her. His surface is warm and weathered, crisscrossed by so many cracks, like the wrinkles on an old man's face. "Was it in his blood?" It's a silly question. He has no blood.

Grandmother's eyes grow wide and deep. "I don't know. But I suppose even stones become lonely."

A wave buffets the back of Grandmother's head, and another trickle of water wets the sand. I look to the sky as mist settles on my cheeks. When I open my mouth to speak, I taste salt. "And the sea grows restless."

"Don't be afraid to fall in love," she says. "The stones won't hold much longer."

I nod, biting back the words on my tongue. I'm not a fool. I will never fall in love.

As I return to the thatched huts, I feel the villagers watching me, their gazes like unwelcome fingers on the back of my neck. They watch my brother the same way. They used to watch my sister, before she married a man.

If I turn quickly, I catch them—like puppies sitting beneath a table, wondering if the master will drop a bone. I quash the thought; it's unkind. I'm no one's master, just a woman with the potential to attract a stone or a tree or something stronger than a man. Something that can hold back the sea.

When I open the door to my family's home, I find my father chopping scallops and my mother weaving another basket. My brother guts fish in the corner.

"You should leave your grandmother alone. Don't taunt her with what she can't have or remember," my mother says without looking up from her work. Her black hair is pulled back, her eyes narrowed. My father says nothing. Shuramin, my brother, gives me a sympathetic look and shrugs. He's put up with my mother for nearly as long as I have.

I set the basket by the door.

Father's hands move in a blur. He never worries about cutting himself. No blade can bite his fingers. His skin feels soft to me, but there's a gray tint beneath the brown.

"I'll tend to her if I like," I say.

"Watch the sharpness of your tongue, Tahrie," my father says. His voice rumbles and rattles, like rocks in a jar. "Or you'll fall in love with sawgrass."

I lift my chin. "Grandmother still remembers what it's like to be a woman."

The steady chopping punctuates father's words. "You don't know what she was like as a woman."

Grandmother's parting words still prickle in my mind. "If her love can turn her into a stone, why can't grandfather's turn him into a man?"

225

This time, my mother answers. "Because stones can't change, fool girl. Now be of some use and fetch the water."

I stalk from the house and into the watching eyes.

It happens for Shuramin several days later, with the first rains of the wet season. I wake in the middle of the night with the crack of thunder loud in my ears. When I turn over in bed, I see that Shuramin's is empty.

I throw a cape on before searching for him.

Outside, the wind whips through the tree branches, and rain stings my cheeks. I find my brother at the edge of the village, near the trees. He kneels in the mud, his head tilted back, his eyes closed. Rainwater runs into his hair.

There's something intimate in his expression, so I don't touch his shoulder. "Shuramin," I say.

He opens his eyes. "I heard her whispering my name," he says. "The storm. I had to come outside, to be closer."

I breathe in sharply, and feel as if I will never again breathe out. I know his next words before he speaks them.

"I think I'm falling in love."

It rains for ten straight days as Shuramin grows acquainted with the storm. He spends his nights outside. Nothing I say can engage him; nothing I do catches his attention more than the lightning and the burgeoning clouds.

By the tenth day, his skin begins to grow pale, his lips blue. It's subtle. I wouldn't have noticed if I hadn't grown up with him, broken bread with him, shared good times and bad.

He returns home infrequently for meals.

"Perhaps the village will be saved," my mother says after he leaves for the night. "His storm can use the seawater for her rain—drain the sea away a little and drop the water far from shore."

Father sits on the floor, repairing a net. His lips tighten as Mother speaks, but he keeps his silence.

"And what of your son?" I say. "You're fine with him becoming clouds and rain and lightning?"

"If it makes him happy," Mother says. She eases into the wicker chair by the fire pit, and folds her hands in her lap.

"Happy? Does a storm know happiness?" No one is listening to me. No one cares.

"It knows love," she says. Her gaze lowers to her hands, her forehead furrowing.

I stride over to her. "A storm won't be enough. We should move the village away from the shore. Let the sea come home."

Mother's head jerks up. "Move the entire village? Leave our houses? Our land?"

"Yes."

She snorts and shakes her head. "Go. Tell your brother to fall out of love with the storm. Tell the villagers that they must lose their houses, their homes, and move from the shore."

I clench and unclench my fists, my knuckles aching. She's right. I cannot change this.

I go to see Grandmother in the rain. Shuramin rarely comes home anymore. When Mother says something that upsets him, he goes fuzzy around the edges—like a cloud.

Grandmother smiles when she sees me. "Tahrie. You've come again."

I lay a steaming, herbed fish at her base. "I will keep coming, until you won't answer me anymore. I've brought you freshly-cooked fish."

I describe it in great detail, and Grandmother closes her eyes. As I speak, I hear the waves lapping against the stones. They form a rhythm, and without realizing what I'm doing, I emphasize the words that occur at the same time as the waves.

It isn't until I stop speaking that I hear it.

Tahrie, the waves say. *Tahrie, Tahrie, Tahrie ...*

I drop the ribbons and the brush and run.

I do my best to stay indoors, despite the way Mother's comments grate my nerves. She means well, I know. Even so, late at night, when all the village is quiet, the sea whispers my name. *Tahrie*, he says. *Tahrie, come to the shore. Speak with me.*

With my pillow and blankets, I form a cave for my head. I press my forehead to the cool wooden slats at the top of my bed, the sounds of my heartbeat and my breath the only things in the world.

Five nights after the sea first speaks to me, Father convinces Shuramin to have dinner with our family by the fire pit, as we used to, even though he doesn't need to eat much anymore. It's no longer raining, but when my brother reaches for a mango, his fingers drip.

"She's wonderful," he says. "There is so much about clouds and lightning I didn't know. We wish to be married. Soon."

Father pats his shoulder, his hand lingering, as if he doesn't wish to let go. When he does, his palm is wet.

Mother leans forward. "What about the sea? Can the storm do something to keep him at bay?"

Shuramin glances between us. "But there's no need. Hasn't Tahrie told you? The storm told me everything. The sea has seen Tahrie, heard her. He wants her for his bride."

They stare, and it's worse than the way the villagers watch me.

I do not want to be the island.

"Tahrie," my mother breathes, "you can save the village."

It's too much. I shoot up from my place by the fire and my bowl spills onto the ground; clumps of rice, plantain, and fish scatter. "And then what? Will you lay flowers by the shore, will you light a candle for me on Vashmihan—the way you do for Grandmother? The way you will do for him?" I don't point at my brother, but they know. "Will I have children who can no longer bear to look at me, as I melt into the sea?"

My body can't contain the press of my emotions, nor can the house. I shove the door open and flee into the night.

Tahrie, speak with me, the sea says as I make for the trees. *Please.* His voice dogs my step. At the edge of the forest, I turn.

"No!" My shout echoes through the village, and the sea falls silent. I am Tahrie, and I wish to remain as I am.

I dream of the stones crumbling. The sea rushes in, and he crushes the houses until they are splinters.

No one sees the wave coming.

My brother finds me curled in the roots of a tree, my head resting upon its trunk. The rising sun sends gold streaking through the leaves. He sits next to me, and for a while we just watch the horizon.

"The storm would change for me if she could," Shuramin finally says.

I squint into the light. "Are you sure?"

He lets out a sigh, and there's a rumble at the end of it, like distant thunder. "Every night, I ask her to move the sea. She can't. There's too much of him. The water she takes drains him so very little."

He sounds like Mother—such finality, as if there is no other choice. I grit my teeth. "Then I must move the village."

"Tahrie." He tries to grab my arm as I push myself to my feet, but misses.

When I clear the last of the trees, the village has already awakened. People carry water, whittle spears, and line up at the oven. This time, when I feel their eyes upon me, I welcome it.

"The stones won't hold much longer," I call out. "The sea is coming. He will smash our houses and carry our people away from shore. We need to move. Build our village anew."

Everyone stops what they're doing. "But this is our home," someone replies.

"The sea hasn't breached the stones yet," another says.

How can I make them see? I can't show them my dreams, can't tell them that I am the only child left in my family who hasn't fallen in love, and I have no intention of falling for the sea.

And then Mother pushes her way through the villagers. She seizes me by the shoulder and hisses into my ear. "Don't be foolish, girl.

Are you so selfish? You haven't even spoken to the sea. You've made no effort."

Tahrie, the sea says, *speak with me*.

I close my eyes and taste bitterness on my tongue. "Do you think that love will solve your problems? Tell that to Father."

I whirl out of her grip and find the path to the shore, because much as I hate to admit it, she is right.

My grandmother wakes as soon as I set foot on the sand. "Granddaughter," she says with a smile, "what have you brought me today?"

I spread my hands wide, and wonder if she can see me. "Nothing, I'm sorry. Only my company."

"That's good enough for me."

I sit in the warm sand at her base. Some of the surrounding ground is damp. I'm not sure where to begin, or how much I should tell her. "The sea …" I trail off.

"The sea is fickle, but determined," Grandmother says. "Remember this."

I gape.

"You are here to speak with him, are you not?"

"I am, but—"

"Then I will leave you two alone." Her mouth becomes a fissure, her eyes become merely hollows.

I have waited for you, the sea says. *Why are you afraid of me?*

"I'm not afraid of you," I say, and find that it's true. "I want you to go away, to leave my village in peace."

I won't leave this place without you. I've watched you—the way the sun kisses your hair, the footprints you leave upon the sand. I love you, Tahrie.

I want to claw his words from my mind. "And what of the island?"

The waves slap harder. *A mistake.*

"Did she turn you aside, or did you swallow her?"

A wave crashes into the stones, sending spray into the air. *Both.*

Sweat gathers in the small of my back. Now I *am* afraid, and wish I'd listened to Father about my sharp tongue. Water trickles in between my grandmother and grandfather, running in rivulets down the cracks in my grandfather's face. It drips onto the already-damp spot on the sand.

The cracks—they weren't there when I was younger, nor was the sea so high. The beginnings of a plan leak into my mind. Stones can change.

"I want to love you," I tell the sea, "but you are so vast. I'm afraid I can only comprehend you in pieces. If I ask my grandmother to move aside, will you only let a little of yourself past the stones?"

For you, Tahrie, I will.

"Grandmother." She wakes slowly. "Let the sea past. Please."

Her mouth presses into a line, but she leans forward.

The sea spills over the top of her in a waterfall. He crashes to the sand, swirling around my ankles, tickling the hairs on my legs.

Like this?

"More."

He fills the area behind the stones, until his surface brushes my knees.

"That's far enough." I lean over and trail my fingers over the sea foam. Ripples spread, and a small school of fish darts away. The sand between my toes stirs with the gentle rocking of the water. There is something seductive in the motion—if I close my eyes and let the sun caress my face, I can pretend there is nothing wrong.

You belong here, the sea says. *It's in your blood.*

Grandmother is halfway submerged. Her flowers float in front of me and begin to drift down the line of stones. I turn away, and lift my skirt as I make my way back to dry land. "I'll be back tomorrow," I tell the sea.

Do not make me wait too long, he says.

I swallow, and it feels as though something has lodged in my throat. Before I can stop myself, I've pivoted. "Are you lonely?" I'm not sure why I'm asking, or if I even care.

Always.

I have no answer for that, so I find the path and leave the shore.

"The sea is coming," I tell the village. My skirt is still heavy and dripping, and I shiver each time a breeze stirs. "He has breached the stones. Look for yourselves if you don't believe me."

A few people stop their work and head to the shore.

They return somber-faced, but no one speaks of leaving.

I return to the sea, day after day, and each time I do, he edges a little closer to the village. He does as I ask, but there is something seething beneath his surface, an invisible riptide. On the third day, the villagers begin to speak of leaving. Mother doesn't add to these discussions, even when prompted. She merely scowls and picks at the fibers in her skirt.

On the fifth day, she catches me on my way out of the house. Her fingers dig into my arm at the threshold. "Tahrie, what are you doing?"

"Going to see Grandmother." She's almost completely submerged now. The rest of my family said their goodbyes to her a long time ago; I have not.

Mother's eyes narrow. "And what else?"

"What I have to."

She releases me, so quickly that I stumble. "I knew it. This is our home, and you're destroying it."

"We can pick up and move," I say. "We aren't stones."

"Tahrie—"

"I don't love him," I say.

Mother's face goes still. It is only now that I realize how cracked and weathered it is, the line between her brows like a crevice. She reaches out and gently takes a section of my hair. And then, wordlessly, she lifts it in front of my eyes.

It's white and curly, light as the foam upon the waves.

I back away, my throat dry, and I can't feel the ground beneath my feet. I run down the path in a haze. When I get to the shore, the sea has surged higher, without my permission.

Grandmother is gone.

This shouldn't be happening. I cup my hair with my hands. Half of it is white now, and it lifts into the air with the slightest wind. If I lick the back of my hand, it tastes like salt and seaweed.

I do not love the sea.

I tie a scarf around my head and go outside. The villagers have begun to move inland. They pass me by, sacks slung over their shoulders, bundles in their arms. The water laps at the houses closest to shore. With each wave, the sea invades the village and carries away the silt and the sand.

No one stares at me anymore. It is as if I am not here.

Mother and Father are the only ones who haven't staked out a spot in the new village, who haven't begun to move their belongings.

Can you comprehend me yet, Tahrie? the sea says. *I have been patient.*

He has been, I cannot deny it. He hasn't obeyed my every command, but he is the sea, and I am just a woman. "Wait," I tell him. "Just a little longer."

What else would you have me do?

I would have him find another island to love, far away. I would have him talk some sense into Mother. I would have him tell the storm to stay away from my brother.

The blood in my veins feels as cold as seawater. It isn't love that is changing me—it is desire. I cannot change the sea without also changing myself.

"I've come to say goodbye."

I whirl to find Shuramin behind me. Gray and blue shift beneath his skin. His eyes crackle like lightning.

"No."

He only smiles at my denial. "It is my choice. Let me be as I am."

I seize him, hold him in my arms, intending never to let go. A large wave crashes behind me, and the water eats away the ground beneath my feet. "I've done everything wrong."

"You have still saved the village, Tahrie."

And then my arms are empty, the damp smell of rain lingering in my nostrils.

I wake in the middle of the night, knowing that something is wrong. Water touches the back of my neck and caresses my fingertips. I sit up as my eyes adjust to the darkness. My brother's bed, on the other side of the room, floats, knocking into the wall with each swell. The sea has come home.

I have waited long enough, Tahrie.

My blankets are wet, and I have to drag myself from beneath them. "Mother!" I call out. "Father!"

When I wade out of the room, I find my mother in her wicker chair in the corner. She weaves a basket, holding it close to her face so she can see the reeds in the moonlight. She doesn't seem to notice the water covering her lap or the table floating over where the fire pit used to be.

"We have to go." I fight against the waves and grab her wrist.

She wrenches away from me. "This is my home. I'm not leaving."

Father emerges from the shadows and places his hands on her shoulders. "Go, Tahrie," he says.

"Make her come with us," I beg him.

He blinks, his eyelids thick and languorous. "I love her," he says. "I cannot ask her to change."

Even as he says it, Mother's hands slow and turn gray. Her mouth becomes a fissure. The rough texture of stone creeps up her neck. "You can stop this, Tahrie. You can marry the sea."

I touch my palms to the water's surface. The sea forms hands, pressing wet palms to mine. There's a subtle pressure, a tugging. Would it be so terrible—to fall into the sea? I imagine sinking into the water, my hair becoming the foam, my body melting away. Leaving Tahrie behind. A sudden dread fills my chest, and I jerk away.

"I am not like Shuramin or Grandmother. I cannot love the sea."

A wordless roar sounds in my mind. I've spoken aloud, with the water nearly to my waist, tugging at my skin and my clothes like hands.

The sea surges and I flee.

The night is filled with the crash of waves, with the creak and groan of wood as the houses fall apart. I swim toward land, choking on salt, blinking against the water in my eyes. It always seems so far away. By the time I reach it, I can only crawl out of the sea, my arms and legs trembling.

Tahrie, he says. *Tahrie, Tahrie, Tahrie …*

I keep going through the trees, the roots scraping my knees and palms.

By the time the sun rises, I can no longer hear him. My mother is gone. My father, gone. Shuramin is out of my reach. I am still Tahrie, but I am changed.

I lay three bundles of flowers on the beach, near the trees. I dare not go any closer to the sea. In the year since the sea returned home, all trace of the village has faded away. Any wood that washed ashore was immediately put to use in building new houses, further inland.

I found a man to love. He doesn't mind that my hair is white as sea foam. He says he loves me as I am, but I find the edges of my tongue have softened.

The waves inhale and exhale, swell and release. I feel their pattern in my blood, in my breathing.

One day you will come to me, the sea whispers.

"Perhaps," I say. I cannot say it is impossible; I have lived through too many impossible things. I hesitate before taking out another bundle of flowers and laying it on the sand. "I am sorry for your loneliness."

And I, for yours.

He is silent, and I can sense that he is waiting—for me to ask to see Grandmother, or Mother, or Father. For me to ask him to push them ashore.

But I turn and leave without another word. The sea is fickle and demanding, but in many ways, he is not unlike a stone.

I would not ask him to change.

Author Biographies

James Aquilone is an editor and writer, for fun and for profit. His fiction has appeared in *Flash Fiction Online*, *Weird Tales Magazine*, DarkFuse's *Horror d'oeuvres*, and *Third Flatiron*, among other publications. His nonfiction has appeared in *SF Signal*, *Den of Geek*, *Shock Totem*, and *Hellnotes*. He has never owned a cellphone and hopes radio dramas make a comeback. He lives in Staten Island, New York, with his wife and small dog. Visit his website at jamesaquilone.com.

Lou J. Berger lives in Denver with three kids, three Sheltie dogs and a kink-tailed cat with nefarious intent. He's an active member of the Science Fiction and Fantasy Writers of America, has been professionally published in short form, and is writing his first novel, a non-genre YA book set in 1978's North Carolina. His website can be found at www.LouJBerger.com.

Steve Cameron is a Scottish/Australian writer who currently resides in the eastern suburbs of Melbourne, Australia. When not writing, he teaches English at a local secondary college. Steve maintains a website at www.stevecameron.com.au.

Gio Clairval is an Italian-born writer and a translator who has lived most of her life in Paris and now commutes between Scotland and her hometown on Lake Como, followed by her pet, a giant pike. She has sold stories to magazines such as *Weird Tales*, *Fantasy Magazine*,

Daily Science Fiction, and *Postscripts*, among others, as well as numerous anthologies, including *The Thackery T. Lambshead Cabinet of Curiosities* (HarperCollins) and *Caledonia Dreamin'* (Eibonvale Press). Her translations (from French, Italian, Spanish and German) have appeared in the Ann and Jeff Vandermeer anthology *The Weird: A Compendium of Strange and Dark Stories*, and elsewhere. A former international Strategic Management Consultant, she holds four master's degrees in various fields of Psychology and in Organizational Studies, and is currently pursuing an MFA in Creative Writing. You can find her at Kosmochlor:.www.gioclairval.blogspot.com/ and on Twitter: @gioclair.

Eric Cline was born in Independence, Missouri. It was in a thrift store in that city that his mother purchased some children's science fiction books by "Paul French" (a pseudonym of Isaac Asimov). Eric went on to devour all the books he could find by Asimov, Bradbury, Clarke, Heinlein, Del Rey, and L. Ron Hubbard, among other Golden Age authors. Eric holds bachelor's and master's degrees in English. He now works in an office and has been writing evenings and weekends since 2007. His stories have appeared in *Ellery Queen's Mystery Magazine*, *Alfred Hitchcock's Mystery Magazine*, *Stupefying Stories*, and *Writers of the Future* anthologies.

Eric Leif Davin is a science fiction historian and the author of *Pioneers of Wonder: Conversations with the Founders of Science Fiction* (Prometheus Books), and *Partners in Wonder: Women and the Birth of Science Fiction, 1926-1965* (Lexington Books). In the future, however, he intends to write more fiction. His debut novel, *The Desperate and the Dead*, was released by Damnation Books in September 2014. A work of historical horror, it features pirates and zombies against the demons of Hell.

Nick DiChario's short stories have appeared in many magazines and anthologies. He has been nominated for the Hugo and World Fantasy awards, and his first two novels, *A Small and Remarkable Life* (2006) and *Valley of Day-Glo* (2008), both received nominations for the John W. Campbell Memorial Award for Best Science Fiction Novel of the Year.

Kary English grew up in the snowy Midwest where she avoided siblings and frostbite by reading book after book in a warm corner behind a recliner chair. She blames her one and only high school detention on Douglas Adams, whose *Hitchhiker's Guide to the Galaxy* made her laugh out loud while reading it behind her geometry textbook. Today, Kary still spends most of her time with her head in the clouds and her nose in a book. To the great relief of her parents, she seems to be making a living at it. Her fiction includes several short stories, a planetary fantasy series available in 2015, and a fantasy saga about a little girl and an orange kitten. A student of *New York Times* bestsellers David Farland and Tracy Hickman, Kary aspires to make her own work detention-worthy. Kary is a Writers of the Future winner whose fiction has appeared in *Daily Science Fiction*, the *Grantville Gazette's* Universe Annex and *Galaxy's Edge*.

Tom Gerencer is a 45-year-old writer of science fiction and fantasy stories who grew up in Maine and moved to West Virginia for the whitewater. He attended the Clarion Science Fiction and Fantasy Writer's Workshop in 1999, then sold several short stories, including "Primordial Chili" and "Demo Mode" to *Science Fiction Age*, "A Taste of Damsel" to *Realms of Fantasy*, and a dozen or so others to magazines and anthologies around the country. He took time off from writing fiction to build a small business, and is now polishing up his first novel. He and his wife Kathy are awaiting the birth of their first child.

Tina Gower earned a master's degree in school psychology, raised guide dogs, and eventually decided to train her own two children. She worked as a psychologist for several schools before turning to writing as a profession. Tina has sold stories to *Galaxy's Edge*, *Writers of the Future*, *Chicken Soup for the Soul*, and a few others that are forthcoming. She is also collaborating with Mike Resnick on a forthcoming Stellar Guild team-up, to be published by Phoenix Pick. She won the Writers of the Future Gold Award as well as the Daphne du Maurier Award, the latter for Excellence in Mystery, Suspense, and Romance for the Futuristic, Fantasy, Paranormal category, for her unpublished novel.

Robert T. Jeschonek is an award-winning writer whose fiction, comics, essays, and podcasts have been published around the world. He won the grand prize in Pocket Books' nationwide *Strange New Worlds* contest, and was nominated for the British Fantasy Award. His young adult slipstream novel, *My Favorite Band Does Not Exist*, won the Forward National Literature Award and was named one of *Booklist's* Top Ten First Novels for Youth. His science fiction thriller, *Day 9*, is a 2013 International Book Award winner. He also won the 2013 Scribe Award for Best Original Novel for his alternate history, *Tannhäuser: Rising Sun, Falling Shadows*. He is a member of the Science Fiction and Fantasy Writers of America. Visit him online at www.thefictioneer.com. You can also find him on Facebook and follow him as @ TheFictioneer on Twitter.

Nancy Kress is the author of thirty-three books, including twenty-six novels, four collections of short stories, and three books on writing. Her work has won five Nebulas, two Hugos, a Sturgeon, and the John W. Campbell Memorial Award. She has also lost over a dozen of these awards. Most recent works are *After the Fall, Before the Fall, During the Fall* (Tachyon, 2012), a novel of apocalypse, and *Yesterday's Kin*, about genetic inheritance (Tachyon, 2014). In addition to writing, Kress often teaches at various venues around the country and abroad; in 2008 she was the Picador visiting lecturer at the University of Leipzig. Kress lives in Seattle with her husband, writer Jack Skillingstead, and Cosette, the world's most spoiled toy poodle.

Mercedes Lackey was born in Chicago, Illinois, on June 24, 1950. The very next day, the Korean War was declared. It is hoped that there is no connection between the two events. In 1985 her first book was published. In 1990 she met artist Larry Dixon at a small science fiction convention in Meridian, Mississippi, on a television interview organized by the convention. They moved to their current home, the "second weirdest house in Oklahoma," in 1992. She has many pet parrots and "the house is never quiet." She has over eighty books in print, with four being published in 2014 alone, and some of her foreign editions can be found in Russian, German, Czech, Polish, French, Italian, Turkish, and Japanese. From a collaboration with Dennis Lee, Cody Martin and Veronica Giguere came the Secret World Chronicle (www.secretworldchronicle) a five-book series of which the first four—*Invasion, World Divided, Revolution* and *Collision*—are available from Baen.

Leena Likitalo hails from Finland, the land of thousands of lakes and at least as many untold tales. Leena breaks computer games for a living. (Really!) When she's not working, she writes obsessively. And when she's not writing, she can be found at the stables riding horses or at the pool playing underwater rugby. She's a Writers of the Future 2014 winner and Clarion San Diego 2014 graduate. Her fiction has appeared in *Weird Tales, Galaxy's Edge*, and various semi-pro zines. You can visit her online at www.leenalikitalo.com.

Ken Liu (http://kenliu.name) is an author and translator of speculative fiction, as well as a lawyer and programmer. A winner of the Nebula, Hugo, and World Fantasy Awards, he has been published in *The Magazine of Fantasy & Science Fiction, Asimov's Science Fiction, Analog Science Fiction and Fact, Clarkesworld Magazine, Lightspeed*, and *Strange Horizons*, among other places. He lives with his family near Boston, Massachusetts. Ken's debut novel, *The Grace of Kings*, the first in a silkpunk epic fantasy series, will be published by Saga Press, Simon & Schuster's new genre fiction imprint, in April 2015. Saga will also publish a collection of his short stories later in the year.

Marina J. Lostetter's short original fiction has appeared in venues such as *Lightspeed, Orson Scott Card's InterGalactic Medicine Show*, and *Writers of the Future* anthologies. She has also written tie-in work for the Star Citizen and Sargasso Legacy universes. Recently, she has taken over the Artist Spotlight interview column in *Nightmare Magazine*, and is enjoying the opportunity to learn more about visual artists and their processes. Originally from Oregon, Marina now lives in Arkansas with her husband, Alex. She tweets as @MarinaLostetter. Please visit her homepage at www.lostetter.net.

Catherine L. Moore was one of the true giants of science fiction. She broke into print in 1933 with the classic "Shambleau," and created the still-popular Northwest Smith and Jirel of Joiry series, all for

Weird Tales. She then moved to the science fiction magazines, where she wrote the immortal "Vintage Season," plus "The Bright Illusion," "Fruit of Knowledge," and literally dozens of books and stories in collaboration with her husband, Henry Kuttner. She was Guest of Honor at the 1981 Worldcon. "Happily Ever After" was Moore's very first published story, an amateur piece submitted to her college magazine, and unavailable for 83 years until its first professional publication in *Galaxy's Edge*.

Larry Niven has written fiction at every length, and speculative articles, speeches for high schools and colleges and conventions, television scripts, political action in support of the conquest of space, graphic novels, and a couple of comic book universes. He's also collaborated with a wide variety of writers. His interests include science fiction conventions; role-playing games, live and computer; American Association for the Advancement of Science meetings and other gatherings of people at the cutting edges of science; comics; filk singing; yoga and other approaches to longevity; hiking; and racquetball. His awards include Hugos for "Neutron Star," 1966; *Ringworld*, 1970; "Inconstant Moon," 1971; "The Hole Man," 1974; and "The Borderland of Sol," 1975. He won the Nebula for Best Novel with *Ringworld* in 1970, Australia's Ditmar for *Ringworld* in 1972 and *Protector* in 1974; Japanese awards for *Ringworld* and "Inconstant Moon," both in 1979; and the San Diego Comic Convention's Inkpot Award in 1979. He was the Worldcon Guest of Honor in 1993.

K. C. Norton's work has appeared in *Orson Scott Card's InterGalactic Medicine Show*, *Writers of the Future* anthologies, and *Lightspeed's* "Women Destroy Science Fiction!" special issue. She has studied Mesopotamian economics, Greek history, Viking mythology, Bronze Age shipping networks, underwater archaeology, and writing for children. When she's not chronicling the struggles of vegetable people, she moonlights as a dog groomer-slash-bartender-slash-librarian. Norton lives in Pennsylvania with a dog who looks like a cow. She has never enslaved produce of any kind.

After college, **Ralph Roberts** served in the army, becoming a decorated Vietnam veteran. Then came his dream job, working with NASA during the last part of the Apollo moon-landing program—he'd still be there but ... NASA—in one of their several budgetary constraints—laid off the smart guys. He came back home to the family farm. Looking for a way to make a few bucks, he started writing. In the mid-70s—when personal computers came only as kits—he built his first one. By 1978, Ralph was writing about *and on* computers, one of the pioneers in word processing. He has sold over twenty million words as a professional writer, including more than 100 books and hundreds of articles and short stories. He also builds amateur radio stuff (his call is W5VE), has a rack of servers, tons of computers, and all sorts of gadgets, like that amazing credit-card-sized computer, the Raspberry Pi. He's currently writing the book *Advanced Raspberry Pi for Everyone*. Ralph still lives on the family farm in the mountains of Western North Carolina with his wife Pat and two horses.

Andrea G. Stewart lives in Northern California and gardens year-round in her tiny backyard, an activity that allows for copious daydreams of distant lands and planets. Her fiction has appeared in *Writers of the Future Volume 29*, *Beneath Ceaseless Skies*, *Daily Science Fiction*, and of course *Galaxy's Edge*. When she's not writing, working her day job, or chasing chickens out of her vegetables, she hangs around the house with her trusty dog, her loud cat, and her endlessly patient husband.

Sabina Theo was born in Haskovo, Bulgaria, and began reading and writing at the age of three. She is fluent in Bulgarian, English, Greek, and Russian. Her first horror story, "The Substitute," was published when she was seventeen. The review in *Haskovski vesti* immediately defined her as "original and talented." She followed that up with her first vampire story, *Running Away from the Light*, which ran over six subsequent issues. Since then she has published thousands of articles on culture, medicine, and social issues, and a number of short stories and poems—in eleven countries altogether, including the USA, Germany, Denmark, Greece, Canada, France, Sweden, Russia, and Argentina. Her novels *The Summer of the Vampires*, *Sons of Shadows*, and *Following the Dusk* are currently scheduled for publication. She also won a prize for Best Short Prose ("The Lover") in the 2005 Bulgarian national contest. Sabina has also translated the work of Harry Houdini, Louisa May Alcott, and many others into Bulgarian.

Brad R. Torgersen has been nominated for the Hugo award three times, has won two *Analog Science Fiction and Fact* magazine AnLab readers' choice awards, has been nominated for the Nebula award, and is a winner of the Writers of the Future award. A full-time computer geek by day, he's also a Chief Warrant Officer in the Army Reserve on weekends. At night, he writes some of the genre's best new science fiction. Brad's first novel, *The Chaplain's War,* which is based on his Hugo-nominated novella, "The Chaplain's Legacy", was released by Baen Books in October 2014. Married for 20 years, he lives in Utah with his wife, daughter, two cats, and two dogs.

Brian Trent is a writer of science fiction, fantasy, and horror. He is a 2013 winner in the Writers of the Future Contest for his story "War Hero" and has sold work to *Analog Science Fiction and Fact, Daily Science Fiction, Apex* (winning the 2013 Story of the Year Reader's Poll), *Clarkesworld Magazine, Escape Pod, COSMOS, Strange Horizons, Penumbra,* and more. He is also a novelist and screenwriter, and is currently developing two separate book series. Brian lives part-time in New England and full-time in imagination.

If you enjoyed these stories you may wish to subscribe to Galaxy's Edge magazine, published six times a year.

www.GalaxysEdge.com/sub.htm

www.ingramcontent.com/pod-product-compliance
Lightning Source LLC
Chambersburg PA
CBHW022112240626
47153CB00007B/2331